THEY ALWAYS WIN

By Anthony M. Pesare

Inspired by a True Story

They Always Win is a work of fiction. All of the characters, organizations, and events portrayed in this novel are either products of the author's imagination or are used factiously.

ISBN: 1463753233
ISBN 13: 9781463753238
Library of Congress Control Number: 2011913144
CreateSpace, North Charleston, South Carolina

To Mary, Jen, and Amy

ACKOWLEDGMENTS

This book and my experiences investigating organized crime are the result of the great fortune I've had in my life to work with members of the law enforcement and prosecution families. I am truly blessed to have worked with such talented and dedicated individuals, including the late Colonel Walter E. Stone, a legend of law enforcement, who gave a grateful young man the opportunity of a lifetime.

There are many people responsible for this book and they have my heartfelt thanks: Mary, Jen (co-author), Amy, Papa Joe, Andy, Don, Eileen, Vin, Ted, Joe, Bob, Solange, Tim, Matt (marketing), Kristy, Maria, Lisa (fact-checking and proofreading), Guy, Sue, Stu and Karen of Book Architecture, and the production team at CreateSpace.

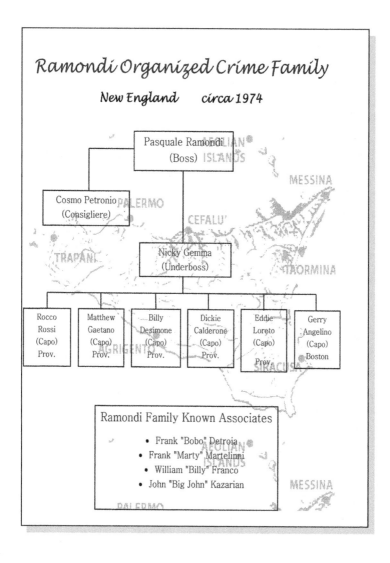

Ramondi Organized Crime Family

New England   circa 1974

Pasquale Ramondi
(Boss)

Cosmo Petronio
(Consigliere)

Nicky Gemma
(Underboss)

| Rocco Rossi (Capo) Prov. | Matthew Gaetano (Capo) Prov. | Billy Desimone (Capo) Prov. | Dickie Calderone (Capo) Prov. | Eddie Loreto (Capo) Prov. | Gerry Angelino (Capo) Boston |

Ramondi Family Known Associates

- Frank "Bobo" Detroia
- Frank "Marty" Martelinni
- William "Billy" Franco
- John "Big John" Kazarian

CHAPTER 1

Most men would do anything for their families—even sell their souls.

The old sailor was exhausted as he wiped away the fatigue from his eyes with wrinkled hands. He pulled off his cap. His long gray hair fell onto his shoulders as his eyes scanned the horizon.

The seas were calm as he surveyed the coastline, looking for the small skiff he would meet in the murky waters of the Bay of Palermo.

His fishing boat had been at sea for two days hauling its cargo, but this was no ordinary cargo. From stem to stern, bricks of heroin filled the boat, leaving just enough room for the old man and his one-man crew.

As he waited to see the lanterns, which would be his signal the skiff had arrived, he thought of being caught and spending the rest of his life in an Italian prison, but the fear was outweighed by the tens of thousands of dollars the Mafia paid him to haul its cargo of death and destruction to Sicily. The money allowed his family to live in relative ease in his small village. Although the old man felt the pride of providing for his family, he knew there was a price to pay. His life was not his own— he belonged to the Mafia...

CHAPTER 2

The Town of Rehoboth, Massachusetts, was mostly farmland and old homesteads. The main road, Route 44, was an old stagecoach route between Providence and Fall River. With a population of about seven thousand people, it was a quintessential New England town.

Dan Kelly, a Rehoboth patrolman with two years' experience, was on the midnight-to-eight shift. Most of his time was spent either patrolling back roads or parked on the side of Route 44 in the hope of catching a stolen car or one full of drugs.

Around one o'clock in the morning, he drove by an open patch of old farmland that had been recently cleared for a new housing development. The clearing was surrounded on three sides by streams and thick woods. It was known as a dumping ground for stolen cars and a refuge for lovers looking for privacy.

Tonight the clearing was empty, and as Kelly drove away, a light snow started to fall. The snow became more intense as the early morning hours wore on.

Around three thirty, Kelly decided to make one more pass through town. By that time, four inches of snow had fallen. As he passed by the clearing, his eyes were drawn to a fresh set of tire tracks etched in the snow.

Kelly eased the Crown Victoria onto the tracks; they ended next to a large patch of thick woods. Kelly got out of his cruiser. Using his flashlight, he saw the tracks formed a large circle. He assumed a car had pulled in, turned around, and left. Kelly tried to turn his cruiser around, but the tires began to spin in the snow. The car did a 360 and Kelly grabbed the steering wheel until his knuckles turned white holding his breath as he waited to smash into one of the large oak trees. Instead, the spinning cruiser came to an abrupt halt as the back tires sank into a soft patch of ground.

Kelly released his death grip on the wheel and smashed it with open palms out of a sense of relief and a bit of frustration. *Fuck,* he thought, *how am I going to explain this one? I'm better off trying to dig myself out than get my balls busted if I have to call the station for help.*

Every cruiser carried a small shovel and some dirt for helping stranded motorists. Kelly popped the trunk, took the shovel out, and tried to free his car. As he began digging, he was drawn to something red illuminated by the cruiser's taillights.

At first, Kelly thought the red might be a reflection of his lights against the white snow. He stopped shoveling and grabbed his flashlight to take a closer look. He got down on his knees and looked directly at the bright red spots in the snow. Blood!

A trail of blood could mean several things to a cop: a wounded victim, a body, or, worse, a wounded adversary who would strike out from the darkness. In spite of the early morning frost, beads of sweat formed on Kelly's forehead, and the sharp pains in his lower back told him his flight-or-fight instincts had kicked in. Despite his fear, he carried on. Kelly followed the trail of blood as it moved into the thick woods. His heart raced as he saw drag marks and two sets of footprints leading deeper into the woods.

In a clearing approximately twelve feet from his cruiser, the blood trail and drag marks ended. Kelly saw the rough outline of a grave marked by the snow.

He ran back to the cruiser for a pry bar. If this was not a grave, the still-frozen ground would resist a thrust from the bar. If it was a grave, the bar would move smoothly through the dirt. He plunged the bar into the soil; it sank down nearly two feet. Kelly pushed the talk button on his portable. "Dispatch, I need assistance at the lot on Mason right away. I think I've found a grave."

• • •

By eight o'clock the next morning, the gravesite was crawling with police officers. As the rising sun started to melt the snow, the grisly work of the Massachusetts State Police forensic unit began. Methodically, they removed the soft earth. Eventually, the parts of a body emerged: first the face, legs, arms, and, finally, the torso.

The sharp features of a white male appeared. He was dressed in a green checked jacket, green tie, white shirt, and green pants.

Kelly watched intently as each layer of earth was removed until the body was fully exposed. Nearby, Detective Victor Peron, the lead forensic tech, briefed Lieutenant Gil Gonzales.

"There's a slash across the face and several stab wounds in the chest and stomach area. When we turned him over, there were at least six gunshot wounds in the back."

"Any ID on him?" the lieutenant asked Peron.

"Just about to go into his pockets, Lieutenant."

Kelly watched as they turned the body on its side to retrieve a plain brown wallet.

"I got cash, charge cards, and a license. It's for Richard Calderone, 12 Bond Street, Providence, date of birth February 3, 1939," Peron told his lieutenant.

Gonzales recognized the name immediately.

"Dickie Calderone," he swore. "This is a Mob hit. Call Providence and the state police."

Calderone's brutalized body was put on a gurney and lifted into the medical examiner's van for the trip to the morgue. Patrolman Kelly gave his statement to the Massachusetts State Police. It would be the last anyone would hear about the case for years.

CHAPTER 3

As Calderone had been tortured the night before, Recruit Gino Peterson endured his own kind of torture.

"Get up, you son of a bitch!"

Gino heard the voice, but only faintly. The ringing in his ears drowned out the shouts coming from the instructor standing over him. Last night's snow failed to provide any cushion as he fell to the turf, knocked down for the third time. Struggling to his knees, he noticed spots of blood on his boxing gloves. Gino could see his opponent waiting to finish him off.

This was no ordinary boxing match. Gino Peterson was a young recruit at the Rhode Island State Police Training Academy. Housed in a former missile site given to the state by the government, it was hidden deep in the woods of Foster. Three buildings painted in drab military gray made the surrounding area a stark and cold setting for the young troopers.

In a small snowy patch, the other recruits pressed in, forming the circle that made the boxing ring.

Lieutenant Gilbert W. Shea, commandant of the training academy, was still screaming. "Recruit Trooper Gino Peterson, get up, you half-breed motherfucker!"

Gino looked in Shea's eyes. He could see nothing but hatred.

"That's right, Peterson. I know you're half a WOP. The only thing you've got going for you is you don't look like one of them—you're a tall, skinny fucker, aren't you?"

Gino knew the slur was meant to enrage him, to break him down and make him quit; Gino would never show this kind of weakness to Shea or anyone else. *I'll never quit, you sadistic son of a bitch,* he thought.

He was fighting his third fellow recruit in a row. He held his own with the first two, but he was taking a beating from the third.

The taunts and brutal fighting were what separated those who truly wanted to be troopers from those who had signed up for the sharp uniform and cop groupies. It tested Gino's resolve in a way he never could have imagined when he applied for the state police.

Gino struggled to his feet as the fight continued. He swung wildly, missed, and fell over from exhaustion. As his opponent moved in to finish him off, Lieutenant Shea screamed, "Time!"

As Gino limped back to the circle, Shea got in his face and spat, "Peterson, if you make it through this academy, it'll be a fucking miracle."

• • •

The year was 1974. Richard Nixon was embroiled in the Watergate scandal. Everywhere, people were questioning authority—but not Gino. He craved the structure, prestige, and power of a career with the state police. Rather than question the Man, Gino wanted to be the Man. It was not an easy decision—he had grown up in a neighborhood controlled by the Mob, and the temptation to lead a life of crime was always great. Ultimately, he decided he would try to uphold the law instead of breaking it.

Gino came to the decision slowly, but once made, he was driven by his own stubbornness and a will to succeed that bordered on desperation. It began when he got a summer job at the Seekonk Twin Drive-In, just over the state line in Massachusetts. He started out working at the concession stand, doling out hotdogs, hamburgers, popcorn, and the ever-popular egg roll. The manager took a liking to Gino, who received more responsibility as the summer wore on. Gino eventually moved up to collecting money and selling tickets at the admission booth. After the initial rush, all of the booth cashiers would count receipts at the main office; Gino would be left to collect money from customers who arrived late.

An off-duty police officer would always be there to guard the money. The detail was manned by a different officer every night, and eventually, Gino got to know them all. Since there was not much activity after the movie began, Gino and the officers would be free to talk for hours. Whenever he explained that his uncle was a state trooper, they always seemed to open up to him. They would tell him things they probably never would have if he were not considered part of the extended law enforcement family.

As Gino got to know the different officers, he realized they were just regular men trying to do the best they could—not corrupt men whose only intent was to put innocent people in jail, talk he'd heard around his neighborhood. If not for his uncle, he would have believed it completely.

The officers told him stories about responding to domestic disputes, checking homes and businesses for burglaries, and talking to kids who got out of line. By the end of the summer, he was convinced it was the life he wanted. His mother and uncle would be proud of him. And even more important, maybe, just maybe, the neighborhood would realize there was a certain nobility in upholding the law.

Gino's uncle, Lieutenant Earl Peterson, spent twenty-one years with the Rhode Island State Police. His last few years were spent urging his bosses to give his nephew a spot in the training academy.

Two weeks before the start of the academy, Uncle Earl stopped by Gino's house to visit his brother,

Albert, and sister-in-law, Teresa. Earl was in full uniform: boots, breeches, and a brown felt Stetson. He had a .38 caliber revolver mounted in a cross-draw style, and a leather belt containing handcuffs and extra ammo. The leather of his brown boots was shined to a high gloss, and every button gleamed. To Gino, he looked ten feet tall.

After dinner, Uncle Earl asked to speak with Gino.

"I know you'll do well in the academy, but you need to know what life will be like on the job."

"I understand, Uncle Earl. I'll do whatever it takes," Gino replied eagerly.

Earl continued. "Being a trooper is different, Gino. It's not just a job; it's a way of life. You'll live and work in barracks all over the state. Our days begin at eight in the morning and don't end until eleven at night. If you're on nights, you work eight to eight. There's little time for a social life."

"Is that why you never married, Uncle?" he asked.

"Part of the reason, but that's a story for another time. I want you to understand: no hint of corruption has ever invaded our world. The Mob, and even the state government, will compromise the state police if they get the chance.

"In 1960, a popular state rep from East Providence was elected governor. He was Italian, and right after the election, the rumors started," Earl said.

"What kind of rumors?" Gino asked.

"That he was connected to the Mob. We weren't sure, of course, but he fired Colonel Smith after he was sworn in. There was no explanation—just showed him the door. It shocked us all.

"The new governor took a lot of heat from the press, so he appointed one of our captains as the new superintendent. For two years, we watched, guarded. We were hoping this governor wasn't in the Mob's pocket."

"Was he?" Gino asked.

"I don't know. In '62, a swamp Yankee Republican ran against the governor. One of his campaign promises was to return Walter Smith to the state police. He won by a landslide, and immediately reappointed the colonel.

"What I'm trying to say is that there will always be someone who'll want to control the state police. People will also try to corrupt you. Don't let it happen."

"I won't, Uncle. I promise," Gino said.

CHAPTER 4

G ino grew up in the Italian section of Providence known as Federal Hill. It was the epicenter of organized crime in New England. The Hill was populated by Italian immigrants who arrived in the States thinking the streets would be paved with gold. It was a time when neighbors spoke Italian and a form of English affectionately called "broken."

Everyone adhered to the Southern Italian philosophy of mistrust toward the government. From an early age, you were taught to rely on the respected men of the community to settle disputes, rather than the police. The community elder was the one you went to with problems—when your neighbor owed you money, when someone was sleeping with your wife, if someone molested your child. Essentially, they were there when you needed muscle.

The rule in the neighborhood was "never react to a situation"—you were to seek out these men of respect. If you were wronged by an ordinary citizen and felt retribution was in order, you were required to ask the permission of the elders. If for some reason this person was protected (an associate or a made man), then the outcome would be decided by the Mob.

Once, a member of the Raimondi crime family made a pass at Gino's mom. Albert wanted to deck the guy for hitting on his wife, but Teresa stopped him—the guy was a mobster. Gino's dad wasn't Italian, and even if he had won the fight, there would be retribution.

During the '60s when Gino was growing up, it was well known that Ray "The Referee" Lombardozzi settled all disputes. Albert brought his grievance to Ray, and after explaining the story, he was assured he would receive an apology. When it happened, Gino was there and took note that his father was careful not to do anything more than graciously accept the wiseguy's apology and handshake.

Although Albert would never be accepted by the wiseguys, it didn't mean that he wasn't accepted by his Italian in-laws. Eager to please his mother-in-law, he spent hours perfecting his own pasta sauce, and after numerous attempts, it finally passed muster.

Even though Albert was warmly accepted into his Italian family, he was shunned by his own parents after he took an Italian as his bride. The resentment they held for their new daughter-in-law ran deep. She was of "inferior stock," part of the waves of Jewish, Irish, and Italian immigrants who polluted their county. They would never accept her as part of the family.

Gino's family lived on the second floor of a three-decker tenement house, one of many in the neighborhood. The apartment sat over a small grocery store across the street from a pizza place and a barbershop.

Gino attended the local public school, where every Wednesday morning, he and his classmates would be marched down to St. Anthony's Catholic School for religious education. It was called released time, and the nuns of the parish educated the public school kids in the tenets of Catholicism.

In Gino's world, everyone was Catholic, or so he thought. He took notice that one of his classmates, Deborah Bolash, was always absent from religious education. He asked his teacher, and she explained that Deborah was a Methodist and therefore not required to go. Gino was shocked—he couldn't comprehend that there was more than one religion in the world.

Gino's dad worked in a jewelry factory during the day but had a second job to make ends meet. Albert worked at the Atlantic Mills building as a janitor from six o'clock until midnight.

Gino watched each night as his dad ate quickly and rushed out of the house with a quick kiss from his wife and a squeeze of his son's cheeks. Gino would lie in bed and wait for his father to come home. He couldn't sleep until he returned.

It was a Friday night just after Gino's fifteenth birthday when his life changed forever. Before he left for work that fateful night, his dad promised that tomorrow they would go to Tim's Barbershop for haircuts, and then off to Pete's Spa for breakfast. The afternoon would be spent playing catch in the backyard. The prospect of a full day with his dad made Gino even more restless than usual.

One o'clock passed, and then two. Still no footsteps on the stairs, no reassuring turn of the lock signaling the return of his hero.

There was a loud knock on the door shortly after two o'clock in the morning. Gino climbed out of bed and saw his mother hesitantly walk across the kitchen floor toward an uncertain future.

As she opened the door, Gino saw her knees buckle. It was the parish priest and a policeman. Gino remembered his mother's wails of anguish as the police officer explained that her husband had been killed in a car accident.

"Seems he fell asleep at the wheel, jumped a curb, and hit a telephone pole." His words were cold and direct and pierced Gino's young heart.

The parish priest said, "Maybe it was all the hours Albert was working, but that doesn't really matter. It's God's will, Teresa, and you have to accept it."

They said it was an accident, but Gino knew his father would never fall asleep behind the wheel of a car. He was too strong and invincible, and nothing would keep him from coming home to his family.

Gino's feeling of helplessness was overwhelming, and he was so shaken that he went numb. He rushed to his mother, but his embrace did little to comfort her. As she rocked him in her arms, her tears fell onto his cheeks like sheets of rain.

They buried Albert Peterson three days later. Albert's parents attended the church service and left as soon as it was over.

After the obligatory month of wearing black, Teresa went to work at a local bakery to support her son. Some normalcy returned to their home, but for Gino, it was more like sleepwalking than actually living.

CHAPTER 5

On a warm day in May 1974, Gino graduated from the academy in an outdoor ceremony.

"Gino, you look so handsome in your uniform! Your father, God rest his soul, would be so proud of you," his mother said as she looked toward the sky. He saw pride in her smile and a hint of sadness in her eyes.

"You've filled out, son. You look like Bobby Orr," Uncle Earl said.

"Who's Bobby Orr?" his mom asked.

"Bruins hockey player, Teresa."

"I don't know who that is, but he must be very handsome."

Gino began his career as a uniformed trooper making the rounds of each barracks, fine-tuning his police skills. One moment would be boring and robotic; the next would be filled with sheer terror. He survived high-speed chases, bar fights, robberies, and gunfire through instinct, training, and a dose of good luck.

Gino's ultimate goal was to become a detective in the intelligence unit, the unit charged with investigating organized crime. It was small, secretive, and elite—the CIA of the state police. Being assigned to the unit meant much more to Gino than most. For him, it was an opportunity to rid his old neighborhood of a cancer—an opportunity to demonstrate that not all Italians were in the Mob or tolerated its existence.

Gino spent his off-duty time reviewing organized crime reports from the department. He also used the microfiche machine at the library to read old newspaper articles about the Mob's activities.

He learned that the New England crime boss, Pasquale Raimondi, was doing time in a federal prison in Atlanta for tax evasion. *It's always the taxes that get these guys,* thought Gino. *They never learn.* Acting boss Nicholas Gemma was in charge of the family while the Old Man was away. Gemma had four crews of mobsters under his control.

The crews were headed by four capos: Matthew "Midnight" Gaetano, Billy "Aces" DeSimone, Rocco Rossi, and Eddie Loreto. Dickie Calderone, murdered at the same time Gino entered the training academy, was on his way to becoming a capo until his death. The remnants of Calderone's crew were divided up among the remaining four capos.

The Providence crews were into everything: gambling, financing drug deals, extortion, loan sharking, stolen goods, strip joints, and exacting "street taxes." Every criminal had to pay a street tax for the privilege of committing crimes in the Mob's territory.

Richard "Moon" Capelli was the Mob's lead gambler and managed all of the gambling operations in New England. It was his job to determine the Old Man's cut of the Providence and Boston action.

Gino was very familiar with Moon from the old neighborhood. As Gino read, his mind drifted to a time when he was seventeen, when he was still awash with grief from the loss of his father. He was searching for answers—something, or someone, to fill the hole in his heart.

The gangsters of the neighborhood were always an option, but Gino had little respect for them. They were thieves and bullies who hid behind the word respect.

Moon was different than the rest of the gangsters Gino knew from the neighborhood. He was a gambler who didn't seem to have any violence in him. Moon was smart and respected for treating his customers honestly.

As a kid, Gino spent his time delivering papers and playing stickball and football on side streets. Sewer caps and telephone poles were used for bases and goal posts.

Sometimes he would sit on his J. C. Higgins bike and stare across the street at the wiseguys as they hung out in front of Mr. Raimondi's store.

One day, Moon summoned him across the street. Gino cautiously crossed Atwells Avenue, and the man introduced himself.

"Hi, kid. My name is Richard, but everyone calls me Moon. You can call me Moon, all right?"

"Yes, Mr. Moon," Gino answered.

"Just Moon is fine, kid. Listen, I got a little proposition for you. I know it's probably been tough since you lost your old man, but I got a way for you to make some money. You interested?"

"Sure, Moon," Gino answered. Thoughts of purchasing cases of baseball cards danced in Gino's head.

Moon explained to Gino that all he had to do was deliver an envelope to the bartender at the Social Club. If he did, there would be twenty bucks in it for him each time. Gino knew the envelope had to be part of Moon's gambling operation, but he didn't care. It would take him eight months delivering papers to earn twenty bucks.

"Twenty bucks for that? Are you sure, Moon?"

"Here's the envelope and the twenty. Take care of this for me today, and next week, you can make the delivery again."

Gino peddled furiously to the club. Without much air left in his lungs, he jumped off his bike, ran in, and handed the envelope to the bartender.

He performed his duties for three weeks and bought dozens of packets of baseball cards—so many, his jaw ached from all the gum he was chewing. Gino decided it was time to do something for his mother with his newfound riches. He went to the local drug store and bought six bottles of Miss Clairol #5 Chestnut Brown. It was a hair dye she would often send him to buy, so he knew exactly what to order from the clerk. He rushed home to present her with a six-month supply and receive what would surely be appreciation.

When he arrived, she was standing over the oven, stirring the red gravy that she would pour over pasta that night. Gino beamed as he presented the hair dye and explained how he was helping Moon in order to earn extra money.

"Gino, Mr. Capelli asked you to do this?"

"Yes, Mom, Moon. You know him; he's a bookie. Everybody knows Moon." Gino still had no idea he'd done anything wrong.

"Yes, he's a bookie, and because of that, you had to know there was money or betting slips in those envelopes. Do you understand that's wrong? It's against the law, and you're just seventeen! Do you know what kind of trouble you could get in? And you want to be a trooper like your uncle."

"But Mom, everybody gambles in the neighborhood. Even Dad used to—"

He didn't even feel the slap cross his face at first. Her dark eyes narrowed, and he saw the disappointment.

"You will not deliver anything else for Moon, and you will not have anything to do with those gangsters. Do you understand me, young man?"

Gino could see a small tear in her eye, and he nodded. He retreated to his bed and curled up in a ball.

• • •

As Gino reminisced, he gently rubbed his cheek and swore he could still feel the sting of that slap. He refocused and started reading about some associates of the Mob, and Moon's name was prominently mentioned as the Mob's chief bookmaker. He thought back to his father and how he'd played the numbers and placed an occasional wager on a sports team. He vividly remembered his family struggling to make ends meet and the endless calls from bill collectors.

Were they in debt because of his father's gambling? Gino wondered. Were bills left unpaid because the bookie always got his money first? Ignoring phone calls from the gas and electric company was less painful than a visit from two of Pasquale's goons. Was there some connection between his father's gambling and the car accident? Questions he would probably never be able to answer.

Whenever Gino had a question about the Mob, he turned to Detective Lou Reynolds of the intelligence unit. Lou instructed Gino's academy class on organized crime and was a wealth of knowledge when it came to the Raimondi crime family.

Although Gino learned the mechanics of gambling and betting on the numbers during his short stint as Moon's assistant, he never understood how the Mob made money from sports betting. He decided to call Lou and ask.

"Gino, the Mob doesn't make money on taking more losing bets than winning. Bookies charge the bettors a vig, or vigorish, of ten percent on all losing bets. Let's say you make a hundred-dollar losing bet. You pay the bookie a hundred and ten dollars," Lou explained.

"What if the bookie takes all winning bets? He's screwed, right?" Gino asked.

"A bookie's entire life revolves around making sure equal amounts of money are wagered on both sides of the ledger. If the wagers are balanced, the losing action pays off the winners, and still leaves a ten percent profit for the Mob. And that's how it's done, my young friend."

"Thanks, Lou," Gino said.

"Hey, kid, listen to the wiretap of Moon taking action on the Pats–Jets game in October. It's a pretty good lesson on laying off bets."

Gino found the tapes in the evidence room and listened to the wiretaps of Moon spending hours laying off action to other bookies to balance out his bets. The Pats were favored by only three points, and Moon was struggling with a great deal of action on the Patriots' side of the ledger. He started calling bookies in New York who were obviously taking heavy action for the Jets. They were able to exchange bets, ensuring both would make money.

The Pats eventually won the game 24–0, and both Moon and the bookies in New York made money.

Moon was an "earner," Mob slang for a moneymaker. It was the greatest compliment one mobster could pay to another.

CHAPTER 6

G ino turned his attention to Dickie Calderone. The thought that Calderone had been murdered at the same time he was in the academy fascinated him. As he read each police report and read interviews of his associates, Calderone seemed to come to life.

Calderone was a good earner and it should have been smooth sailing for him in his quest to become a capo. He started his Mob career as a thief—stealing was a way of life for him. If he could get his hands on it, he would take it and fence it.

He got Pasquale's attention when he kicked the shit out of one of the Mob's fences. Calderone and his partner, Tommy LaTola, broke into a fancy house on the east side of Providence and made a major score. They took about ten grand worth of swag to Angelo "The Blind Pig" Suffrette. He told him he'd give them five for everything.

A few days later, Calderone went back to collect, but Suffrette said he had no money. He said he had to give it back to Pasquale. Supposedly, the house they hit belonged to a friend of the Boss.

Calderone said, "Bullshit. I checked with Nicky before we hit it. He said the owner wasn't connected."

"Look," Suffrette explained, "I'm telling you, this guy is tight with Pasquale. The swag is going back to him."

Calderone snapped. He jumped over the counter and kicked the shit out of Suffrette. Calderone knew that if he was right and the owner was not connected, he was safe; if not, he would be dead. Either way, he knew he was going to cross paths with the Old Man.

Within a few days of the beating, Pasquale's men called Calderone to the religious items store he used as a front. He figured he would end up stuffed in a trunk, but he had no choice but to show up; they would find him one way or another.

Pasquale's headquarters was housed in a cinder-block building with large front windows. The black stenciling, "Pat's Religious Supplies," was peeling off the glass. The windows were dark with dirt and grime. The showroom was filled with bibles, candles, chalices, and enough religious clothing to outfit the Vatican.

When Calderone walked in, two of the Old Man's goons searched him. They took him to a back room and sat him at a small card table; the room was cut in half by a blanket drawn across a rope. As Calderone sat down, his eyes were drawn to a large pile of cash on the table. He didn't dare do anything but stare straight ahead.

Pasquale Raimondi made a slow and deliberate entrance into the room like an actor walking to center stage. He was five foot five, small framed, with hands that could palm a grapefruit. His jet-black hair was slicked down, and he was dressed in the most expensive suit Dickie had ever seen.

He could have passed for anybody's grandfather—except for the eyes. They were as dark as pools of oil, and looking into them told Calderone this man was responsible for many deaths.

When Raimondi spoke, each of his carefully chosen words made Calderone understand why so many men shook at the mere mention of his name.

"I understand the Blind Pig agreed to pay you five Gs for the score?" Pasquale said.

"Yes, sir, Mr. Raimondi." Calderon's voice cracked.

"What happened when you went to collect your money? The Blind Pig says you robbed him."

For a second, Calderone forgot who he was talking to.

"Well, he's a fucking liar. He told me the guy was connected to you and the stuff had to go back. I knew it didn't work that way. I know if he was connected, Nicky would have told me, so I kicked the shit of him."

Oh, fuck, he thought, *time to save my ass.*

"I apologize, Mr. Raimondi. I know the Blind Pig is your guy. I'm not the brightest guy in the world, but I know I'd be dead if I stole from you. You know me from the neighborhood, Mr. Raimondi, and I know the rules."

Raimondi grinned. He slowly slid the money across the table and said, "Listen, kid, here's your money. The Blind Pig made a mistake, but that's the end of it, understand?"

"Yes, sir," he answered. For the first time since he arrived, Calderone felt he just might walk out alive.

"Screw," Raimondi said.

Calderone folded two one-hundred-dollar bills from the stash and handed them to one of Pasquale's goons. He looked at Raimondi and said, "As a sign of respect."

Pasquale Raimondi smiled.

CHAPTER 7

After his meeting with Raimondi, Calderone started working for Underboss Nicky Gemma. He slowly worked his way up the ladder in the family, from thief to hijacker, bookie to loan shark, leg breaker to hit man, all under the guidance of Nicky. In less than ten years, he had gone from a small-time thief to a wiseguy. The brass ring of being a made man was right around the corner.

Calderone's next step would be taking part in a murder, so he could "make his bones." This would cement him in the life, and allow him to be "made." He didn't have to wait long. Nicky told him that the order had come down from the Old Man to take out Ralphie Baccari.

Baccari was a thief and a junkie who'd made the mistake of breaking into the house of one of Pasquale's bookmakers. Baccari knew who it was but just didn't give a fuck; all he wanted was money for heroin. Sealing his fate, the stupid bastard refused Nicky's order to return the money. Nicky gave the hit to Gerry Almy, one of many non-Italians Pasquale used to do his dirty work.

Gerry and Calderone caught Ralphie nodding off in his apartment with a needle sticking out of his arm. He pleaded for his life as Gerry pumped five bullets into his chest with a .38 caliber revolver. He handed Calderone the gun and said, "Shoot him once in the head."

Calderone took the gun and pulled the trigger. The slug flew into Baccari's head and made a thumping sound; it was easier than he thought.

"You just made your bones, you lucky guinea bastard. They'll probably make you a made man, and I'll always be an errand boy, cleaning up their shit."

Two weeks later, in the back room of Pasquale's store, Calderone pledged his life to the family and sold his soul to the devil. His dream had come true: he was a made man.

Calderone spent most of his time as a made man putting together a crew. They worked out of the Madonna Social Club in Johnston, a suburb of Providence; he conducted business from the back office of the restaurant. Calderone was paranoid about the police bugging the back room, so he installed a jukebox. Whenever he conducted Mob business, he would crank up the volume, hit K5, and Eric Clapton would begin singing "I Shot the Sheriff."

His crew committed the crimes, he collected the money, and he always made sure he passed 10 percent along to Nicky.

Calderone's nightly routine consisted of booze and broads. Quaaludes and Valium soon became part of his repertoire. He thought he was on top of the world; the only thing keeping Calderone from moving up was Pasquale being away in federal prison. Pasquale would not be making any new capos until he got out, so Calderone had to be patient.

On St. Patrick's Day in 1974, Calderone stopped into Montebello's to pick up a suit he had ordered to celebrate the occasion. It was a green checked jacket and solid green pants, all in the latest material, polyester. He wore it with a white shirt and a green tie.

Calderone said good-bye to his wife and headed to the Madonna Social Club to celebrate. His crew ate swordfish, fried sliced potatoes, and broccoli mixed with olive oil and garlic, and they toasted the Irish with shots of Johnnie Walker Red. After coffee with anisette, Calderone popped two Quaaludes and left to visit his girlfriend.

Sue Restive loved movies, and earlier that week, Calderone had taken her to see *One Flew Over the Cuckoo's Nest*. He loved to have her play out scenes in their lovemaking, and tonight, Sue would play Nurse Ratched. He entered her apartment around midnight, entered her at twelve fifteen, and was out the door at two o'clock in the morning.

He was still fucked up from the booze and the pills when he left Sue. Calderone did not want the night to end, so he thought he would check out the Hill. He noticed that Frank "Tiger" Detroia's club was open, even though it was well past closing time. Calderone hated him and was convinced that someday he would have to take Tiger out. Even though he knew it was a bad idea, he decided to walk in, have a drink, and taunt Tiger with his mere presence.

He parked his Caddy and walked to the front door. He knocked, and someone peeked through the shade. Slowly, the door opened, and Tiger greeted him.

"Welcome to my club, Dickie," Tiger said.

"Open kind of late—aren't you afraid the cops will pinch you?" Calderone asked.

"I got it covered. I've been slipping the beat cop a C-note every week, and they leave me alone. Come in, please," Tiger offered.

Inside, Tiger was bartending. His crew was sitting at the bar: Marty, Billy, and Big John. Alonzo Regent, Tiger's cousin, was passed out in a corner from too much booze. There were a couple of old-timers playing cards at a table in the corner.

Tiger asked, "What can I get you, Dickie?"

"Amaretto on the rocks, and set up the bar," he answered.

Tiger set the drink in front of Calderone. "Dickie, this is on the house as a sign of respect."

"Ah, salute," he said.

The rest chimed in, "Ah, salute."

The Amaretto slid smoothly down his throat, and the conversation in the room picked up. Even in a haze of alcohol and pills, Calderone could sense Tiger moving out from behind the bar. Tiger placed his hand on his shoulder, and Calderone relaxed. The last thing he heard was the click of a revolver's hammer.

CHAPTER 8

The Calderone case was as cold as his dead body. Eight years had passed, and the investigation had not produced any solid leads. With each dead end, enthusiasm for the case waned. Soon, the case became lost among the files of other unsolved Mob hits. Although Calderone's dream had ended, Gino Peterson's dream of fighting the Mob was beginning to take shape.

Gino spent time at each of the barracks: Chepachet, Lincoln, Howard, Hope Valley, Portsmouth, and Wickford. At each, he adapted to the new commanders and noncommissioned officers who would rule his life. He learned that each barracks presented different policing challenges. Chepachet and Hope Valley and Lincoln were rural areas, Howard handled the interstate highways, and Wickford and Portsmouth covered Rhode Island's coastline.

After six years of working on the road, Gino thought it was time to apply for a transfer to the intelligence unit. He was working out of the Hope Valley barracks, which covered the southwest corner of the state and the roads leading into Rhode Island from Connecticut. His boss, Lieutenant Ray Neil, hardly ever said a word to him—he just gave the occasional grunt or raised eyebrow when Gino would walk a prisoner through the door of the barracks. Over the next year, Gino applied whenever there was an opening in the intelligence unit but was never selected.

He expressed his disappointment to Lou each time he was passed over. They usually met at a '50s-style diner in Scituate filled with customers sporting long hair and beards. Long hair was in and short hair was out in the early '80s, and the locals easily pegged Gino and Lou as cops.

Lou could see the physical changes in Gino since the academy. "I guess we can't call you the Italian string bean anymore—you've really filled out since the academy."

"I've been lifting weights," Gino replied. "You know what it's like out there. Alone in a cruiser in the middle of nowhere, with the closest trooper thirty minutes away—I'm doing everything I can to keep from getting my ass kicked," Gino said.

"Quite the stud, aren't you?" Lou joked.

"A lean, mean, fighting machine," Gino said, and they both laughed.

Lou began, "Look, Gino. I know you're frustrated. But remember, it took me nine years before I got in. Keep your eyes and ears open and your mouth shut. It will eventually happen, trust me," Lou said.

"I know it's going to take time, but patience isn't something I was ever very good at," Gino said.

They continued to talk over coffee about some of the arrests Gino had made on the road. Lou told him the key to getting into the unit was making an arrest that was connected to organized crime.

A month after their conversation, Gino was sitting on the side of Route 95 at the Connecticut line when his passport to the intelligence unit drove by. He was listening to John Cougar sing about Jack and Diane when a beat-up Ford Econoline van drove by. The van caught his attention because it was riding low, and the driver kept glancing at him while he drove by.

Gino stopped the van and asked the driver for identification.

"License and registration, sir."

"Did I do something wrong, Trooper?" the driver asked.

"You're riding really low. Can I ask what you're carrying back there?"

"I'm going to be straight with you, trooper," the driver replied. "I'm bringing magazines from New York to my boss, Frank Martelinni."

"What kind of magazines?" Gino asked.

"Porn," the driver said sheepishly.

Gino recognized the name. Martelinni was a wiseguy who hung around with Tiger Detroia and Big John Kazarian.

Finally, Gino thought, *all that reading about the Raimondi crime family might pay off.*

Gino asked dispatch to notify the intelligence unit of the traffic stop. He was ordered to accompany the van back to headquarters so that members of the unit could interview the driver.

When Gino pulled up to the intelligence unit with the van, he was greeted in the parking lot by Lou and Sergeant Michelle Urban. Urban directed Lou to interview the driver and inventory the contents of the van.

The boss, Sergeant Urban, was a fifteen-year veteran of the state police. She was in her thirties, with crystal green eyes and black hair, which she wore pulled back in a tight bun. It gave her a harshness that detracted from her natural beauty.

Throughout the state police, Urban was known for her knowledge of the Mob and her fierce loyalty to Colonel Smith. Rumors swirled around her personal life: was she single, married, or a lesbian? Whatever Gino knew about her, he learned from the rumor mill. Unless he got a chance to work with her, all he would ever know about her was the gossip that cops were only too happy to spread.

What Gino did know was that Michelle Urban was the daughter of retired Lieutenant Theodore Urban,

Colonel Smith's former partner. She spent a mere three years on the road before being selected for the unit; she made corporal in five years and was promoted to sergeant and head of the unit in ten years. It was a meteoric rise that most assumed was a favor to her father.

Michelle made a CIA agent look like a gossiping housewife; everything about her was a mystery. Unless you were actively involved in one of her cases, you never knew what she was working on.

"Nice work, Trooper Peterson," she said.

"Thank you, Sergeant. Do you need anything else from me?"

"Just do an activity report and get it to Detective Reynolds."

"Will do," he said. Behind her, he could see Lou grinning.

A week later, Michelle waited in the colonel's office while he retrieved his second cup of coffee of the day from the kitchen. She marveled at the wood-paneled office with the deep shag rug vacuumed in the required north-south pattern. The walls were barren except for a photo of the former director of the FBI. It was signed, *To Walter, Warmest Regards, J. Edgar.* Not one piece of paper cluttered his desk; the telephone, pen, and small tape recorder were all neatly arranged in a row.

She was staring at the picture when he walked back into the office. An imposing six feet, four inches tall, at age sixty-five he still maintained the physique of a boxer. The only concession to age were gray hair and wrinkled hands.

"There was something else you wanted to ask me, Sergeant?"

"Colonel, we've been short a detective since Corporal Morrison retired, and I was wondering if we could transfer someone in from uniform."

"I don't have a lot of bodies to spare—manpower is down across the department," he said.

"I understand, sir, but you know how active Pasquale's family has been lately, and we could use the help."

Michelle let the colonel process the information. She knew he hated Pasquale. If she was going to get another body, that would be the reason. He sat down in his chair, put his coffee on the desk, and chewed on the earpiece of his eyeglasses.

"Who do you want?" he asked.

"I was thinking of Peterson," Urban replied. "He seems to have good instincts, and Detective Reynolds says he's been studying the Mob since he got on the job. Last week, he stopped one of Pasquale's guys making a delivery of porn."

"He grew up in Pasquale's neighborhood, you know that?"

"I know, sir, but that might work to our advantage—"

"Or it might bite us in the ass, Sergeant," he said.

"Colonel, with all due respect, I think the kid gets a bad rap because he's Italian. I know a little bit about what it's like for people to assume something about you because of your family—"

The colonel held up his hand, "All right, enough. You know you're always going to have the albatross of your father around your neck. This is different. Peterson's uncle was a good man—that's why I gave the kid a shot at the academy—but I'm not so sure about him. You can have him, but keep an eye on him. Understood?"

"Understood, sir. Thank you."

On March 31, 1981, the teletype machine typed out the order. Trooper Gino Peterson was transferred from the uniform division to the intelligence unit.

CHAPTER 9

By the fall of 1982, Gino was a salty yearlong veteran of the intelligence unit. On this sharp fall day, he cruised to work in his undercover Cadillac Seville, listening to "Bette Davis Eyes."

He drove through the village of Scituate, which was made up of several white houses; the only contrast was a small brick fire station. The state police headquarters was a half mile west of the village. It was located on the former Coggeshall property, which had been forfeited to the state by its owner, a victim of the Great Depression.

The Coggeshall mansion, horse barn, and servant quarters were converted by the state police into offices and a garage for vehicles. In 1960, the state erected a fourth building to house the communications center.

The intelligence unit was housed in a stone building at the rear of the complex that once served as the servant quarters. Six detective desks were jammed into one room; a second was reserved for the sergeant running the unit.

The intelligence unit was made up of Detectives Lou Reynolds, Tim Sullivan, and Mike Quinn, the unit's electronic and forensic expert.

Lou was the consummate debriefer and interviewer. The confessions he obtained were legendary in their detail and ability to stand up against any defense attorney's challenge. A shade over six foot five, he was built like a linebacker with a no-nonsense face that radiated competence and confidence.

When Gino was first assigned to the unit, Lou took him to interview a witness in Woonsocket. This northernmost city in Rhode Island was made up of old mills and rows of tenement houses.

Marcel Beausolieu was a small, greasy man with an attitude. They approached him as he was working on his car and displayed their credentials.

"Mr. Beausolieu, I'm Detective Reynolds, and this is Detective Peterson from the state police."

"What the fuck do you guys want?" he said.

"Listen, Mr. Beausolieu," Lou said. "We just want to ask you a few questions about a murder investigation. You're not a suspect, but you could know something that might help us."

"Murder? You've got to be fucking insane. I don't know anything about a fucking murder. You state cops are all alike, trying to jam someone up for something they didn't do. Why don't you go fuck yourselves," said the arrogant little man.

Lou answered, "Mr. Beausolieu, we know you don't have to talk to us, and we don't want to spend a lot of time on this. It's just some background stuff. Why don't you just come back to the barracks? We'll ask you a few questions and have you back here in less than an hour."

"Listen, I don't know anything, and I'm not going to the barracks with you pigs."

There was no reaction from Lou, just calm determination.

"Mr. Beausolieu. We already know you deal a little weed, and that you're into Tiger for a couple of Gs you borrowed. We hear you're a little behind in your payments, but to be honest, we don't care. We're just interested in what you might know about this murder. So it's your choice. You can come back to the barracks with us and answer a few questions, or Detective Peterson and I can leave here and tell Tiger you spilled your guts about his loan-sharking operation. I'm sure he'll be anxious to talk to you after our visit."

"OK, OK," the little man said. "I'll go, but you fucking guys better have me back in an hour."

"Certainly, Mr. Beausolieu," Lou responded. Gino still couldn't believe the shit they were taking.

Once they arrived at the barracks, Lou invited Beausolieu to sit in a chair in the conference room. As soon as he sat down, Lou slapped Beausolieu across the back of his head with such force that it knocked him out of the chair and across the room.

As he lay on the floor moaning, Lou stood over him.

"Listen, asshole. The next time the state police come to talk to you, put on your tuxedo, top hat, and tails, and act like you're going to the fucking Ritz Carlton. You ever talk to a trooper like that again, I promise you, I'll find you and beat you senseless. Now, I'm going to put you back in the chair, and Detective Peterson will ask you some questions, which you *will* answer."

Sonny had been missing for three weeks, and his family feared the Mob was responsible. The unit was trying to confirm it was a gambling habit that had gotten him in trouble with the Mob.

When Gino began to question Beausolieu, Lou stood behind the little man.

"Tell us what you know about Sonny Burgess," Gino said.

"He owns a bar near Rhode Island Hospital, and I stop in for a drink every once in a while."

Whack! Lou's hand slapping the little man across the back of his head sounded like a clap of thunder.

"OK! OK! He let me deal a little weed out of the bar; some of his customers wanted more than a drink."

"Was he a gambler?" Gino asked.

"I didn't know him that well."

Whack!

"Jeez, yeah, he had a gambling problem. He was into the Mob for some big numbers. Someone at the bar saw him leave with some wiseguys, and that's the last time anyone saw him."

"Do you know who the wiseguys were?" Lou asked.

"No," he answered.

Beausolieu raised his hands to protect his head, but there was no slap.

"That's all I know, sir, I swear," he said as he slowly lowered his hands.

"Thank you," Gino said.

"You're welcome, sir."

CHAPTER 10

One of the first intelligence-gathering techniques Gino learned when he joined the unit was interviewing inmates. Detectives would wait until a mobster or drug dealer had been sentenced for a crime, and then pay him a visit in jail. The logic was the weight of a heavy sentence might loosen the lips of those who previously would never have dreamed of talking to the police.

What the state police could do for the inmate depended on what he had to offer. If it was valuable information and led to an arrest, the state police would go to the attorney general's office and ask for a sentence reduction or early release.

About a month after his transfer into the unit, Michelle took Gino to the adult correctional institution in Cranston to visit Arnold Sweet. Sweet was a drug dealer and extortionist who stayed friendly with the Mob by paying them a percentage of his ill-gotten gains. He was doing time for murdering a drug dealer who had tried to infringe on his territory.

Sweet was in the maximum-security unit of the prison, where the worst of the worst were housed. Michelle explained that since he was doing a life bid, he might be inclined to part with some information in return for an easier life inside the joint. If what he had to offer was valuable, they would arrange increased visitation, conjugal visits, and even a transfer to a less restrictive unit.

Before they left the unit, Michelle called the warden and arranged the visit. As they drove from Scituate to Cranston, Gino asked for permission to turn on the radio. He tuned in to WPRO, the local rock station, and the refrains of Donna Summer's "She Works Hard for the Money" echoed in the Crown Victoria. When he boosted the volume, Michelle told him to turn it down.

"Sorry, Sarge, but isn't this your theme song?" He hoped the lame joke would loosen her up a bit. Much to his surprise, she laughed, and he sensed a small crack in the hard shell of Michelle Urban.

They arrived at the prison and reported to the visitors room, which was located off the main block of maximum security. After showing their credentials, they were buzzed in and escorted into a small office that was used by the correctional officer in charge of the shift.

Sweet was pulled out of the block under the pretense of an emergency family visit.

As Gino and Michelle sat in the sparse office with the bolted-down furniture, Sweet was led in by two correctional officers. He was dressed in a khaki jumpsuit with his prison number on his chest and ACI printed across his back in large block letters.

Gino took note that he was tall and muscular with short blond hair and a pencil-thin mustache. Looking at Sweet, Gino saw the look most cops could spot a mile away— the look of someone who had spent most of his life in jail. It was unmistakable—a body sculpted by continuous weightlifting, cropped hair cut unevenly to make the inmate unattractive. A hardened look produced by an environment of constant violence.

When Sweet walked in, he looked at the two correctional officers and said, "Family visit? You guys are always messing with our heads."

Michelle asked the officers to leave them alone, and they shackled Sweet to an eyebolt in the wall.

There was no need for introductions; Michelle and Sweet had crossed paths many times. As Michelle began to speak, Gino remained silent; he knew better than to interfere.

"Arnie, I think we might be in a position to make your life a little more bearable."

Sweet was slow to respond, and Gino knew he had to weigh his response carefully. If he chose to cooperate, this would be the first of many meetings. If he chose not to, he had to be sure to remain respectful. Sweet knew that as well as making his life more bearable, the state police were more than capable of making his life miserable if he was disrespectful.

"Sergeant, with all due respect, I'm not interested. I'd appreciate it if you let the screws take me back to the block as soon as possible. I'm sure by now everyone knows you're here, and if I spend more than a few minutes with you, I'll be labeled a rat, and rats don't last very long around here," Sweet said.

Michelle tried one more time. "But we can have you moved off the block right now and put you in protective custody. We just want some information on your contacts with the Raimondi family. You won't even have to testify—"

"Excuse me, Sergeant, I don't mean to interrupt, but you know my record, and you know I've never ratted on anyone. I'm not about to start now just because I'm doing a life bid. I just want to do my time and be left alone."

"Are you sure, Arnie?" she asked.

"I'm sure, Sergeant."

"Well, if you change your mind, just reach out to me, and we can talk," she said.

"Please, Sergeant, call the guards."

Michelle stood and knocked on the door. The correctional officers returned Sweet to his cell.

CHAPTER 11

Michelle was silent as she got into the car, but Gino couldn't resist asking about the visit.

"I guess we didn't accomplish much," he said.

"It doesn't matter what I accomplished today. It's what will happen down the road. What's important is for you to learn how this works."

"What do you mean?" he asked.

"Today was just the start of a slow process. We'll wait a few months and pay him another visit, and we'll visit him again and again and again, until he gives us what we want," she answered.

"When does that happen?" Gino asked.

"Maybe not today, but you never know with these guys. Something happens, and they end up giving you a call. That's why reaching out to them is all part of turning someone into a cooperating witness."

"I don't know. Sweet seemed pretty hard core. I can't see him reaching out."

Michelle continued the lesson. "Agreed, but all that it takes is a crisis at home, or another inmate who decides to stab him with a shiv, and he'll be on the phone in a New York second. Sometimes it happens quickly, and sometimes it takes years. The point is that you have to be persistent, and never take no for an answer."

Gino thought of what it must be like to be in prison: to be in constant fear, never being able to enjoy the simple things, things he took for granted.

As they pulled out of the prison parking lot, Gino decided to ask a favor.

"Sergeant, there's a small record shop on Pontiac Street right around the corner. Can we stop in for just a minute?"

"What for?" she asked.

"I go in there a lot and flip through the old 33s and 45s. Sometimes the owner will order something I can't find. He called me yesterday and told me a 45 I was looking for came in."

"How long is this going to take?" Urban asked. "We've got a lot of work to do."

"It'll take just a minute. I've just got to run in and pay for it."

"All right," she mumbled, and with a shrug of her shoulders, they headed to the record store.

The record store was a converted cottage in a residential neighborhood. It sat on a quiet, tree-lined street, across from an Episcopal church and light-years away from the chaos and mayhem of the prison just around the corner. Except for the **PONTIAC RECORDS** sign over the front door, it looked like many of the small homes in this section of Warwick.

When they pulled up, Gino invited her to come in and look around; he was surprised when she agreed.

Gino was greeted by the owner, an older man with a jovial attitude borne of his dedication to something he loved singularly—music. He quickly disappeared into his back room to retrieve Gino's record.

As Gino waited at the counter, he noticed Michelle flipping through the classical music section. She seemed lost in what she was doing; it made her more human. The stern exterior was stripped away as she flipped through the records.

He walked over. "Classical music fan?"

She spoke gently as she continued to flip through the records. "My dad used to play it all the time. I got hooked."

"My mom was a big opera fan, but I could never get into it."

She looked up. "Let me guess. Rock and roll?"

Gino laughed. "Exactly! That's why I'm here. I've been looking for a 45 of the Young Rascals, and it finally came in."

"The Young Rascals? You must have been a teenager when they were big."

"I can remember watching them on the Ed Sullivan show. I think it was '67. My friends and I were instantly hooked," Gino said.

"I'm sure the fact that they were Italian didn't hurt, either."

He was impressed that she knew, and they both laughed. "OK, maybe that had a little to do with it, but you have to admit, they're good."

They were interrupted by the owner, who reemerged from the back. "Here you go, Gino. "How Can I Be Sure?" by the Young Rascals."

"Thanks. How much?" Gino asked.

"Just give me two bucks, and we're square. Lord knows you spend enough in here."

"Deal," Gino replied.

CHAPTER 12

Richard "Moon" Capelli stood in a Massachusetts courtroom as a young female prosecutor outlined the facts that led a jury to convict Moon and Frank "Marty" Martelinni of assault with a dangerous weapon.

"Your Honor, on the night of June 21, 1980, Manny Costa, president of Local 251 of the Laborers Union, was viciously beaten in Fall River. This defendant, along with Mr. Martelinni, beat Mr. Costa because he wouldn't sign a labor contract filled with no-show jobs."

What was it about Costa that would lead him to defy the Mob? Simply, he placed his workers' interests first and the threats of violence second. In his world, defying the Mob paled in comparison to betraying his people.

Frank "Tiger" Detroia picked Marty for the job; he was the perfect enforcer, all brawn and no brains. Marty was small, but his frame was packed with two hundred pounds of solid muscle. He was a tried-and-true leg breaker, a part of Tiger's crew for over ten years.

What the prosecutor didn't know was that Al Pontarelli, not Moon, went with Marty that night.

She continued, "On January 15, 1982, Mr. Costa pulled into his driveway. The defendant and Mr. Martelinni approached him as he was closing the door of his pickup truck. The defendants then beat Mr. Costa with baseball bats until he was unconscious. The beating left Mr. Costa with a broken jaw, three cracked ribs, and countless bruises. Two neighbors noticed the men sitting in a car with Rhode Island plates directly across the street from Costa's house shortly before the attack."

Marty was stupid enough to use his own car to travel to Fall River that night. A simple registration check by the police showed the car belonged to him. It was only a matter of time before the second individual was identified.

The Fall River Police Department knew the beating of a union official was no ordinary assault. It was common knowledge that the Raimondi crime family controlled all of the unions in New England.

The Fall River Police Department contacted the Rhode Island State Police and asked about Marty's associates. One name appeared over and over again:

Richard "Moon" Capelli. Detectives prepared two six-picture photo lineups for Costa to view. The first lineup had a picture of Frank "Marty" Martelinni, and the second, Richard "Moon" Capelli. Fall River detectives showed a reluctant Costa both lineups. He identified Marty without hesitation. Some gentle prodding led to the misidentification of Moon as the second individual.

"On behalf of the Commonwealth, the district attorney recommends the maximum sentence of twenty years." The prosecutor sat. She nodded to Mr. Costa, who watched from the gallery.

Moon's lawyer made a plea for leniency, but the judge had no mercy.

"The Commonwealth of Massachusetts sentences you to twenty years at the Massachusetts Correctional Institute at Walpole."

The events leading up to this miscarriage of justice came flooding back to Moon, and the judge's words became white noise.

The prosecutors had offered them both five years in prison in return for pleading guilty. Although he wasn't guilty, Moon was more than willing to take the plea and do the time. He figured with good behavior, he would be out in three, but if the case went to trial, he could face a longer sentence. Marty wanted to go to trial; he thought they could beat the charges.

As was the Mob's custom, they took their disagreement to their boss, Tiger, who told them to go with

Marty's instincts and rely on the lawyers. The result was two guilty verdicts.

I'm looking at twenty years in prison, he thought as he sat in the holding cell after the sentencing. *I just turned sixty-five; this is a death sentence.*

Moon was put in a van with the usual collection of drug dealers, child molesters, and robbers, all on their way to the living hell called prison.

At Walpole State Prison, Moon went through the same processing he had been through a dozen times; he was no stranger to the prison system. But this time it was different: he was innocent.

Yeah, right, he thought, *who the hell is ever going to believe me? Every fucker in here says they're innocent.*

CHAPTER 13

Intelligence unit, Detective Peterson."

A female voice asked, "Will you accept a collect call from inmate Richard Capelli at Walpole State Prison?"

"I'll accept the charges, operator," Gino said.

"Go ahead, Mr. Capelli. Your party has accepted the charges."

"Moon, to what do I owe this pleasure? It's been a few years," Gino said, but there was no reply. He tried again. "How's it going, Moon?"

Finally he spoke. "Pretty shitty. How do you think it's going? You fuckers put me here."

Gino could hear the venom, but there was also a slight quiver, a hint of vulnerability.

Gino remembered him not only as a bookie, but also as a young man who left the neighborhood to become an airborne ranger. He tried to escape the neighborhood; instead, it ripped him back with the siren song of money, women, and fancy cars.

"If you're looking for an apology or sympathy, you're barking up the wrong tree, Moon."

"No, just called to catch up on old times. I wanted to know if you were like the rest of your cop friends. You know, putting guys in jail for things they didn't do. I figured you were better than that."

"What are you trying to say, Moon? That I'm not a stand-up guy because I'm a cop?" Gino said.

"I'm just saying, you took a different path. You chose a way of life that's the total opposite of what we were taught in the neighborhood. Maybe it's because you're only half Italian. I don't know."

"Listen, Moon. I don't really have time to walk down memory lane, and I bet there are about twenty guys who would kick your ass to get to that phone."

"They can wait," Moon said. "Just one more thing, Gino. Say hello to my friend Dickie." The line went dead.

CHAPTER 14

G ino thought about Moon's parting words. *Say hello to my friend Dickie. What the hell does that mean?* The unit had recently arrested a low-level drug dealer named Dickie Palazzo, but Gino knew of no connection with Moon. Gino remembered some intelligence the unit had gathered on a Dickie Sanchez who was running a Mob-sanctioned gambling operation, but it was small-time, and he could not fathom that Moon would waste a phone call to the cops about something that insignificant.

The rest of the unit gathered around his desk, and the banter began. Tim Sullivan chimed in, "Dickie? Is it a code name for someone?"

Sullivan stood about six feet tall and carried 225 chunky pounds. He had sandy-colored hair and a freckled face that gave him a youthful look. He was a legacy; his father retired as a lieutenant, and Sully followed in his footsteps. He graduated from Boston College, joined the state police, and then was transferred into the intelligence unit after eight years as a uniformed trooper.

"Remember the wiretap we did on Moon's gambling operation when you first came into the unit, Gino?" Quinn asked.

Quinn was the forensic and wiretap expert and looked nothing like the prototypical trooper. He was short and round and looked like the Gerber baby. Peach fuzz substituted for a beard, and a small wisp of hair sat on the crown of his bald head.

Gino was always amazed at the analytical approach Quinn took toward investigating crime. Most detectives were all about banging on doors, interviewing witnesses, and interrogating suspects in the hopes of getting a confession. They would interview dozens of witnesses and suspects before solving a crime.

Quinn was different. He would narrow down the suspects and witnesses to be interviewed by examining records relating to the victim. He would carefully pore over phone records, bank and credit card statements, and prison visitors lists, anything that related to the crime or victim. They were pieces of a puzzle, and Quinn put them together so he could pinpoint who to talk to, and who was the most likely suspect. When he confronted the suspect, he usually had enough information to elicit a confession.

Gino thought Quinn was ahead of his time, but his peers often criticized him because in the '80s, brawn still trumped brains in the macho world of police work.

"Sure, how could I ever forget that? It was my first wire, and I was paranoid about the minimization."

Courts required officers to shut off the recording device when the conversation was not criminal in nature to "minimize" the intrusion of privacy. The courts also allowed an officer to periodically turn on the recording device to ensure the conversation had not turned back into something criminal. The trick was how often to check and how long you should listen until you determined the conversation was not criminal.

Failure to minimize could result in all the evidence from the wiretap being excluded at trial. As a result, turning the recorder on and off was tricky—but it also led to hearing some interesting conversations.

Quinn started his story.

"Moon had all his customers use code names. Remember the guy who'd call and say, 'It's me, the Italian Stallion'? Sometimes Moon would be in a ball-busting mood. 'Who is this again?' 'The Italian Stallion,' the reply would come. 'Who?' Moon asked him again. 'The Italian Stallion, Moon. Come on, Moon, it's me, Mario.' 'Oh, Mario! Why didn't you say so?' 'What the fuck are you trying to do, Moon, get me arrested?' 'So what if you get arrested, Mario?

That's the chance you take when you bet over the phone.'

Mario tells Moon, 'Well, if I get arrested, I'll just plead the Fifth Commandment.'" The room burst into laughter.

Quinn told the story of another wiretap. "'So how's your kid doing?' one mobster asked another. 'Great,' replied the other. 'How old is he now?' 'He's seventeen and growing like a tree stump.'" More laughter. "So the mobster continued, 'Wow, that's great. He's still in school?' 'Yeah, he's a southpaw in high school.'"

"Hey, Quinn," Sully jumped in, "remember that time the inmate escaped from work release at the prison? Listen to this. We got a call that an inmate had an argument with his girlfriend during visiting hours and bolted from the building. We caught him hiding under a small plastic kiddy pool in the backyard of a house off Reservoir Avenue. After we cuffed him and threw him in the backseat, he asks Quinn, 'Hey, what are you guys going to charge me with?' Quinn says, 'Escape from the adult correctional institution.' 'Escape?' the guy says. 'Escape? The best you got me for is breach of promise. I promised not to run away.'"

Michelle came out of her office. "What's going on, gentlemen? Not enough work to do?"

"Gino got a call from Moon at the prison, and we were just trying to figure out what he meant when he mentioned the name Dickie," Sullivan answered.

"What exactly did he say?" Michelle asked.

"Say hello to my friend Dickie," Gino answered.

Gino was still trying to make a connection to either Palazzo the drug dealer or Sanchez the bookie.

"Dickie?" Michelle said. "Maybe he was talking about Dickie Calderone. A rival of Tiger's who got whacked in '74. His body was found in Massachusetts, but the case was never solved. It sounds like Moon is trying to deliver a message."

Gino tried not to show his excitement. Could it be Moon wanted to talk to him about the Calderone case? After all, they had a history together—sometimes the ties of the old neighborhood still held.

"Pull the Calderone case, Gino," Michelle said. "Read it, because we'll be paying Moon a visit."

CHAPTER 15

Buried in the small closet that masqueraded as the unit's records room was a box marked **CALDERONE HOMICIDE (74-128)**, covered in dust. It hadn't been touched in years.

It was late in the afternoon, and Gino wanted to go home to read the file. But he couldn't leave yet, because no one left work until Colonel Smith made his nightly drive through the parking lot to make sure everyone was still working.

Colonel Walter E. Smith ruled the Rhode Island State Police with an iron fist. He had grown up on the streets of Providence and became a trooper in the late '20s.

Smith earned his reputation as a fearless cop when he and his partner, Detective Theodore Urban, gunned down two bank robbers. As the robbers entered the bank on a snowy December day, Smith and

Urban were waiting. Detective Smith yelled, "Merry Christmas, motherfuckers!" and a hail of buckshot brought the robbers down like a driving rain.

Many in the press would allege Smith and Urban planned an execution, not a stakeout. Their rants fell on deaf ears; it was, after all, the Roaring Twenties. Smith would rise steadily through the ranks to become colonel. Urban became head of the detective division, a post he held until his retirement.

Smith was incorruptible, uncompromising, and a man whose entire life was police work. He spent his career battling the Mob and keeping the state government out of state police business. The colonel used his power as a weapon, keeping politicians at bay and his troopers in line.

He controlled every aspect of a trooper's life: assignments, schedules, vacations, and the most coveted prize: promotions. The colonel was fond of saying to his command staff, "I have a very simple philosophy, gentlemen. If you work hard, uphold the reputation of the state police, and avoid booze and broads, you'll have no reason to fear me. If you fail to follow these simple rules, I will drive you from my state police."

Those who chose to work for Colonel Smith made a total commitment to police work. Their personal lives came in a distant second.

At about seven thirty, the colonel's black Crown Victoria moved slowly through the parking lot and out of the driveway. Gino heard the blinds in Urban's office snap into place, and a few minutes later, she walked out of her office and out the door. Gino and the others watched as she pulled out of the lot and followed suit.

CHAPTER 16

G ino's apartment was on the second floor of a two-family house in Cranston, a working-class suburb of Providence. His widowed landlord, Esther Ricci, charged him two hundred dollars a month rent. Gino appreciated the cheap rent, even though he had to endure a nosy landlord.

Gino entered the sweltering apartment and turned on the air conditioner. His mother had furnished his apartment in a style that could only be described as "tolerable" for a young bachelor. He had obediently paid for the furniture his mother picked out, and he suffered in silence as she decorated his apartment.

Gino's sanctuary was a small room he converted into a makeshift office. Inside, he was surrounded by his most prized possessions, Yankee memorabilia. Surrounded by Red Sox fans at work, he was forced to become a closeted Yankees fan. Framed pictures of his heroes—Ruth, Gehrig, DiMaggio, and Berra—hung on the walls. Most prized, however, was a large framed picture of Maris, Mantle, and Berra standing on the steps of the Yankees dugout, bats in hand, ready to do battle.

On a card table, stacks of photo albums were filled with scores of baseball cards collected in his youth. Magazines and books about the storied franchise sat neatly in a roll top desk Gino had picked up at a flea market.

From the refrigerator, he took out some veal parmigiana and pasta wrapped in aluminum foil. The attached note read, *Gino, 350 degrees for thirty minutes. Love, Momma.* As the veal heated and the room cooled, he began reading the Dickie Calderone case.

After a few hours, Gino finally succumbed to the weariness of a long day. His last thought as he drifted off to sleep was what the connection could be between Moon and the Calderone homicide. Selfishly, he could only think that if Moon took part in this gangland slaying, and he was reaching out to Gino, it could be a career maker.

CHAPTER 17

As he got into his Caddy the next morning, Gino was greeted by Mrs. Ricci as she headed off to morning Mass at St. Lucy's on Providence's Federal Hill.

"Did you have a quiet night, Gino?"

"Very quiet, Mrs. Ricci. Don't forget to say a prayer for me," Gino replied.

She smiled and nodded as they parted for two different worlds. As Mrs. Ricci continued on to church, Gino wondered if she knew about the women she knelt and prayed with every morning, old women who prayed for their offspring, hoping for health, success, and long lives. Did Mrs. Ricci know that some of the children of these women were in the Mob and responsible for the misery caused by drugs, gambling, prostitution, and murder? Her only clue had to come when they passed the collection basket and these so-called pious women dropped in hundred-dollar bills.

He took the slow drive up Route 116, and as he passed the Scituate reservoir, a hint of fall air blew in the windows. Tall pine trees stood guard around the waters of the reservoir, and the watershed represented a purity and tranquility foreign to the world of cops and mobsters.

Michelle was at her desk when he arrived around nine. Gino had come to learn that you waited at least half hour to gauge her disposition before you even thought of asking her a question.

At nine thirty on the button, he approached her. "Sergeant, I started to read the Calderone file last night, and I have some questions."

"Did you read the entire case?" Michelle asked.

"Not really. I fell asleep around two, but I got through the reports of Kelly finding the body and the Mass State Police reports of the scene."

"All right, gather round, gentlemen. I'm going to give you a little history lesson on the Calderone case," Michelle said.

Despite what they might have felt about her personally, the entire unit knew she was a wealth of information when it came to the Mob.

As she began speaking, some of the guys took out pads and wrote down notes, while others just listened.

"Back in the '70s, the wiseguys were in a bit of disarray," Michelle said. "Pasquale Raimondi ruled all of New England ruthlessly. He commanded fear among his soldiers and a great deal of respect in the neighborhood.

"Raimondi had two small-time bookmakers shot to death for failing to kick back a percentage of their operation. The two bookies were gunned down as they picked up some groceries in a small market. Nicky Gemma was the shooter.

"Even more amazing was the reaction of the neighborhood. There was no outcry about the violence, no concern that some innocent person would be hurt; they knew the Mob would never harm them because they were considered 'civilians.'"

Gino listened as Michelle moved on to her scouting report of Frank "Tiger" Detroia and his crew. She explained that Tiger's crew was made up of criminals anxious to please him; they were willing to do anything to help him achieve his goal of becoming a made man. The crew was made up of Moon, Frank "Marty" Martelinni, John "Big John" Kazarian, and William "Billy" Franco.

Big John Kazarian was about six foot five and weighed well over three hundred pounds. He had a full head of black hair, a pockmarked face, and a nose as crooked as Rhode Island's coastline. Big John knew he could never become a made man because he was Armenian; he was content to be an enforcer.

Marty Martelinni was as stupid as he was short, and he was the perfect enforcer. When Marty and Big John teamed up, they looked like Danny DeVito and Arnold Schwarzenegger. Their specialty was shaking down nightclubs for Tiger.

Michelle explained the shakedown was accomplished by the two posing as doormen for the owner, collecting a cover charge. The money they collected went to Tiger, not the owner, and this was only after the duo skimmed an appropriate amount off the top for themselves. In return, the owner received the services of Marty and Big John as bouncers.

This was just one form of extortion Tiger's crew used to make money. Extortion was the Mob's "street tax" on strip club owners, bookies, drug dealers, and burglars. For criminals, it was the cost of doing illegal business. You either paid with cash or broken body parts. A simple set of rules, enforced by individuals devoid of any sense of humanity.

Gino respected Moon; he had a reputation for treating his customers fairly and giving many a losing bettor extra time to satisfy his debt. He, unlike his other Mob friends, served in the Army, which Gino found admirable.

William "Billy" Franco was not your typical wiseguy. He was more of a pretty boy than a gangster; he hung around Tiger in the hope of living off Tiger's reputation.

Billy's father died when he was only five, and he was constantly looking for a father figure. Billy spent half his life trying to be a tough guy, and the other half, a family man.

Michelle sounded like a psychologist as she talked about Billy. She told them Billy continued his search for a father figure when his uncle died, and unfortunately, he found Tiger. He worked a series of menial jobs during the day and spent his nights following Tiger around like a puppy.

Michelle described Billy as small and rugged. She compared his looks with Fonzie from *Happy Days*. Tiger used him for hijacking trucks, fencing stolen goods, and loan sharking.

Gino decided to impress his boss. "I remember when I was in uniform stopping Tiger, Moon, Frank, and Billy as they were leaving a nightclub in Providence. Billy was pretty meek, even with his crew around."

"Yeah, Peterson, we remember the mountain of field intelligence reports you sent in when you were campaigning to get into the unit. Suck-ass," Sully said.

"I was just doing my job," Gino shot back.

Sully was angered by Gino's response. "You're lucky you're even on the job, never mind in this unit. I don't give a fuck how many arrests you've made or how much you've studied. I still don't trust you, and as far as I'm concerned, you're just a cleaned-up version of one of them."

The room went silent as the resentment and distrust that Gino had hoped he had erased with hard work reared its ugly head.

"All right, knock it off," Michelle said. She was pissed, and they knew enough to shut up. "I don't want to hear any more of that bullshit. Let's get to Tiger and finish this up. Everyone knew Tiger's reputation—a psychopath with a twisted sense of humor. He's two hundred and fifty pounds, easy, with thinning hair and bushy eyebrows. Only in Tiger's case, his eyes aren't the gateway to his soul, because the fucker has no soul."

"Pretty profound, Sarge," Lou said. Even Sully laughed, and the tension broke.

"Back then, he wasn't a made guy—just an up-and-comer with a decent crew—but something changed after the Calderone murder. We all assumed Tiger became a made man because he carried out the contract to kill Calderone. There just wasn't any evidence to connect him to the hit. Enough story time for one day. Gino, stay on the file, and tomorrow we'll talk about what our next move will be."

CHAPTER 18

G ino arrived at his apartment around seven thirty, took off his suit, and slipped into a pair of Bermuda shorts and a T-shirt. He popped a piece of his mother's lasagna in the oven and opened a beer. As he stretched out on his small sofa, he read the autopsy report of Dickie Calderone.

Bristol County Medical Examiner Dr. Arnold Katz's autopsy was written in the sterile medical language of a man who cuts open dead bodies for a living.

The report read, *This white male suffered six gunshot wounds to the back from a .38 caliber revolver. Deceased was stabbed seven times in the chest and slashed once across the face. There is post-mortem evidence of trauma to the body, most likely caused by it being moved from one point to another.*

The autopsy photos showed that Dickie Calderone had been sent to his maker in an exceedingly vicious manner. Riddled with bullet holes and knife wounds, this was no ordinary Mob hit—this was personal. No report could describe the horror of how Calderone was executed, but the photos spoke volumes of the brutality.

Gino found the detective activity reports and surveillance photos taken by retired State Police Detective Francis McCaffrey. The reports contained all of the intelligence gathered on Tiger's crew. The photos were mostly of the Pineapple Social Club, the crew's hangout, a small bar located on Spruce Street, just off Atwells Avenue on Federal Hill.

Although the legal age to drink alcohol was twenty-one by then, Gino remembered going to the Pineapple when he turned eighteen and treating himself to his first legal beer. It was a place where old men gathered during the day to drink and play cards. There was sawdust on the floor and a bathroom consisting of an old, stained commode hung on a wall of slate. As day turned into night, young hoods replaced the old men.

The photos depicted a one-story brick building with glass windows and a large bar stretching along the entire back wall. Photos of the inside showed sports memorabilia from the Red Sox, Celtics, and Bruins hung in a haphazard fashion. Prominently displayed was an autographed picture of former heavyweight champ Rocky Marciano. The native New Englander, a hero in the Italian community, was treated with the same reverence as the pope.

One of the detective activity reports written by McCaffrey indicated that during the course of the murder investigation, McCaffrey reached out to one of his confidential informants. The informant offered a story of a sit-down requested by Calderone because of disrespect shown to him by Tiger.

About six months before Calderone's murder, his brother Rico was out on the town with two friends. Around two o'clock in the morning, after visiting several nightclubs, Rico and his buddies decided to stop into the Pineapple Social Club for a nightcap. Rico knew it was Tiger's club, but stopped in with a sense of security since he was the brother of a made man.

Tiger was bartending that night and gave the trio their drinks on the house as a sign of respect. At one point, Rico became unhappy with the time it took Tiger to bring him a second drink, and he called him a "fat fuck."

Tiger's temper flared, and he came across the bar with a club and hit Rico on the side of the head, knocking him off his stool. Tiger continued to hit Rico until his crew dragged him off; Rico limped out of the bar, vowing to tell his brother.

The informant told McCaffrey the sit-down was held at the club a few days later. The word had come down from Pasquale for Nicky Gemma to mediate the dispute. Tiger and his crew sat at one end of the club, Dickie and his crew at the other. Nicky sat alone at a table, sipping a glass of his favorite Scotch, Chivas Regal. Nicky slowly finished his drink and with the wave of a hand called the two to join him at the table.

According to the informant, the meeting ended abruptly. Gino wondered what was said during the sit-down, but there was no escaping the fact that six months later, Dickie Calderone was dead. There was only one explanation: Tiger killed Calderone, and Moon knew it.

CHAPTER 19

G ino arrived at the intelligence unit around eight the next morning. Despite the golden rule of waiting a half hour, Gino approached Michelle as soon as she arrived. He told her that he thought Moon held the key to cracking the Calderone murder, and after listening to him, she agreed. His conversation with Michelle produced a flurry of phone calls and a meeting with the colonel.

The next day, Michelle called the unit together.

"We're going to try to flip Moon. He's obviously got info on the Calderone murder, and if he wants to get out of prison, he's going to have to cooperate. We're going to get Gino into Walpole, posing as a lawyer, so that he can talk to Moon."

As she spoke, Gino became nervous at the thought of walking into the prison.

"The only ones who'll know that Gino is a cop will be a Mass trooper and the warden. They'll get you inside, Gino, and give you a place to speak to Moon. We go tomorrow afternoon."

Gino returned to his desk, dreading that his worst fear would soon come true: being held hostage in prison. The prison riot of Attica was still fresh in his mind, and he recalled the grainy video of correctional officers held hostage by rioting inmates. They were bound and blindfolded and put on display in the yard. Behind each officer, an inmate held a makeshift knife to his throat. When one thousand New York state troopers entered the facility to end the riot, the ensuing gunfire killed eight correctional officers and thirty inmates. Tragically, the guards were killed not by inmates, but by friendly fire.

Gino showed up the next day in his best preppy suit, with slicked-back hair, sporting a pair of horn-rimmed glasses. He prayed it would be enough to fool men who'd survived life on the streets and in prison by not being fooled.

Michelle called him into her office.

"Gino, you're going to meet Trooper Mike Newton of the Mass State Police at the warden's office. Lou and Quinn will go with you, but then you're on your own."

He tried not to show any fear, but it was radiating up from the pit of his stomach. His only hope was that she didn't see it in his face.

"Gino, be careful," she said, as she gently touched his forearm. Her lingering hand on his forearm seemed to be more than a simple expression of concern. There was something in her touch that made him believe she was trying to send a subtle message, a message there could be more between them.

The trip to Walpole took about forty-five minutes from Scituate. As Gino drove in a seized BMW, Quinn and Lou followed. Thoughts of Michelle invaded his mind like hundreds of arrows flying into a target. He tried to concentrate on the visit to the prison, but he began to think of her as more than his boss. For the first time, he thought of her as a woman.

He met Newton and the warden, Harold McDonald, in the warden's office. Newton was a twenty-year veteran who took the Walpole assignment because the investigations didn't require much legwork, since all of his suspects were a "captive audience."

The warden, a nondescript civil servant, had acquired the mentality of those working and living in a prison: a chip on the shoulder combined with an inherent mistrust of government.

Detective Newton presented Gino with credentials for fictional attorney Richard Lovett. Gino walked the short distance from the warden's office to maximum security. The unit was housed in a stone building with guard towers at each of its four corners. Built in the early 1900s, it looked more like a European castle than a prison. However, in this castle, there were no knights or ladies-in-waiting, only the dregs of society.

He went to the visitors desk and identified himself as attorney Richard Lovett. The correctional officer asked him to wait until an escort was available. As he waited, he sat among the wives, girlfriends, and children of Walpole's inmates.

He thought back to a time when he was in uniform and there was a riot at Rhode Island's prison. Troopers moved into the prison to supplement the correctional officers. The original visiting room had been destroyed in the riot, and a makeshift visitors room was set up in the prison cafeteria.

No physical barrier separated visitors from inmates as they sat across from each other. Gino sat in awe, as female visitors masturbated their significant others, their hands furiously stroking away under the table without a hint of shame.

A voice bellowing, "Attorney Richard Lovett!" snapped him out of his daydream. A correctional officer with **WALL** on his uniform nameplate looked around the room until Gino got up. Gino sensed that Wall was not interested in anything other than putting in his eight hours and getting home.

Wall said, "Moon is housed in D block. Since this isn't a regularly scheduled visit, you're going to meet your client in a room just off the block."

"Sorry for messing up your schedule, but the judge asked for a motion by tomorrow," Gino said.

"Part of the job," Wall grumbled.

Gino put on a visitor's pass and took a deep breath as he passed through the first set of cell doors. They entered the bullpen, a room that allowed access to the three separate cellblocks that made up the maximum security unit.

"Ready?" Wall asked.

"Sure," he said, trying to sound like he had done this a hundred times. He prayed a silent prayer, because Wall did not impress him as the type of CO who would protect him if things went bad.

As they entered B block, Gino glanced at the three tiers of the block, each containing about twenty cells. The inmates were out of their cells and hanging over the rails, watching the show. Obviously, any distraction from the routine of prison life was welcomed.

As he walked the corridor from the entrance of the cellblock to the rear of the tier, the catcalls began. "Hey, I paid for that suit!" one inmate called out.

"If it wasn't for you, I wouldn't be in here, mouthpiece," another chimed in, and finally, the ever-popular "fucking lawyers" resounded.

Gino continued to walk with eyes straight ahead, hoping that no one recognized him as a cop.

CHAPTER 20

The walk to the end of the cellblock seemed to take forever. Gino entered the small holding room, and there stood Richard "Moon" Capelli. There was instant recognition in his eyes, but he didn't say a word to Officer Wall.

"Inmate Capelli, you have thirty minutes with your attorney. He'll let me know when you're done. Do you understand?" Wall said.

"Yeah, no problem," Moon replied.

Wall left the room, and Moon spoke first. "I haven't seen a lawyer since the trial, so I couldn't figure out what the fuck was going on till I saw you walk through the door."

"Look, Moon, we don't have a lot of time. The colonel sent me to find out if you want to cooperate."

"Gino, here's the story. I didn't beat up Costa, and I'm not going to rot in jail for the rest of my life for something I didn't do."

"Well, if it wasn't you, then who was it?"

"It was Al Pontarelli. Just show his picture to Costa—he'll tell you it wasn't me."

"That's for your lawyer to do, not us. If you have new evidence, that's your problem, not ours," Gino said.

"How the fuck can I go to my lawyer with this? He's wired to Nicky and Tiger. If I try to give up one of Tiger's guys, they'd kill me right here in prison."

"What are you talking about?"

Moon explained that just before the start of the trial, Tiger got them together with their lawyers, Richard Silverman and Americo Salvatore, to talk about the plea offered by the district attorney. The Massachusetts prosecutors were offering a straightforward deal: if both pled guilty, they would receive five years in prison.

"I begged Tiger, please, let us take the deal. But Marty tells him the lawyers are going to muddy up the identification and we should roll the dice with the jury. What the fuck, I said to Tiger. I wasn't even there, and this guy wants to roll the dice with my future. Tiger tells us, go with Marty's gut feeling."

"What did you do?" Gino asked.

"What the fuck was I going to do at that point? He's the boss," Moon explained.

"So you went to trial?" he asked.

"Right, we go to trial, and we're both found guilty. Now I'm here doing twenty years for something I didn't do. Salvatore and Silverman are right up Tiger's ass, so how can I turn to them?"

"So what do you want to do?" Gino said.

"I'm telling you, I'm not doing the rest of my life in prison because of that asshole Marty. He got thirty years because of his record and what he did, and he deserves every day of it. But I'm innocent. You get me out of here, and I'll give you Tiger, Marty, Billy, and Big John for the Calderone murder," Moon said.

"How can we be sure you're not lying?" Gino said.

Moon became angry. "Because I was there when Tiger shot him. I was there when Marty and Big John loaded him in the trunk for his last ride to Rehoboth. Only someone who was there would know all of that. Is that enough for you, half-breed?"

Gino's instinct was to strike back, but he knew a fistfight in a cellblock didn't exactly scream "attorney visit."

"I'll deliver your message to my boss," he said.

Gino knocked on the heavy metal door and waited for Wall to take him back.

When Wall opened the door, Gino tried to sound like a lawyer. "I'll start on that motion as soon as I get back to the office, Mr. Capelli."

Wall and Gino made the slow walk back through the block. He turned his pass in at the visitors desk and walked out of the prison. Gino drove about a mile and radioed Lou and Quinn that he was clear.

Gino's ride back seemed like fifteen minutes, not forty-five. He rushed up the long cement walk that led to the intelligence unit. Michelle was behind her desk when he walked in.

Michelle cradled the phone to her ear. "As soon as Lou and Quinn get here, we'll talk." No sooner had she uttered those words than the duo appeared, anxious to hear the outcome of the interview.

He caught himself staring at her, wondering what she would look like with her hair down and a glass of wine in her hand. Pure fantasy, but her touch had earned him the right.

They gathered in Michelle's small office, and Gino began. "Sergeant, Moon's willing to give up Tiger, Big John, Marty, and Billy on the Calderone murder. He just wants us to get him out from under the beef he's doing for the beating of Costa. He still says it was Al Pontarelli, not him."

Michelle said, "Do you believe him?"

Gino spoke carefully. "Yes, Sergeant. I remember him from the old neighborhood. He was a lot of things, but he was never a bullshitter."

Urban pulled at the bun on top of her head. "I have to go see the colonel."

CHAPTER 21

After two days of meetings with the colonel, Michelle called the unit together. As she spoke, Gino noticed she was fingering a diamond earring, and the small circular motion of her finger became hypnotic. Since she'd touched his arm before his prison visit, any subtle movement she made seemed to pull his attention to thoughts of a relationship.

"We've made arrangements for Moon to be brought to the Bristol County Courthouse on a phony motion for a new trial. Once he's there, the judge will transfer him into our custody. He's still a sentenced inmate, so we're going to keep him in the cellblock at headquarters," Michelle said.

"What about security when we get him back?" Gino asked.

"Security for Moon will be provided by uniformed troopers from eight at night until eight in the morning."

"An overtime detail without a lot of heavy lifting; the troops will be happy," Gino said.

"The rest of the time, he's our responsibility. That means Lou, Quinn, and Sully will work on the debriefings and running down the leads. Gino, you'll be providing security for Moon during the day."

The words went through him like he was standing in a pail of water and someone dropped in a hair dryer. He had just become the most expensive babysitter in the state of Rhode Island.

Michelle continued, "We go to court tomorrow, so be prepared to bring Moon back and lock him up. We'll start working on the Calderone murder and the Costa beating as soon as he's tucked away."

"What about the gambling wiretap we've got going?" Lou asked.

"We're going to shut down the wire. There's enough evidence on it against Billy to get an arrest warrant. That's the leverage we'll use to flip him if we decide to make a move on him."

Gino walked back to his desk, pissed. Moon had reached out to him—he should be working the case, not babysitting. He tried to rationalize the decision by telling himself he was the newest member of the unit and had no reason to bitch. In Mob vernacular, he hadn't "made his bones." No big cases under his belt, no murders solved, not enough on his resume to even begin to complain—but it still stung.

Gino wanted to say something to Michelle, but she was talking to Quinn about ending the wiretap. Gino was sent to North Providence to disconnect the large reel-to-reel tape recorders and clean up the apartment. The phone company would be notified to disconnect the line after the court order to end the wiretap was issued.

Gino finished collecting the equipment and cleaning the apartment around seven o'clock. He headed home, grabbed something to eat, and hit the sack early. He was determined to plead his case to Michelle in the morning.

CHAPTER 22

G ino arrived at seven o'clock the next morning and waited for Michelle to arrive. Usually the first to get there, she was surprised when she saw him sitting at his desk.

"Can I speak to you?" he asked.

"Sure, just give me a minute to get settled," she said.

Michelle hung up her coat and dropped the tea bag from her Styrofoam cup into the wastebasket.

"What's up?" she asked as she took her first sip.

"Sergeant, with all due respect, I feel like I should be working these cases, not just babysitting."

"Really?" she said, and Gino sensed this wasn't going to end well.

He started to backpedal. "I'm just saying. Moon called me, and I think I should be more involved." Then he became just plain stupid. "You know, Sergeant, maybe it's because I'm half Italian, but I always get the feeling I'm not trusted, and I have to work harder than everybody else just to prove I belong. Now I got Sully on my case."

Gino hadn't told Michelle, but he had a rocky history with Sully. When he was a young trooper, he had investigated a car accident involving Sully and a young woman. Sully was driving to work in his detective car and collided with the woman at an intersection in Scituate.

After Gino investigated the accident, he issued the woman a ticket for failing to control her vehicle. She was livid. As she protested, Gino mentioned that if she wanted to contest the ticket, she should hire an attorney. Sully overheard the conversation, and as soon as the woman drove away, he started berating Gino about not being a stand-up guy. He made it clear that Gino had no clue how to protect another trooper and that he was disloyal by suggesting she hire a lawyer.

From that day on, he never let Gino forget the incident and never missed an opportunity to tell other troopers that Gino had tried to fuck him. Gino might have understood Sully's initial reaction, but as the years passed and the abuse continued, he realized the venom went far beyond giving someone advice about fighting a traffic ticket.

Before he could utter another word, she shut the door. Her breathing became more rapid, her cheeks flushed, and her eyes narrowed.

"Work harder? You've got to be kidding. I'm the first female supervisor in the history of the state police.

Not just any supervisor, but the boss of the intelligence unit. It doesn't get any more boys-only than this unit. Three-quarters of the troopers out there think the only reason I'm on the job in the first place is because of my dad," Michelle said.

"But…"

"Half Italian? Give me a break. Try being a woman boss who has to show every day that I can command. You don't think I've heard the rumors? You don't think they bother me? A lesbian? A baby born out of wedlock? Give me a break. And if you can't handle Sully, then maybe you *don't* belong here." She took a deep breath and her voice lowered. "Go back to your desk, get to work, and earn the right to come in here and bitch to me. Understand, Detective?"

"Yes, Sergeant."

As soon as Gino left the room, Michelle's feelings about him came rushing back to her. The reason she had reacted so harshly was that she had feelings for him—feelings she was trying to hide. She desperately tried to will them away, telling herself she couldn't possibly be falling for someone she worked with, someone she was supposed to supervise.

As strong as she knew she was, the feelings were stronger. Gino possessed all the qualities she wanted in a man. He was smart and funny, with a stubborn streak that reminded her of her father. He was easy on the eyes—wavy black hair and green eyes that betrayed a hint of loneliness. All she could think about was what it would be like to lie in bed with him. *Shit.*

CHAPTER 23

Gino arrived home that night looking forward to a quiet night. He had just put the Beatles' *A Hard Day's Night* on his record player when the phone rang.

"Gino, I need you to take me to a wake at Sardella's. Mrs. Petronio was going to take me, but her grandson's sick, and she had to take care of him."

"A wake tonight, Mom? Do you have to go?" he asked.

"Yes, I have to go. And the more I think about it, you should come inside with me and pay your respects," she said.

"Why, who is it?" he asked.

"Mr. Lombardozzi. He was ninety-six," she answered.

"Ray Lombardozzi, the mobster? You want me to go to a mobster's wake—"

"Whatever he was, that was a long time ago," his mother interjected. "More importantly, he was good to me—especially after your father passed away."

"Wasn't he the guy who straightened out the beef Dad had with the guy who made a pass at you?" he asked.

"That was just a misunderstanding, and yes, Mr. Lombardozzi corrected the situation. He also helped me get a job after your blessed father passed. We owe him the respect."

She was suddenly silent, and Gino knew it was her way of insisting. *What would be the harm if I slipped in and out with my mom?* he thought. If anyone saw him, he would just say that he was accompanying his mother. Lombardozzi was so old, he doubted anyone would pay much attention to his passing.

Gino relented and picked up his mom at her tenement house on Federal Hill. They drove to Sardella's, just a few minutes away, a large Victorian house that was converted into a funeral home.

As Gino had suspected, at age ninety-six, Lombardozzi did not have much family to mourn him, just two grandchildren. He had been out of the rackets for so long, Gino did not even see anyone inside who remotely resembled a wiseguy.

They knelt at the coffin, said a quick prayer, and paid their condolences to the grandchildren. Gino and his mom sat in the chairs in front of the coffin and used the time to catch up. It was a curious place to speak to each other of his job, family, and her aches and pains, but that was life.

Having arrived at seven o'clock, the start of the calling hours, Gino convinced his mother that by seven-twenty, they had satisfied their obligation. They left, and he drove her home.

As Gino left the funeral home and headed toward his car, he was unaware that he had drawn the attention of the detective inside the surveillance van parked across the street. The white panel van was plastered with signs indicating it was a Bell telephone truck. In reality, it was no phone truck, but a state police surveillance van manned that night by Detective Tim Sullivan.

Earlier that day, Urban had assigned Sully to survey the Lombardozzi wake. She did not share the assignment with Gino or any other member of the unit. If pertinent info was obtained, it would be shared in due time.

Sully was sipping on stale coffee and dying to relieve himself through the periscope that masqueraded as a vent at the top of the van.

Attached to the periscope was a camera, and Sully clicked away furiously when he saw Gino walking the old lady into the funeral home. Until Gino's appearance, it had been an uneventful night, just a collection of old-timers that Sully didn't recognize as players. He was there because Urban knew that Pasquale would have to send someone to represent the *family* out of respect. She was right, and before the wake officially started at seven o'clock, Sully got some photos of capo Matty Gaetano, accompanied by his driver Tiny Albanese, ducking in and out of Sardella's.

Two days later, Gino was called into Michelle's office, where she and Sully were waiting for him. Spread across her desk were several photos of Gino and his mom arriving and leaving the Lombardozzi wake.

Gino looked at them and immediately felt sick to his stomach. He gazed into Michelle's puzzled eyes and Sully's look of disdain.

"Can you explain this, Detective?" she asked.

"I took my mom to the wake. He helped my family after my dad died. He helped my mom get a job, that's all. She had to go to show her respects, and I agreed to go with her."

"So you think it's all right for a member of this unit to go to a mobster's wake?" Sully continued the cross-examination.

"I didn't say it was right, and I know it doesn't look good. You have to understand, when I was growing up, Lombardozzi was the guy you went to when you had a problem. We didn't know he was a mobster. All we knew is that he was respected. It was just the way it was when I was growing up." Gino was pleading his case, but it was falling on deaf ears—at least as far as Sully was concerned.

"That doesn't excuse you being there. You, of all people, should know better," Michelle said.

Sully jumped on him again. "What the fuck are you trying to do, embarrass us? Or is there something else going on?"

Gino struck back. "Listen. I don't expect you to understand why I had to take her. You'd have to understand what respect is. If you did, you would have had enough respect to come to me with this, not run to the Sergeant—"

"You've got to be kidding me. You want to bust my balls about going to my boss about a trooper going to a mobster's wake? If you're dirty, I'm supposed to come to you with it? You're the one who doesn't understand."

Michelle ended the confrontation. "All right, enough! Gino, don't you ever do anything this stupid again. If you do, you're out of here. Understand?"

"Yes, Sergeant," he said meekly.

"Sully, this stays right here. File a report about Matty and his bodyguard, but that's it. Understand?" she said.

"You're the boss," Sully said and left the office.

When Sully was gone, Michelle closed the door and turned her attention to Gino.

"Nice move. What the hell were you thinking?"

"I'm sorry. Obviously I wasn't thinking," he said.

She was not about to let him off the hook that easily.

"It's bad enough Sully doesn't trust you. Now he'll have the rest of them watching you. You screwed up, and I just went out on a limb for you. Let's be perfectly clear: you screw up again, I go to the colonel, and you're out of this unit—and probably off the job."

He could tell she was exasperated, but he was astonished she was not kicking him out of the unit. He knew he had dodged a bullet, and after all the bitching and moaning he had done about not being allowed into the "club," he had almost caused her to throw him out.

He regretted it, of course, but it just reinforced for him how hard it was, trying to live on both sides of the tracks. Living in one world, whether it was being a police officer or loyal to the neighborhood, would have been simpler. Straddling two worlds was a constant struggle, and it was times like these that made him wish he had picked one over the other.

CHAPTER 24

The next morning, the unit assembled for the trip to the Bristol County Superior Court in Taunton, Massachusetts. Gino avoided Michelle and jumped into one of the Crown Victorias as soon as the unit was ready to leave.

The court was an ornate stone building located off the Taunton Green. They were greeted at the courthouse by Detective Darren Mousseau of the Massachusetts State Police and Phil O'Hara, a prosecutor from the Bristol County District Attorney's office. After the obligatory introductions, they all proceeded into the courtroom of Judge Thaddeus Bulman.

O'Hara told Gino, "Bulman is a crotchety old bastard, but he's a friend of law enforcement."

Moon was escorted into the courtroom by Bristol County sheriffs. He was dressed in gray prison garb and shackled by his wrists and ankles. A long chain joined the cuffs, and it caused him to shuffle as he walked to the front of the judge's bench. The district attorney made a motion to transfer custody of Richard "Moon" Capelli to the Rhode Island State Police.

O'Hara explained to the judge that the purpose of the transfer was twofold: to clear a homicide and to develop evidence that would be the basis for proving Moon innocent of the Costa beating.

Standing before the judge, Gino noticed that Moon appeared frail and more like the sixty-five-year-old man he was, rather than the confident, cocky mobster Gino remembered from his youth.

"Mr. Capelli, are you represented by counsel in this matter?" Bulman asked.

"No, Your Honor. I don't wish to be represented," Moon replied.

"Mr. Capelli, do you voluntarily waive your rights to a full hearing and agree to be transferred into the custody of the Rhode Island State Police?" he asked.

"Yes, Your Honor," Moon replied.

"Motion granted," Bulman barked.

The hearing took less than five minutes, and Gino was sure most observers in the courtroom must have been wondering what the hell had just happened.

A Massachusetts State Police cruiser took the lead for the ride back to Scituate. It took them to the state line, where a Rhode Island cruiser took them the rest of the way. Moon sat silently in the back with

Gino, his newly appointed babysitter, while Sully drove.

Gino thought that Moon, like many other criminals, had spent his life constantly trying to screw the system. Now he was thrown into the system he had battled against his entire life. When the government was done with him, he would be put in the Witness Protection Program, sent to some unsuspecting community, and given a mundane job.

Most criminals, despite the opportunities the program gave them, seemed to always revert to a life of crime; they just could not change a lifetime of behavior. Gino thought it was akin to having a pit bull as a house pet and wondering why it suddenly attacked you.

Moon, always the loyal soldier, had been left to rot in jail for a crime he didn't commit. Becoming an informant was his only choice, because the Mob didn't reward loyalty.

Gino had heard the stories of loyal Mob soldiers having great going-away parties after keeping their mouths shut and being sentenced to jail. Everyone got hammered and promised the poor bastard they would take care of him and his family while he was away.

Soon, envelopes full of cash would flow to the new prison widow, and there would be plenty of money in his prison account. It would last a few months, and then the envelopes would slow to a stop, and the inmate account would go dry.

It did not matter what you'd done for the Mob. You were considered dead until you were released from prison. The wiseguys who survived prison time were smart enough not to rely on their so-called friends. They were the ones who stashed away money to support their families until they got out.

Moon, however, was like many before him: he spent his money on women, gambling, and entertaining his friends at restaurants and nightclubs. With an active social and criminal life, he never prepared for a long prison term.

Moon broke the silence. "Gino, haven't seen you since our little visit in prison. You still get your jollies off by putting your friends from the old neighborhood in jail?"

Gino wasn't about to start his babysitting assignment by being verbally abused, especially in front of Sully.

"Listen, you fuck," Gino started. "You're in my world now, and your ass is mine. You think prison was tough? Well, stand by, because prison is going to be a walk in the park compared to what we've got planned for you. So from now on, I'm Detective Peterson, and you'll do exactly what I tell you to do, because your life depends on me. If you fuck with me, I'll dump you on Atwells Avenue and let Tiger know where to pick your ass up, understand?"

"All right, all right," Moon said. "Just fucking with you, Detective. Come on, you know me. I know your family from the old neighborhood. I didn't mean any disrespect—just busting balls."

"Don't fuck with me, Moon, and we'll be fine," Gino said.

Moon sank deeply into his seat, and they rode in silence for the rest of the trip.

CHAPTER 25

The months passed quickly with Moon in custody, and 1982 soon became 1983. The duo fell into a familiar routine: every morning, Gino would take Moon out of his cell for a shave, shower, and breakfast. Around nine, the debriefings would begin and, after a lunch break, continue till around five.

After dinner, Moon and Gino would take a walk around the grounds of the headquarters complex, and then Gino would turn security over to a uniformed trooper.

Gino knew that debriefing a cooperating witness was a like peeling an onion. As each layer was pulled away, more and more of the truth was revealed, but not without the accompanying tears. It was exhausting, frustrating, and trying—even for the most patient investigator.

A cooperating witness would tell you just enough to suit his purposes. If he had to give up only one of his accomplices instead of three that was what he would do. To get the entire story, the debriefing process had to be deliberate and methodical—each facet of the story verified, each discrepancy challenged, and each lie thwarted with the threat of a return to prison.

Lou started the debriefing process by taking copious notes and questioning about every detail of Moon's criminal life. He started with the Costa case, and then moved to the Calderone murder.

"All right, Moon. Let's go over the Costa case again," Lou said.

"Costa was a pain in the ass. He wouldn't go along with a union contract that included no-show jobs. Tiger had it all worked out with the major construction companies in Fall River, but Costa balked. Tiger tried to talk to him, but he wouldn't listen. Tiger tried to bribe him, and that didn't work, either, so he decided a beating was in order."

"Who did he give the job to?" Lou asked.

"He talked to Marty and offered him four hundred bucks to beat the shit out of the guy. He didn't want him killed; he just wanted him to sign the contract. Marty asked if he could take Pontarelli along. Tiger said he didn't give a shit as long as the job got done," Moon said.

"All right, if you weren't there that night, where were you?" Lou asked.

"I was with my girl. I never left her apartment," Moon replied.

"What's her name?" he asked.

"Cynthia Carnesville," Moon answered.

"All right, we'll interview your girl, and then show Costa a photo lineup with Pontarelli's picture. I hope to God that you're telling the truth. Otherwise, we're bringing you back to Walpole," Lou said.

Moon never flinched. "Check it out, go ahead. I'm telling you, I was with her."

The next day, Lou returned from a trip to Providence and told Gino he had confirmed that Moon was indeed with Cynthia.

"How did you make out with Costa?" Gino asked.

"We showed him a photo lineup with Pontarelli's picture, and he identified Pontarelli as the second attacker. You can give him the good news," Lou said.

The Costa debriefing was done; it was obvious that Moon was not involved. Getting his sentence vacated would be relatively easy, but they wouldn't do that until they squeezed every bit of information out of him.

Next would be Moon's debriefing on the Calderone murder, and Gino couldn't wait to hear the story. Driving home that night, thoughts of mobsters, cooperating witnesses, and murder dominated his thoughts.

At the same time, pictures of Michelle flashed in his head. He imagined her away from work, hair down, in jeans and a tight sweater. He wondered what was hiding behind the business attire she wore to work each day and could only dream.

CHAPTER 26

As Gino drove to work the next morning, he took his eagerness to hear Moon's story out on his gas pedal. If Moon's statement led to solving the Calderone case, hopefully he would get part of the credit. The debriefing on the murder was scheduled to begin first thing this morning, and Gino didn't want to be late.

Any guilt he may have felt about "betraying" his neighborhood would be swept away by taking whoever was involved in the killing off the streets. He did not care what his detractors thought about loyalty to a neighborhood; there was nothing nobler than bringing murderers to justice.

Gino, like most from the old neighborhood, was torn between the street life and going straight. Watching wiseguys in their flashy clothes, shiny cars, and wads of cash was tempting, but the death of his father and the respect he had for his uncle drove Gino in another direction.

Whack! Lou's hand came crashing down on the table. He was pressing Moon for more details about the murder. Lou was peeling the layers of the onion away with a sledgehammer.

"I need more on the Calderone murder, Moon, and I need it now."

"Like I told you, Detective, we were all shocked when Calderone walked into the club. We didn't know if he was there to cause trouble or just trying to show us up. Tiger signaled Big John to get the gun out of his car. We never kept guns in the club in case the cops came in, but Tiger always had one in his Caddy."

"What happened after Calderone walked in?" Lou asked.

"Calderone sat at the bar, Tiger gave him a drink, and they started bullshitting. Big John gets Tiger's .38 caliber and slips it to him. I knew what was coming, but I figured Tiger would shoot him out on the street, not in the club."

"What happened next?" Lou continued.

"All of a sudden, Tiger comes out from behind the bar and starts shooting. Dickie falls off the stool and flops on the floor like a fish out of water. Everyone in the bar goes into a fucking panic. Two old men run out, but that drunk, Alonzo Regent, slept through the whole thing. Do you fucking believe that?"

"I'd believe anything at this point. What happened next?" Lou asked.

"Next thing I know, Tiger comes out with a butcher knife and starts to stab and slash at Calderone's body. Calderone stopped moving, and I knew he was dead. Tiger tells Billy to get Calderone's keys out of his pockets, find the car, and pull it up to the side door. He tells Marty to get the Caddy and pull it up behind Calderone's car. He tells Big John to drag the body over to the side door. He tells me to look outside to make sure no one is around."

"Then what?" Lou asked.

"John and Marty come back after getting the cars. They carry the body outside and dump it in Calderone's trunk. Tiger tells them to dump the body and get rid of the car. Marty drove Calderone's car, and Big John followed in Tiger's Caddy. I stayed with him to clean up the mess," Moon said.

"Is that it?"

"No. The next day, Tiger had us all at the club. He was out of his mind because they found the body. He was afraid someone had followed Marty and Big John. When the reports started to come out that a rookie cop traced the snow tracks back to the body, he calmed down. Tiger told us to lay low and keep our mouths shut."

"That's all?" Lou asked.

"That's all, Detective, honest."

Gino thought, *You have to hand it to Tiger; he had the balls and the motivation.*

The debriefing session was over. Gino brought Moon back to his cell, fed him, and turned him over to the uniformed trooper assigned to overnight security.

CHAPTER 27

The next morning, Gino returned to the intelligence unit, where Michelle gathered everyone together. With Moon in custody, it was time to go after the rest of Tiger's crew.

"If the colonel agrees, I'll ask the attorney general to return the indictments for the gambling wiretap. Our tapes and surveillance show Billy was heavily involved. We'll ask for an arrest warrant and pick him up," Michelle explained. "We're going to attack the weakest link: the one who has the most to lose, the one who's never done any hard time. That's Billy."

The next morning, Michelle, Lou, Quinn, and Gino traveled to the attorney general's office. Gino didn't have a clue why Michelle wanted him at the meeting—after all, he was just a babysitter—but he wasn't about to question her again.

The attorney general's office was located on Pine Street in the heart of downtown Providence. A four-story nondescript brick building, it housed lawyers, paralegals, cops, and staff.

They met in a conference room adjacent to the attorney general's private office. It was adorned with a large oak table and walls stacked with leather-bound law books.

Attorney General Thomas Morgan entered the room, and Gino was taken by the size of the man. He was well over six foot five, with green eyes and strains of gray hair zigzagging across a balding head.

Morgan was in his early sixties, a veteran of many political wars as a city councilor, mayor, and now attorney general. Morgan's last election was a breeze; aided by the Democratic machine and vigorous campaigning, he easily beat his Republican opponent.

Morgan was known for his integrity, his Baptist faith, and an ambition for higher office. He walked in flanked by two prosecutors, Criminal Chief Renée St. Pierre and Special Assistant Attorney General Arnold Bernstein.

Gino's attention was quickly drawn to Renée. She was a handsome woman with short black hair, blue eyes, and a shapely frame. Known for her quick wit and ability to curse, she was respected by her coworkers for the fearless way in which she prosecuted cases in the courtroom.

Her companion, Arnold Bernstein, was a mild-mannered career prosecutor from a family of lawyers.

He was small-framed with curly black hair and dark eyes behind frameless glasses. Arnold wore a gray plaid jacket with a silver handkerchief neatly peeking out of the chest pocket. The tie, which screamed as loudly as the jacket, was accented by alligator loafers and red socks.

As the meeting began, Michelle disclosed the events leading up to Moon's transfer into protective custody. She talked about the debriefing sessions and the follow-up work on the Costa and Calderone cases.

"What do you want from us, Sergeant?" Attorney General Morgan asked.

"The colonel would like us to arrest Billy and try to get him to cooperate. We're asking your office to indict him based on our gambling wiretap, and then ask the court to issue an arrest warrant."

"So we're looking at solving the Calderone murder and cleaning up the Costa case?" Renée asked.

Michelle answered, "That's it so far, but who knows how much more we can get from Billy. We need him to back up Moon's statements. Look, you know how these things go. The only way to get Tiger is by turning his own crew against him, jamming them up one at a time until they all fold."

"What do you think, Renée?" the attorney general asked.

Renée paused. "Let's issue the gambling indictments and get a warrant for Billy. Turn up the heat, and see what happens. I don't see a downside here, boss."

"Make it happen," the attorney general said. He excused himself and left the room.

Renée said to Michelle, "We'll go to the grand jury tomorrow morning and return the gambling indictments. You should have your arrest warrant by four o'clock."

The room emptied quickly, and they drove back to headquarters. Michelle met with the colonel, and then returned a short time later and gathered the unit together.

"The colonel said Lou and Quinn will go to Franco's house and talk to him tonight. He wants you to make a soft approach—just let him know he's got some trouble coming. Feel him out—if his wife hears what's going on, I think that helps us. After you visit him, I want Sully and Gino to put him under surveillance. We'll stay on him until we scoop him on the warrant. I want to know if he tries to reach out to Tiger, and I don't want him out of our sight. That's it for now. Lou, call me after you talk to Billy. Work out a surveillance schedule, and *don't* let him get away."

Lou and Quinn planned to make the approach around seven. Sully volunteered to take the surveillance after the approach until midnight. As low man on the totem pole, Gino got the midnight-to-eight shift. With a hectic schedule ahead of them, Lou, Sully, and Quinn headed out to get something to eat. Gino headed home for some rest.

CHAPTER 28

G ino called Lou as soon as he got to his apartment. After three rings, Lou picked up.

"Lou, sorry to bother you, but I'd like to go with you and Quinn." Gino was embarrassed about the desperation in his voice.

"Why? I don't think anything is going to happen. Besides, you've got to take over the surveillance at midnight," Lou said.

"Come on. I'm not going to learn anything sitting at home." He was pleading.

"All right, all right. Meet us at the 7-Eleven on Warwick Avenue just before seven. And Gino?"

"Yeah?" he said.

"If you tell Michelle, I'll kick your ass."

"Got it," he said.

Billy's house was in the Warwick suburb of Providence, a city made up of strip malls, shopping centers, and thousands of single-family homes. At exactly seven o'clock, they pulled up to Billy's neatly landscaped raised ranch house in a development where it was hard to distinguish one house from another.

Billy's blue Corvette was parked in the driveway. They approached the front door, rang the doorbell, and waited.

Billy appeared at the door in black sweatpants and a sleeveless Everlast T-shirt. Looking past Billy, they could see a modestly decorated house; there wasn't a velvet Elvis portrait or a piece of leather furniture to be seen.

Billy knew they were with the state police; he'd watched them drive past the social club a million times.

"Can I help you, Detectives?" Billy asked.

"No, but I think we can help you," Lou said. "Can we talk?"

"Yeah, but can I step outside?" Billy answered.

"Sure," Lou said.

Once outside, Lou spoke slowly. "You know we've got Moon, and we're going to be making solid cases, some against you. You've got a problem because you're involved in Tiger's gambling operation."

Billy said, "Moon's only trying to save his ass. I don't know anything about gambling."

"Really?" Quinn chimed in. "Maybe you should take a look at these." Quinn produced a number of surveillance pictures of Billy collecting betting slips.

"And, to top it off, we have a bunch of your cronies on the wire talking about you and betting." He made it sound like Billy was facing punishment by lethal injection.

"Wire? What wire? I never talked on the phone about gambling," Billy said.

"You're right," Quinn said. "But the other guys had a lot to say about you being the man for Tiger."

"With all due respect, Detectives, I don't know what the fuck you're talking about," Billy said.

Lou pointed a finger at Billy. "All right, asshole, this is what I want you to do. When we leave here, tell your wife and daughter that you're going down for an organized crime gambling operation and the Dickie Calderone murder. Remind them they won't be seeing you for a long time, maybe a lifetime. Then you'll realize what the fuck we're talking about."

Billy stood on the steps of his house. Gino thought he looked a bit stunned, but he still maintained his composure. They left without saying another word. As they drove away, Lou radioed Sully to begin the surveillance.

CHAPTER 29

When Billy walked back into the house, he was met by his wife. The conversation that he knew was inevitable from the moment he started hanging around with Tiger had finally arrived.

"Melissa, why don't you go to your room and watch TV until it's time for bed? I have to talk to your father."

"OK, Mommy," the child answered and quickly left the room.

"Rachel, I can explain," Billy said.

"You can explain? Well, then, by all means, explain. Explain to me exactly what the state police want with you."

"It's about Tiger, but it's all right. Really, I can take care of it."

"Take care of what? You told me they were just friends. You said they were wiseguys, but you weren't involved in anything. That's what you told me," Rachel said.

"They *are* friends. I tried to stay out of their business, but sometimes friends ask you to do things, and you get sucked in. I swear, I thought I could just hang around and not get in trouble. I thought I was smarter than that, but I was wrong."

"You're in trouble! What kind of trouble? What did you do?" Rachel asked.

"The detectives said they got me for helping Tiger with a sports betting ring. I just started picking up money and sports betting cards for him. I didn't think it was any big thing."

Murder, robbery, extortion—what the hell was I thinking? I had a family, a house, responsibilities, and I threw it all away for some fucking wiseguys, Billy thought.

He saw tears in her eyes, but heard anger in her voice.

"What did they say? Are you going to be arrested? Are you going to jail?"

"Rachel, please calm down," he pleaded.

"What are we supposed to tell our families? What do I say to your daughter? How am I going to survive if they put you in jail? How am I supposed to pay for this house and raise Melissa?"

"I won't let them put me in jail, I promise you. I'm sorry. I just got caught up in the life. I just started out hanging around with them and having a few drinks, maybe a bar fight every once in a while. Then someone would bring some hot stuff into the bar, and I'd buy a few things. Sometimes Tiger would ask me to pick up envelopes for him, deliver messages—things like that. Before I knew it, I was hijacking trucks and robbing drug dealers. I was in over my head, and it seemed to happen overnight."

Billy told her about the hijackings, robberies, shakedowns, and murders. They flowed from him like he was making a confession to a priest. He held nothing back, and finally felt a sense of relief; the only dread was wondering what she would do.

"Billy, all those nights I waited for you to come home. Two, three, four in the morning, and I never said a word because I trusted you—and now this. I'm going to ask you this just once, and you better not lie to me. Were there any women involved?"

It was a question he could answer easily; despite his life of crime, he never strayed. Never felt the need, mostly because he feared his wife.

"No, I swear! Those other guys, yes, but not me. I swear on Melissa," Billy said.

"What are you going to do? Tell me!" she demanded.

"I'll do whatever I have to do to keep us together. I just need to know that you'll stand by me. It's the only way I can get through this. Please don't let me go through this alone. I was stupid and did a lot of bad things, but it's over now. You know everything." Billy was crying, and he sought the comfort of his wife's embrace.

Rachel thought, *How could I be so blind as to what was going on, how could I not see that my husband was turning into a monster. I have no place to turn, I have to keep my family together but as a woman I will not stay with him if he's been with whores.*

Rachel held him in her arms. "I'll stand by you, but if you're lying about other women, you'll never see me or Melissa again."

CHAPTER 30

G ino left his apartment at eleven thirty that night and radioed Sully that he was en route. Sully responded that the target was home and there had been no movement. When Gino was in position, Sully drove away without saying a word, leaving Gino responsible for Billy until the morning.

Gino spent most of the night in the 7-Eleven parking lot near Billy's house. It gave him a decent view of Billy's house, but there was nothing going on. An occasional ride through the neighborhood did nothing to alleviate his boredom.

It was about one o'clock in the morning when ego overcame reason. Gino passed by Billy's house, and he could see a flickering TV through the bay window.

He parked his car, walked up the stairs, and lightly knocked on the door. After a few minutes, a sleepy Billy answered.

"Billy, I'm Detective Peterson from the state police. Can I talk to you?"

"Haven't you guys busted my balls enough for one night? Now you're going to bother me at one in the morning?" he said.

"Just hear me out, OK? You and I have something in common: we grew up in the same neighborhood."

"So? What does that make us, brothers or some bullshit like that? You got to be kidding me," Billy said.

Gino decided to plead his case. He knew he was way out of line, but if he could get Billy to flip for him, it would make the case.

"I just want you to know I understand what you're going through—"

"How the fuck could you know what I'm going through?" Billy said.

"I'm just saying that if you want to talk to someone who knows what it's like to grow up with those guys, who knows what it's like to be tempted by what they have to offer, I'm you're guy."

"My guy...my guy...I don't know who I should trust. I don't know if I'm fucking coming or going."

"If you talk to me, I promise to do my best for you, to always have your best interest at heart. You have my word."

"Your word? What the fuck is that worth? You're out here at one in the morning by yourself. What kind of juice do you have? Get the fuck out of here." Billy slammed the door.

Gino went back to his car, knowing his actions would cost him dearly if the unit found out. He had tried to scoop the case, to take the glory, and there was no way he would be able to justify it to them. He had fucked up, and he knew it.

Finally, around eight o'clock in the morning, Lou and Quinn radioed him that they were in position and he could secure. Gino did not want to miss the arrest, so he asked if he could stay. They told Gino to park his car and get in. At eleven o'clock, Billy emerged, dressed in sweatpants, a T-shirt, and a leather jacket. He left his house and made the twenty-minute drive to the Federal Hill section of Providence.

Billy entered Tiger's club. Lou, using binoculars, could see Billy sitting at the bar. Billy had a few drinks and left the club at four in the afternoon. The surveillance continued, and a short time later, Michelle radioed Lou. The warrant for Billy had been issued, and they were free to pick him up.

They followed Billy out of the city and south on Interstate 95. They coordinated with the nearest barracks for a marked cruiser to stop him on the highway. The trooper asked him to step out of the car. As he did, he noticed the trio approaching, and his head dipped.

"William Franco, you're under arrest for participating in an illegal gambling operation in violation of the State Racketeer Influenced Corrupt Organization Act," Lou said. Sully read him his rights, and Billy was put in the backseat with Gino.

At headquarters, Sully photographed, finger-printed, and processed Billy. After processing, Gino escorted him into a small interview room. He asked Billy if he wanted anything to drink.

"Fresca, if you have it," he said.

"I'll check the machine." Gino made the walk down the corridor and dropped a quarter into the Coke machine. As he opened the door and pulled the soda out, another bottle slid into position. He returned to the interview room with the soda.

"I think you're going to need something a lot stronger than this," Gino said.

"No shit," was the reply.

When he walked back out of the room, Michelle was there, red-faced and with clenched fists. Sully was off to the side with a smirk on his face. Lou and Quinn stood there with their hands in their pockets.

"When Sully was processing Billy, he said you went to his house last night after Lou and Quinn were there. Is that true?"

"Yes, but—"

"Yes, but, my ass! Who the fuck are you to approach a potential witness when I gave you specific orders on how this was going to go down?"

"I just thought I could gain his trust because of my background—"

"You thought, you thought. The problem is, you disobeyed my order. I swear to God, if this thing goes sour and he doesn't cooperate because of your half-ass glory grab, I'll have you patrolling the backwoods of this state for the rest of your career," she said.

Sully decided to pile on, "I told you he couldn't be trusted, Sarge, just out for himself, the selfish bastard—"

"Shut the fuck up, Sully," Lou said.

Michelle looked directly at Gino. "I'm going in there now, and you better hope he flips. If not, your career is going down the toilet. Now get in there, and keep your mouth shut."

CHAPTER 31

A s Billy sipped his soda, Michelle and Gino entered the room.

"You know why you're here, Billy. You have some serious problems," Michelle said.

"What problems? Gambling? That's a chump charge. Come on, Sergeant," Billy responded.

Michelle answered, "It's more than that. We're going to indict you for the Calderone murder. We know you got rid of the gun for Tiger."

Billy jumped from his seat. "No way! That fucking Moon's a liar. I told these guys before—he's just trying to save his own ass."

Gino pushed him back down, hard enough that it would not happen again.

"Look," Michelle said, "of course he's trying to save his own ass, but that doesn't mean he's lying. I also know we can prove that he didn't go to Fall River to beat Costa. We've got Marty to back him up on that."

Billy said, "You got Marty? No way. He's still at Walpole, and he'd never flip."

Michelle was lying, but it would keep him off-balance and unsure. She laid it on thick. "Listen, we've got him, and he's talking. And we got you cold on the gambling and the murder. If you cooperate, you got half a chance at a life. Tiger isn't going to take a chance that you might talk. You'll end up stuffed in the back of a trunk like Calderone."

Billy said, "What the fuck do I say to my wife and daughter? How do I tell them I might be going to jail for the rest of my life…"

"Listen, I'll bring your wife up here and talk to her. I'll explain what we can do for you and your family. First, we need to know if it's worth going to bat for you. We're not going down this road unless you can give us Tiger and the rest of the crew."

Billy sat up in his chair and adjusted the handcuffs. "I'll give you the Calderone murder and two others, Jimmy McDonald and Fredo Marchetti, but I can't go to jail. You'll get Tiger and the rest of the crew, but I don't go to jail. My wife would never go for it. I'm giving up everything, and I won't do it without my family."

Michelle paused. She'd gotten what she wanted from Billy, and Gino was relieved that his grab for glory hadn't ruined his career.

"All right, if that's what you can give us, then I'm pretty sure we can make a deal. Let's get the attorney general's office on board. We'll go from there."

As Gino led him out of the interview room, Billy looked Michelle squarely in the eyes. "Sergeant, I'm only doing this because I got nowhere else to turn, but there's something you need to know. Moon's a fucking liar because he wasn't even there when we whacked Calderone."

CHAPTER 32

Michelle was in a frenzy as she raced to Moon's cell. Gino, Lou, and Sully were close behind. As she unlocked the cell door, Lou and Sully rushed in and grabbed Moon, and suddenly, he was flying across his cell. The sound of Moon's soft flesh against the thin metal walls sounded like claps of thunder.

After each thud, there would be a pause while Lou grabbed Moon by the collar. Then he would launch him across the cell, off the opposite wall, and into the arms of Sully. Sully would catch him and toss him back.

As he flew through the air, Moon was screaming. "What the fuck did I do? What happened? Enough already! What am I, a fucking ping-pong ball?"

Finally, Moon fell to the floor. Michelle stood over him. "You weren't even there when Calderone got whacked. I'm going to indict your ass for something—I don't know what for, but I'll figure it out. Then you're going back to Walpole, and I hope that Tiger has you killed."

Moon rose to his knees and held his hands together as if in prayer. "Stop, please, Sergeant. You don't understand. I had to! I had to! What was I supposed to do, rot in jail for the rest of my life?"

Lou grabbed him by the shirt and threw him on his bunk. Moon gasped for air. "I knew that if I convinced you that I could give up Tiger, you'd get me out of the can. I knew you'd investigate my case and prove I was innocent. You were the only chance I had to get out from under something I didn't do."

Michelle screamed, "What am I supposed to do now? You're useless to us. You lied about Calderone; I can't even put you in front of a grand jury. You'll be lucky if I don't get your ass indicted for obstructing justice."

"Listen, Sergeant, I know I fucked up," Moon said. "But what I told you helped you to flip Billy, didn't it?"

How did he know we had Billy? Gino thought.

"And I still got a ton of stuff on Marty. I guarantee with what I know, you'll flip him too."

"You just sit in your cell. I'm going to see the colonel, and then talk to the attorney general's office. We'll let you know what we're going to do."

"Come on, Sergeant, you know what Pasquale and Tiger are like. This was the only way I could get you to listen to me and clear me of this bogus rap," Moon pleaded.

"How did you know we flipped Billy, Moon?" Gino asked.

"Call it an educated guess. Billy never could take any heat—just a pretty boy who thought he was a tough guy. I was right, though, wasn't I?"

After three days of letting Moon worry about having to go back to jail, Michelle finally talked to him. She told Moon they would continue to work with the Massachusetts authorities to get his conviction vacated. Although he was no longer a priority for the state police, they would keep him safe, and eventually, he would be put in the Witness Protection Program. To stay out of jail, he would have to testify to a grand jury and explain why he lied to the state police.

CHAPTER 33

Michelle told Gino that Billy and his family would be housed at the state police training academy. There was no recruit class in session, so it provided an ideal location to hide a witness and his family. Gino, although years removed from being a recruit, still got an uncomfortable feeling reliving his academy days.

It reminded him of the many guest lecturers who liked to begin with a joke. He cringed, remembering how they always asked if there were any Italians in the class. How he would meekly raise his hand before they launched into a story that was invariably about a "dumb WOP." Yet he never protested.

The academy was tucked away in the northwest corner of the state in the town of Foster. The ten-acre compound housed a barracks with offices, a mess hall, and garage.

The trick was to turn this former military post into a home for the Francos and a place for the detectives to debrief Billy.

It was decided that a portion of the barracks would be carved out as a living area for the family, and office space would be used for debriefing. The garage would be converted into living space for the security detail, and everyone would share the mess hall for meals.

In a series of lightning-like moves, Billy was arraigned on the RICO gambling charges, held on half a million dollars bail, and remanded to the custody of the state police. Members of the unit, using rental trucks and undercover vehicles, moved his family out of their house in Warwick. In a mere twenty-four hours after the arraignment, the Franco family became reluctant residents of the town of Foster and members of a select group known as protected witnesses.

At his apartment that night, Gino watched TV, but his mind was elsewhere. He was thinking about what it must be like for the Franco family to have their lives turned upside-down in one day.

His thoughts were halted by a soft knock on his apartment door. Gino wasn't expecting anyone. Instinct kicked in, and he reached for his snub-nose .357 lying on the kitchen table.

"Who's there?"

"Sergeant Urban, Gino," was the answer.

He released his grip on the gun and stumbled over himself getting to the door. *What the hell is Michelle doing at my apartment?* he thought.

He opened the door, and she stood before him in jeans and a gray wool V-neck sweater. Her dark lipstick enhanced her full lips; her eye makeup was applied to draw attention to her blue eyes. Her hair was down and parted in the middle and fell below her shoulders. She was carrying two cups of coffee.

For the first time, he allowed himself the luxury of staring at her body. The sweater struggled to house her abundant breasts, and the belt around her jeans accentuated her thin waist. His face flushed, and he struggled to say something. Luckily, Michelle spoke first.

"I'm sorry to bother you at home. I hope I'm not disturbing you," she said in a soft tone, one he had never heard.

"No, not at all, Sergeant. Is everything all right?"

"Everything's fine. Can I come in?"

"Of course," he said.

She walked in and handed him a coffee. "I just wanted to talk to you away from the office about your new assignment. Look, I know you're frustrated. But you have to understand that to become a good detective, someone who's respected by other detectives, takes time. It doesn't come as fast as you might want. It's my job to get you there, and I want you to know that I will, but you just have to trust my judgment."

"I do, Sarge. I just get aggravated sometimes. I know I can do this. I was born to do this. I can feel it every day I go to work." Gino wasn't afraid to let her know how he felt about work—what was hard to hide was how he felt about her.

"Well, I'm glad we got a chance to talk. I'm going to get going. I'm meeting some friends for dinner at Ghirardi's around the corner," she said.

As she turned and walked to the door, he grabbed her hand and turned her around. They were inches apart, and he pressed his body against hers. She didn't push away.

"Gino, this would be wrong on so many levels. It's dangerous for both of us," she said.

"I know, but I don't think you'd be here if you didn't think it was worth the risk, Sarge," he said, hopeful.

She paused for the briefest of moments, and then pressed her finger against his lips. "Tonight, I think I just want to be Michelle."

He moved her finger away and kissed her. Their lips pressed together with equal force. As mouths parted, he could taste the passion. They continued to kiss as he moved her toward his bed. With each step, clothing was shed.

"I've been fighting these feelings since I first met you. Please tell me this means something to you," she said.

"Of course it means something to me. I just never thought anything like this could ever be possible. I kept trying to put you out of my mind, but I couldn't," he said. He kissed her neck and caressed her back as she clutched at his shirt, pulling it out from his jeans.

They were at his bed and completely naked. She pushed him down and straddled his hips. She gently placed him inside of her. The irony wasn't lost on him that in this position, she remained in control. She was in charge; she was the boss.

CHAPTER 34

As Gino drove to work the next morning, he wondered what it would be like. In less than twenty-four hours, Michelle had gone from threatening to throw him out of the unit to sharing his bed. Gino knew they could not be open about their relationship because it could ruin their careers. The colonel barely tolerated women on the state police, never mind relationships between officers.

To his relief, Michelle acted as if nothing happened, although they would occasionally lock eyes for the briefest of moments. He prayed the rest of the unit did not pick up on the signals that passed between them.

Despite what was going on, there was still work to be done. Addressing it in the same way they handled Moon, Michelle assigned Lou and Sully to do the debriefings. Quinn would do the follow-ups, and Gino would coordinate security.

After the initial debriefing of Billy, Michelle scheduled a meeting with Renée St. Pierre and Arnold Bernstein.

Michelle and Gino brought Billy to the attorney general's office. Renée and Arnold walked into the conference room carrying case files and yellow legal pads. Renée wore a conservative blue dress with a high collar and a hem that reached mid-calf. Arnold was dressed in a blue herringbone jacket with a pattern so tightly woven, Gino had to look away so as not to get dizzy. Blue slacks accented the jacket, and his yellow tie screamed, "Meet me at the yacht club for drinks!"

After they were introduced to Billy, Michelle began to press her case for him. She had to convince Renée that Billy was able to make significant cases against the Mob, but the hardest sell would be Billy's request for no jail time.

"Michelle, tell us what Mr. Franco has to offer." Renée never took her eyes off Billy. Gino was sure she was measuring him up as a potential witness.

"Our initial debriefing of Billy indicates Tiger sent Marty and Al Pontarelli to beat Costa in Fall River. It wasn't Moon."

"Go on," Renée said.

"Billy was in the bar the night Calderone was killed. He can testify that Tiger sent Big John to get the gun and that he saw Tiger shoot Calderone. Tiger made him get rid of the gun after Marty and Big John left to dump the body."

"Anything else?" she asked.

"Billy can testify about two unsolved murders, the beating death of James McDonald, and the murder of Fredo 'The Moron' Marchetti."

Arnold looked up from his legal pad. "Fredo Marchetti, the guy they found buried behind the Old Ranch Restaurant?"

"That's him," Michelle answered.

"Who's this McDonald?" Renée asked. "I don't remember that being a mob case."

Michelle explained that McDonald wasn't connected, just a guy in the wrong place at the wrong time. Tiger and Billy were driving around the city, and McDonald's brother cut them off. They got into a beef, and Tiger smashed the kid's head in with a baseball bat.

"Let me get this straight. Billy can give us Al Pontarelli for a union-related Mob beating in Fall River. He can also give us Tiger and the rest of the crew for the Dickie Calderone, Fredo Marchetti, and James McDonald murders. That right, Sergeant?"

"That's right. We haven't done the debriefings and investigations, but that's what he has to offer."

Renée turned her attention to Billy. "Well, Mr. Franco, that's a lot to offer. I guess the question is, what do you want?"

At first, Billy tried to charm her. "Miss St. Pierre, I'm doing this for my family and to do the right thing."

"Cut the shit, Billy," Renée said. "Don't waste your time trying to con me. Save it for a jury. Just give it to me straight."

Billy was caught off guard by Renée's bluntness. "I am being straight with you, Renée. Can I call you Renée?" She nodded, and he continued. "Keeping my family together is why I'm going to testify. I'll give you three murders, but you have to keep me out of jail."

"Why shouldn't you have to go to jail? You're a murderer," Arnold said.

"If I go to prison, they'll kill me. Please don't tell me about protective custody in prison because there's no such thing. Even if they can't get me in prison, they'll get my family. I know that. Even if I do all of this for you, someday they'll find me. No matter what, they always win."

There was silence in the room. It came from knowing that what he said was true; to argue otherwise would be foolish. Gino knew that their first priority was convicting mobsters; the consequences for Billy ran a distant second.

Renée broke the silence. "All right, Billy, this is what we're going to do. The state police will keep you and your family safe. We'll put you into the grand jury to testify about the three homicides. If what you say checks out and you do well at trial, we'll make a pitch for no jail time to a friendly judge, but no promises until I'm sure about you, understood?"

"I'm not lying," Billy said. "Everything I said is true."

"I didn't say you were lying," Renée said. "We just have to be sure we don't get fooled again, like we did with Moon."

CHAPTER 35

When Gino and Michelle returned to the academy, they we were met by Lou and Sully.

"Sarge, we got a problem," Lou said.

"What's the problem?" Michelle asked.

"Rachel isn't sure she wants to stay here."

"Shit," Billy said. "I knew this was going to happen."

"Do you want me to talk to her?" Michelle asked.

"No, I'll do it," Billy answered.

Rachel was waiting in the living area when they walked in. Gino took note of her long, curly brown hair; soft brown eyes; and delicate features. She was the girl-next-door kind of pretty—not your typical Mob wife.

They entered the room, and Billy tried to speak to his wife. "Rachel," he began.

She cut him off with a palm to his face. "I don't want to hear from you, asshole. You ripped us out of our house and away from our family. Melissa was taken out of school and away from her friends. We're in the middle of God knows where, and our only companions are state troopers. I think you've done enough for one day." She turned toward Michelle. "How do you expect us to live like this? I want to go home."

"I know things aren't good, but you have to give us a chance. Eventually, we'll relocate your family, and you can start a new life. How many people get a chance to wipe the slate clean and start over?" Michelle said.

"What about the rest of our family?" Rachel asked.

"I'll have Gino meet with them. You can exchange letters, cards, gifts—anything you want. We'll arrange phone calls and visits, but they can never know where you're living."

"What kind of life is that for my daughter?" she asked.

"It's the best life you can give her and still keep her safe. It'll be tough at first; I'm not going to lie to you. But eventually, it'll get better. Once you're relocated, it'll get better, I promise. I've seen it happen before with other witnesses. I know one thing: you can't go back home and pretend nothing happened. These people are animals, and if they can't hurt Billy, they'll hurt you or Melissa. If you stay with us, I promise you, no one will ever hurt your family," Michelle said.

"Rachel," Billy tried again.

Rachel tore into him. "Shut up. You're the one who got us into this mess. When you were out playing gangster, did you ever think about your family? Did you ever for a second think about something like this happening, you selfish son of a bitch?"

She turned away and held her hands to her face. Gino thought she was crying, but instead, she had taken a few movements to gather herself.

"All right, Michelle, my daughter and I will stay here, but let me tell you something. If you let anything happen to her, I'll testify for the Mob myself and tell everyone what a sack of shit my husband is."

Michelle said, "Rachel, if that happens, I'll drive you to court myself."

Over the next few weeks, Gino noticed a quiet uneasiness settle in between Billy and Rachel. Rachel did her best to support her husband when others were around, but when Gino was alone with the family, he could sense a reservoir of hurt and resentment.

Gino leased a house in Foster and registered two undercover cars in the phony name of William Ferland of Howard Hill Road. The home and cars were a means of providing a new identity for Billy's family. Melissa became Melissa Ferland, the newest enrollee at Isaac Paine Middle School.

Billy's days were filled with debriefings. After most sessions, Gino would let him blow off steam exercising in a makeshift gym set up in the garage.

The amount of time needed to provide security, debrief witnesses, and investigate the cases put a strain on the entire unit. They were spending more time at work than at home. The strain was evident, especially for those with children.

Gino now understood why divorce ran rampant in police work. It was impossible to stay married when you loved your job more than your wife. The tension of trying to balance two loves was the same anxiety Gino saw as the Francos struggled with being away from their family. It caused them to bicker constantly, and he imagined it was much the same for his colleagues who were trying to balance work and home.

Once, Sully told of the time he tried to discipline one of his daughters after hardly seeing her for weeks because of the hours the unit was working. She turned to her mother and asked if she had to listen to him. Although he told it as a joke, Gino thought it must have made Sully feel like a stranger in his own house.

CHAPTER 36

The spring of 1983 marked a year since Moon and Billy had come into protective custody. The state police investigation into the Mob was pushed to the back pages of the Providence paper by stories about the mayor.

In March, the mayor was accused of assaulting a car dealer who was having an affair with his wife. The mayor summonsed the man to his home and beat him with his fists.

For weeks, a long line of self-righteous individuals clamored for the mayor to be arrested. Gino didn't quite agree. He came from a neighborhood where it was a man's God-given right to, at the very least, beat the shit out of a man who was sleeping with his wife. After all, the state of Texas allowed you to shoot a man if you caught him in bed with your spouse. To Gino's way of thinking, if the offender was any kind of man, he would have taken his beating and left the mayor's wife alone.

Despite providing for some interesting reading, the mayor's predicament was not the unit's concern, and the debriefing of Billy continued. Each day, Gino brought Billy from the living area into the interview room, and Lou handled the debriefing.

Like Moon, Billy would not be totally honest at first. A life of lying to the police would not be changed overnight. Lou began talking to Billy about his initial involvement with Tiger and the rest of the crew.

Billy told them the first time he did anything criminal was the hijacking of a tractor-trailer. The truck was part of a fleet working from a liquor warehouse in Lincoln, a town north of Providence.

The foreman had a huge gambling debt. He walked into the Pineapple Social Club to ask Tiger for more time to pay and walked out part of a criminal conspiracy.

To wipe out his debt, he agreed to leave the keys to a tractor-trailer full of Scotch, vodka, and gin in an unlocked cab. Tiger's crew would take the truck from the warehouse; all the foreman had to do was report it stolen. Tiger would sell the load, give Nicky a piece of the action, and throw some money to his crew.

Billy and Marty were to take the truck from the warehouse and drive it to a garage in Providence; the rest of the crew would be waiting to unload the booze. When it was emptied, they would dump the empty truck in Connecticut.

Billy told them he and Marty drove to the warehouse in a stolen car. What Billy didn't know at the time was that Marty had no clue how to drive a tractor-trailer. After he got into the cab and turned over the ignition, Marty drove out of the lot, and the grinding of the gears pierced the night.

Mercifully, Marty found first gear, and the truck slowly inched its way onto the roadway. At first, Marty's top speed was about five miles an hour because he couldn't get the truck into second gear. Miraculously, he found second and tore down the road at the breakneck speed of twenty-five miles an hour, with Billy close behind in the stolen car.

When they arrived in Providence, Marty refused to back up to the doors of the garage because he couldn't find reverse. Billy, Big John, and Moon were forced to carry cases of liquor from the street to the garage. Marty sat in the truck the entire time, afraid to turn off the ignition.

As Marty drove the empty truck away, the grinding of gears started again, but not quite as loud. The truck slowly made its way through the streets of Providence, and then onto Route 95.

As soon as they crossed into Connecticut, they pulled into the State Line Truck Stop. Marty used a screwdriver to bust out the ignition of the truck and a crowbar to smash the windows to add credence to the foreman's story that the truck had been stolen. He slowly walked over to Billy's car, and they drove away.

Billy spoke of how he admired Marty's lack of fear. He was sure Marty could break into a house, rob a bank, or commit a murder, and his blood pressure would never rise above normal. Whenever Billy heard the words cold-blooded, he told them he thought of Marty.

After the heist, Tiger gave them each two hundred dollars, telling them it was the best he could do because he had to give Nicky a "big taste" of the score. No one had the balls to say anything, so they just bitched and moaned to each other. Anticipating that they would get screwed, they had each grabbed a case of Scotch, and Billy said it eased their disappointment.

CHAPTER 37

After Billy's initial debriefing, it was time to start on the McDonald and Marchetti murders.

Michelle began entrusting Gino with more responsibility, assigning him to interview Toby McDonald with Lou. Toby was with his brother, James, the night James was killed, and it was crucial that his story backed up Billy's version of the murder.

They found him late on a Friday afternoon in Mulvey's Pub, a local hangout in Pawtucket. A grimy industrial city just east of Providence, it was an enclave for working-class immigrants drawn to the textile miles.

An English immigrant, Samuel Slater, founded the industry when he brought British textile technology to America in the 1700s. Slater found the labor he needed by employing entire families; children as young as seven toiled alongside siblings and parents in the mills that dotted the Blackstone River.

Pawtucket had all of Providence's crime, run-down houses, and industrial areas, but none of its affluent neighborhoods or historical charm. Obviously, the bar owner had given up trying to maintain the place years ago. The red leather stools were worn and cracking. There wasn't enough varnish in the world to restore the bar. It was enough for his clientele that he keep the liquor flowing.

They approached Toby as he sat at the bar, nursing a beer and eating a hardboiled egg. Lou explained to him that the state police had reopened his brother's murder case and asked him to come to the Lincoln barracks. He swallowed what was left of the egg and downed his beer.

"All right, let's go," he said.

When they got to the barracks, he told them that his brother had a good heart, that he was a simple kid with a bit of a temper. The brothers lived with their mom in a third-floor apartment on Prospect Street about a block from Mulvey's.

Lou asked about the night his brother was killed.

Toby explained that every Friday night, they played in a darts tournament at the club. The night Jimmy was killed, they played darts and drank until Mr. Mulvey tossed them out at closing. They were both hungry, so they decided to get some hot dogs at the New York System Restaurant in the Olneyville section of Providence.

They drove to the restaurant in Toby's Monte Carlo. They got there around two o'clock in the morning, and the place was packed.

It was a warm night, so they took their food outside rather than fight the crowd for a seat. They sat in the doorway of a bank next to the restaurant. As they were sitting on the step, a big guy smoking a cigar stepped on Toby's foot as he walked up to the restaurant.

"Any words exchanged at this point?" Lou asked.

"I said to the big guy, 'Hey, watch it,'" Toby answered. "Then he tells me, 'Next time, move your feet.'"

"What happened next?" Gino asked.

"Jimmy jumped up and was about to start something when the second guy told him to sit down."

He described him as smaller than the other guy but said both looked like wiseguys. They decided to finish their hot dogs and leave, but they were pissed.

Toby and Jimmy saw the two guys get into a big Cadillac. They got into Toby's car and started to follow them down Smith Street. Toby gunned the engine and cut in front of them, and Jimmy flipped them off as they passed by.

The big guy was driving, and they could see he was jerked, but Jimmy just laughed. "That will teach them to fuck with the McDonald brothers!" Jimmy hollered to his brother.

Toby gunned the engine again and started to head home. The Cadillac suddenly appeared out of nowhere and hit them from behind. Their heads snapped forward, and Toby almost lost control of the car.

Jimmy wanted to stop and fight them. Toby told his brother that they weren't getting into a fight with a couple of goombahs. The only thing they were going to do was head home and call it a night.

Toby buried the accelerator, continued down Smith Street, and passed the statehouse. When he tried to get on the highway to head home, they got ass-ended again. They went into a spin and ended up on the side of the entrance ramp. The Cadillac stopped, and Toby could see the big guy and his friend laughing.

Before Toby could stop him, Jimmy grabbed the softball bat his brother kept in the car and jumped out. He yelled at them, "Come on, you motherfuckers!" Toby screamed at Jimmy to get back in the car. Toby saw the two guys get out of their car and start toward him.

Instead of listening to his brother, Jimmy kept screaming. The big guy got close to him, and Jimmy swung and missed. After he missed, the big guy went after the bat.

Suddenly, Toby's eyes welled up, and he stopped. Lou asked if he needed some time. He said he was all right and just wanted to finish the interview.

"What happened next?" Lou asked.

Toby's face flushed. He looked down and seemed to be studying the laces of his Converse sneakers. Finally, he spoke.

"I was so scared, I dove under the dashboard. Do you believe that I let them beat my kid brother to death, and I didn't do a fucking thing to help him? My own flesh and blood, and I was a coward." He paused again. "After I heard their car drive away, I got out and saw Jimmy on the ground. He was just lying there, not moving, and there was blood coming out of his ears. The last thing I remember was the sirens getting louder and louder."

CHAPTER 38

It was time to get the story of the McDonald homicide from Billy Franco. Gino brought him into the interview room at the training academy, where Lou was waiting.

Lou asked Billy to start at the point Jimmy McDonald confronted them.

"Tiger and I got out of the car just to scare this asshole, but he's holding a baseball bat and yelling for us to come get a piece of him. Tiger takes a few steps toward him, and then stops. 'Forget this chump,' he tells me. 'He's not worth it. Look at the skinny fuck. I'd break him in half.' I said, 'We can't let him get away with this shit. Doesn't he know who you are?'"

Tiger told Billy that was exactly the reason he was going to leave the kid alone. He explained to Billy that if he was ever going to be a made man, he had to start acting like one. A made man would never fuck around with a street punk.

They turned and headed back to the car, but the kid wouldn't keep his mouth shut. Instead, he kept screaming at them about being guinea bastards and going back to WOP land. Something snapped in Tiger, and he turned and was on the kid in a second. He took the bat away from the kid and swung.

Billy told them the next thing he heard was the bat hitting the kid's head. He described the sound like that of a watermelon dropped out of a window hitting the sidewalk. The kid fell to the ground twitching, and then stopped moving.

Tiger headed for the driver, but he was hiding under the dashboard like a scared rabbit. He just turned around and headed back to the car.

They drove to the Pineapple Social Club, and Billy dropped him off at his car. Tiger handed him the bat and told him to get rid of it, turned, and walked away, like they had just spent a pleasant night at the theater.

Billy turned to Lou. "Fucked up, huh?"

"Yeah, fucked up," Lou said.

CHAPTER 39

The intelligence unit was now faced with verifying Billy's account of the Calderone and McDonald homicides.

Lou, Sully, Quinn, and Gino were assigned to interview the witnesses in the McDonald and Calderone homicides. They began by talking to the Providence police detectives involved in the original investigations, and then interviewed the medical examiner and patrons of Mulvey's Social Club.

Most of the cops who originally investigated the cases were still working, and those retired eagerly volunteered their help. No cop likes to leave behind unfinished business; unsolved homicides haunt a cop forever.

The work of reinvestigating the cases took up the bulk of the unit's time. With a limited role, Gino found himself spending most of his time with Moon and Billy, and he was learning more and more about the men he guarded.

Gino concluded that there was not much difference between cops and mobsters, other than the side of the law they chose. They were remarkably similar. Each had a strong allegiance to an organization; they were ambitious and constantly evaluating and measuring up the competition.

Success for police officers was defined by rising through the ranks. For a mobster, it was the same type of progression. Instead of corporal, sergeant, lieutenant, and captain, it was made man, capo, underboss, and boss. Each step brought more responsibility and more chance of failure, but everyone was driven by prestige and power.

He also learned that mobsters and cops had their own groupies. Women attracted to the power and the perks associated with both groups. Tickets to shows, good tables at restaurants, and the sense of security that came with being with a man who carried a gun. All of it seemed to attract women.

It was also apparent, as in any male-dominated group, that the conquest of women was part of the equation. It was a way to demonstrate prowess and deal with the danger they faced on the streets. In their minds, there was a direct correlation between the number of women they could bed and how powerful they were perceived to be on the streets.

In a sense, women made them feel invincible. But to gain that invincibility, they had to expose their vulnerability to a member of the opposite sex—completely surrendering themselves to one person, yet still being able to return to the streets and survive.

Gino found that in Michelle. Their time together reminded him of the first time a woman had ever made him feel that way. He was eighteen and looking for a summer job. Uncle Earl called in a favor from an old friend, and Gino was hired as a state lifeguard.

His first assignment was Beach Pond State Park, located in Exeter. It was 430 acres of forest nestled against the Connecticut state line. The crystal clear pond was a mile and a half wide and three-quarters of a mile long.

Gino considered himself lucky to be sitting on a lifeguard chair rather than sweltering in the city. Most of his friends found summer jobs in small jewelry shops and grocery stores. It was the summer of '70, and Gino's hair was down to his shoulders. Days in the sun produced a deep tan, easy for him to achieve because of his olive complexion.

During a particularly hot stretch of weather, he noticed a woman with two children and a babysitter. Gino set his sights on the blonde-haired, blue-eyed babysitter; she was about eighteen years old, with full lips and ample breasts.

Still, he could not help but notice the mom. She was tiny with long black hair—a Native American look about her. Her frame fit nicely into her two-piece bikini, accentuating her firm breasts and shapely ass.

They usually sat close to the lifeguard chair, and friendly conversations became commonplace. Joyce Moradian introduced herself and her babysitter, Sheila Johnson, to Gino and his lifeguard partner, Mike.

One night around six, Mike was putting the guard boat away as Gino was surveying the last of the swimmers. Joyce approached and took one step up on the lifeguard chair, and Gino instinctively stared down at her breasts. She handed him a note, smiled, and walked away.

When he opened the note, his jaw dropped, and his whistle fell to the sand. He could hear a satisfying chuckle come from Joyce as she gathered her kids and headed for the parking lot.

When Mike returned to the chair, Gino was staring at the note like it contained the map to the Holy Grail.

"What's that?" Mike asked. "You get some chick's number?"

"It's Joyce's number, Mike," he answered. "She handed it to me and just walked away."

Mike laughed.

"What the fuck am I supposed to do? She's old enough to be my mother," he said.

"Listen, Gino, she's not that old, so put that out of your head. She wants you, man, you lucky son of a bitch."

Gino continued, "But what do I do, Mike? I don't know what to do. What if she's married? Where do I bring her? Am I supposed to take her out on a date like she's some teenager?"

"Gino, shut up. Listen to me."

"OK, OK." He stopped.

"Go home and clean up. Tell your mother you're staying at my house. Buy a bottle of wine, drive down here, and call her from the guard shack. Invite her down for a quick drink, and take it from there."

Mike's advice seemed to calm Gino. "Yeah, I can do that. Can you believe this? Me! She wants to see me!"

As soon as Gino got home he rushed into his bedroom took off his swimsuit and T-shirt and jumped into the shower. He scrubbed his skin until it was raw, jumped out of the shower, and shaved. Appling copious amounts of Aqua Velva he was forced to stifle a scream as it hit his skin. Throwing on a pair of jeans and an alligator accented polo shirt, he bolted from the house.

His first stop after home was the liquor store. He didn't know anything about wine, so he bought the most expensive bottle he could afford. Gino thought that the five-dollar corked bottle of Italian wine would impress the hell out of Joyce.

He made the trip back to the beach, pushing his 1960 Ford Fairlane 500 to its limits. The Jackson Five were blaring from the eight-track cassette as he drove in joyful anticipation.

When he arrived, he made the call that would turn the boy into a man.

CHAPTER 40

"Hello, Joyce. It's Gino," he said, trying to hide his nervousness.

"Gino, hi. Where are you?" she asked.

"I'm at the beach. I brought a bottle of wine, and I was thinking—"

"Stay there. I'll be right down." She hung up, and he just stared at the receiver.

Joyce lived in Norwich, twenty minutes away, but the wait seemed like an eternity. As he sat waiting, he cursed himself for forgetting to bring any kind of glasses or even a corkscrew to open the wine.

She pulled up in her Dodge Charger and rolled down the window. "Hop in, Gino. Sheila's watching the kids till I get back. Then she has to go. Leave your car here, and I'll bring you back later." He grabbed the bottle of wine and jumped in the car obediently.

Joyce pulled up to a three-story tenement house that sat high on a hill. She lived on the second floor in a two-bedroom apartment with a large kitchen, a small living room, and a bathroom.

Sheila told Joyce that the kids were asleep and that there were no calls. She rushed past Gino with a quick good-bye and a knowing smile.

Joyce produced a corkscrew and two wine glasses, and they settled on the floor of the living room. She opened the bottle, and after a glass or two, the conversation seemed to flow easily. He relaxed; Joyce made him feel more and more comfortable. It wasn't anything she said in particular; it had more to do with her treating him like an equal, a friend, and a man.

After their third glass of wine, she took him by the hand and led him to her bed. He awkwardly kissed and caressed her, and she responded to every awkward move with assurance. Gino sensed she enjoyed the time he spent kissing her breasts, so he lingered. He slowly worked his way down her firm body and buried his face between her legs; she grabbed the sheets and moaned in delight.

When he entered her, he exploded almost immediately. Instead of humiliating him, she just sighed and stroked his back; his youthful body against hers seemed to soothe her.

Although a bit embarrassed, Gino knew that shortly he would be able to please her again. For what he lacked in quality, he was determined to make up for in quantity. Depending on your point of view, being eighteen was a curse or a benefit.

Their relationship continued throughout the summer. Gino would spend his days at the beach and his nights with Joyce. They stayed together until the summer ended and he returned to college.

At school, he would often find himself in the company of girls his own age, and they paled in comparison to Joyce. They were truly girls, and he had been with a woman; he wondered if he would ever experience that feeling again.

CHAPTER 41

Reminiscing about Joyce made him realize that Michelle was the woman he had been searching for since that glorious summer. Since the night she visited his apartment, he knew he needed her to know that she was the one, the one who made him feel complete.

As he drove to work, he decided that he would tell her exactly how he felt. He wanted to be with her, and he was not about to wait for her to randomly show up at his apartment again.

When he arrived, he found Michelle with Lou and Sully; they were in her office discussing the cases. Gino's hopes of speaking to her in private had to be put on hold; she was obviously all business this morning.

She waved him into the office and explained she wanted to finish debriefing Billy on the capital cases.

Then she wanted to go to the grand jury and use the indictments as leverage against Marty.

"Gino, I just spoke to Lou and Sully. Get up to the academy and help them with the debriefing," she said.

"All right," he said.

Gino arrived at the training academy and brought Billy from the living quarters, where they debriefed him on the shooting of Fredo "The Moron" Marchetti.

Marchetti was a small-time criminal with a streak of insanity that was legendary. A thief, drug dealer, and armed robber, he fancied himself a kung fu expert and enforcer. He earned the nickname "The Moron" because of his arrest for the murder of two black men.

Billy explained to Lou and Sully that on one of the Moron's many trips to Daley's Liquors on Broadway, part of Federal Hill, he noticed two black men buying beer. The Moron was incensed that black men would have the audacity to wander into an Italian neighborhood, so he calmly pulled out a pistol and shot them dead.

The owner of the liquor store stared in disbelief as the Moron, screaming racial slurs, calmly took a bottle of vodka off the shelf and left the store. The owner looked down at the bodies of men who would never know what had caused them to be singled out and executed.

When the police arrived, a large crowd gathered outside the liquor store. The throng pressed forward, straining to look into Daley's Liquors. From behind crime scene tape, they could see the bodies lying on the floor.

Fredo Marchetti returned to the scene and screamed, "I taught those motherfuckers a lesson about coming into our neighborhood! Those black bastards should stay in South Providence where they belong!"

His rant drew the attention of two police officers, who yanked him out of the crowd. A quick frisk revealed a revolver, still warm from the shooting. Thus, the nickname "Moron" was born.

The Moron was paroled ten years into his life sentence. A mere six months after his release from prison, his body was found buried behind the Old Ranch Restaurant in Warwick. One of the chefs stumbled upon the body while searching for mushrooms.

The medical examiner ruled the Moron had been shot at another location, and then dumped in the woods. The year was 1982, and, like the Calderone investigation, the case went nowhere.

The Moron was small-time; he could have been killed by almost anybody for almost any reason. There wasn't much incentive to solve the case.

CHAPTER 42

The debriefing continued with Lou asking Billy about the Moron. They were familiar with the Daley's Liquors murder but wanted more information.

"You have to understand, Detectives, this kid was a stone nut, and he was more dangerous than a hit man because he was a loose cannon. The Moron didn't give a fuck about anything, and for some reason, he was obsessed with Tiger. He really thought he was going to be his bodyguard, but Tiger told him he didn't need him."

Billy explained that at first, Tiger just laughed the Moron off, but after he told Tiger he was going to take *him* out, something had to be done. Tiger went to see Nicky and got the OK to kill him, but before they got a chance, the Moron messed up his parole on the murders by stealing a car and got sent back to prison on a parole violation.

One night after hitting the clubs, Tiger and the crew stopped into Pita's, an all-night restaurant. Billy said they couldn't believe it when the Moron walked in because they thought he was still in prison. He came over to the table and flashed karate stars; he started jawing at Tiger about how he would take him out right there if he had a piece. Tiger just laughed at him, and the Moron walked away.

Tiger decided he'd had enough and they'd take him in the parking lot. The plan was for Big John to pin his arms behind him, and Billy was going to sucker-punch him. Marty and Big John were going to stuff him in the car, drive him someplace, and whack him.

"Is that the way it went down?" Gino asked.

"No. The Moron got his food and headed out the door. I don't know what got into me, but before he got out of the restaurant, I made a move…"

"Why didn't you follow the plan?" Sully said.

"I don't know, Detective. I was hyped up, and I didn't want him to get away," Billy answered.

Billy then gave a bizarre explanation of the shooting. "I went for my gun. As I was pulling it out, I tripped over the doorjamb. The gun went off and hit him. After he went down, I just kept pulling the trigger until the gun was empty."

Billy described how Tiger came into the hallway and started screaming because he had just shot the Moron in a restaurant full of people. By then, Big John and Marty were in the hallway. Tiger told them to lug the Moron out to the car and throw him in the backseat.

Billy gave the gun to Tiger, got Tiger's Caddy, and pulled up to Big John and Marty. They threw the Moron into the backseat and peeled out of the lot.

Billy said, "It was impossible to hide what we were doing, but we had no choice because I jumped the gun."

"Jumped the gun? No shit. Good choice of words," Sully said.

Billy explained that Tiger told him there were some woods behind the restaurant where they could dump the body. It was about three o'clock in the morning when they pulled into the parking lot of the restaurant. They dragged the body into the woods, dumped it, and drove away.

Sully asked, "You're telling me you shot this guy in front of a restaurant full of people, dragged him across the parking lot, threw him in a car, drove away, and no one ever said a thing?"

"I'm telling you, Detective, that's the way it went down; people just knew you didn't fuck with Tiger."

In this case, he was right, because no one ever came forward. When the cops found the body a few months later, the investigation went nowhere.

"Unbelievable," Lou said.

"Unbelievable," Billy repeated.

CHAPTER 43

F rank "Marty" Martelinni lay in his bunk at Walpole State Prison, thumbing through a girlie magazine smuggled in by a prison guard. Although he heard the rumors Billy and Moon had flipped, he knew if he continued to be a good soldier and keep his mouth shut, he would have nothing to fear, or so he thought.

Over his bunk, disguised as a light bulb, was a silent assassin. The hit man had skillfully pierced the cardboard portion of the bulb with a needle and syringe and filled it with a mixture of cooking oil and liquefied butter. The lethal bomb was called California napalm by the inmates.

As the lights in the cellblock flickered, Marty drooled over Miss March, and as each second passed, the filament in the bulb heated the murderous liquid to the boiling point. Soon it would explode, covering its unsuspecting victim; the sticky substance would adhere to his skin and inflict severe burns, immeasurable pain, and, ultimately, death.

Marty heard a crackle above his head and felt something bad was about to happen. He threw himself under his bunk as the light bulb exploded and liquid death painted his cell. As flames engulfed the cell, he curled up in a ball.

He screamed like a little girl, but he did not give a fuck. He was trapped in an inferno, and only the hacks could save him.

From under his bunk, he looked across the floor and saw the girlie magazine go up in flames. He heard the boots of correctional officers slapping down the catwalk and the sudden spray of a fire extinguisher. A correctional officer pulled him out from under his bunk and out of danger.

As correctional officers wheeled him to the infirmary, he felt searing pain in his arms and legs. The "napalm" had found its mark as he scurried under the bunk. Only his instincts gave him the few seconds he needed to dive under his bunk and save his life. As the nurse used a solution to remove the deadly mixture from his arms and legs, Marty drifted off into a morphine-induced haze.

The next day, an antibiotic cream had been placed over the burns, and an IV was slowly dripping pain medicine into his veins. The prison doctor told him he was a lucky man. Marty said, "You call this lucky?"

The nurse asked if she could get him anything. "A phone with an outside line," was his reply.

"Intelligence unit, Detective Peterson."

"Collect call from Walpole inmate Frank Martelinni," the operator said. "Will you accept the charges?"

"Absolutely," Gino answered. He motioned to Michelle, and she picked up the line.

"Gino?" Marty asked. His voice was strained.

"Yes?" he answered.

"It's me, Marty." Gino remembered him from that traffic stop many years ago and the many reports in which he was mentioned as a member of Tiger's crew. He also remembered him from the old neighborhood.

"You sound strange," Gino said.

"That's because they tried to set me on fire last night. The fuckers tried to cook me like a piece of meat. You've got to get me out of here," he said.

"Marty, Sergeant Urban on the line. Who set you on fire?"

"Who do you think?" Marty shot back. "The same cocksuckers who are always telling you they'll take care of you if you keep your mouth shut."

Michelle played coy. "We can have the prison put you in protective custody. We've already got solid cases against you, Tiger, and Big John. I can't see what you can do for us."

"Julio Lanni," Marty said.

"Who?" she asked.

"Sergeant, you know who I'm talking about. Tiger's cousin. He disappeared in '79, and everyone thought he took off for Germany with his Kraut girlfriend.

Well, we killed him. Get me out, and I'll take you to the body."

Michelle said, "Hang tight. We'll get you some more protection, and I'll talk to the colonel and the attorney general's office. I'll see what we can do."

"Hurry the fuck up. Get me out of here, and you get everything." Marty hung up.

"Gino, call the prison. Ask them to assign extra correctional officers to guard Marty. I'm going down to see the colonel."

Michelle arranged a meeting with Renée and Arnold at the attorney general's office.

"What does he do for our cases?" Renée asked.

"Well, he definitely helps us lock Tiger into the Calderone and Marchetti murders. He'll also confirm Al Pontarelli was with him when he beat Costa."

"What about Julio Lanni?" Arnold asked. "I never even heard of the guy."

"He's been carried as a missing person since 1979. Marty says they murdered him, and he can take us to the body," Gino answered.

"All right, Sergeant. We'll work with the Bristol County DA and get him transferred into your custody. He stays locked up until we sort it all out," Renée said.

"Make sure you don't put Marty and Billy together until we get them into the grand jury," Arnold added.

"Will do," Michelle said.

"Listen, if we take Marty, we'll have three witnesses in protective custody," Renée added.

"I know that. What's your point?"

"My point is, you better come up with a body and some convictions; otherwise, we're done with these assholes."

"Oh, you'll get a body. If it's not Lanni's, it'll be Marty's." There was no hint of humor in Michelle's voice.

CHAPTER 44

Marty was silent on the ride from Taunton Superior Court. He was still in pain, and every bump in the road caused him to grimace. Gino explained that they were taking him to the Chepachet barracks, where he would live and be debriefed.

The barracks was located on Route 44, the main route between Providence and Hartford. It sat halfway between the capital city and the state line. A solid brick building with attached garages, the middle portion of the barracks contained office space, a dispatch center, and cellblocks. Two small cells were located directly behind the radio console, which allowed the desk trooper to watch prisoners. The cellblock would become Marty's new home.

When they arrived, Marty slowly exited the cruiser. He carried a bag full of painkillers, antibiotics, and some clothes. Gino placed him into a cell, and with a turn of a key, his life as a protected witness began. At least for now, he wouldn't have to worry about being burned, stabbed, or thrown off a tier.

Marty was like newfound money for the unit. He would bolster Billy's testimony about the Calderone and Marchetti murders, and he would deliver another murder. He would also confirm that Al Pontarelli, not Moon, accompanied him to Fall River to beat Costa.

Michelle called the unit together.

"Lou will continue to work with Billy and Moon. Sully will work with Marty. Quinn will continue to do follow-up interviews and subpoena any records we might need. Gino will help with the interviews and be responsible for security of all three."

Gino now had to adjust from working with Lou to working with Sully, and given their history, he was apprehensive. Gino had no illusions that he was going to be treated as an equal; he could only hope Sully did not try to make his life miserable.

Sully was known as a brutal interrogator, not afraid to use his fists to get answers. Despite his heavy-handed tactics, he had a knack for getting the most out of mobsters. For some reason, wiseguys opened up to him more easily than they did to other members of the unit. Gino thought it had more to do with fear than Sully's people skills, and fear was something mobsters understood.

Gino attempted several times to talk to Michelle about coming over, but they were always interrupted by members of the unit with questions about cases. He was finally able to talk to her by waiting for her in the parking lot in the morning, and she agreed to stop by his apartment. She stopped by with Chinese takeout and a six-pack of Heineken. Gino wanted to take the opportunity to have the conversation he had rehearsed in his head a thousand times. He wanted to tell her about how she made him feel, and how their time together kept him going, but Gino sensed Michelle wanted to talk about the case. It was all-consuming for her, and he was smart enough to let her vent. After they talked about how difficult it was to get Moon and Billy settled and debriefed, they talked about Marty coming forward.

"The odds of having three Mob guys in protective custody are one in a million," Gino said.

"I know…"

"What's the matter?" he asked.

"Do you realize how important it is for me to convict Tiger's crew? If I don't, I'll be back in patrol," she answered.

"Just give me more to do. I promise I can handle it. I want to convict these bastards for you as much as for the unit."

"We'll see. Can we stop talking about the case now? I just want to forget about it for a while."

"OK. What do you have in mind?" Gino asked playfully.

Michelle drained the last of her beer, shot a glance at the bedroom, and smiled.

CHAPTER 45

The next morning, Gino woke to an empty bed. Michelle had slipped out sometime during the night, and he never heard a thing. *Some detective I am,* he thought.

Gino drove to the Chepachet barracks and prepared Marty for his first debriefing. Gino was anxious to watch Sully interview Marty; he had learned a great deal from observing Lou and expected he would learn as much from Sully.

Each detective brought his own strengths to an interview. There were a thousand ways to get the most out of a witness; the trick was finding what method worked best with each witness. Lou used finesse with a hint of intimidation. Gino would soon learn Sully used intimidation with a hint of finesse.

It was obvious to Gino that Marty was a brutish man; his only schooling came from the streets.

Beating, robbing, and murdering were his ABCs. In spite of his crudeness, the initial briefings went well; he corroborated Billy's account of the Calderone and Marchetti murders and confirmed that Moon wasn't with him when he beat Costa.

"All right, I think it's time we talked about Julio Lanni," Sully told Marty.

"Wait a minute," Marty said. "What about my deal?"

"Listen, the Sarge already told you we don't fucking need you," Sully said. "Here's how it's going to go: you tell us everything. You testify, and then we work out a plea."

"What kind of a deal is that?" Marty asked.

"It's the best deal you're going to get. Unless you want me to take you back to prison," Sully said.

"I wouldn't last there a week, and you know it," Marty said.

"I know, so let's stop dicking around and get back to the statement," Sully barked.

A defeated Marty told his story.

Julio Lanni was a punk living off his reputation as Tiger's cousin. He used it to get free meals and drinks at places Tiger was shaking down.

One of the clubs was called Disco Mania. The first time they approached the owner about paying, he said no. Tiger sent them back to bust up the place.

Disco Mania had huge fish tanks built into the walls. When they went in, Billy took a stool and smashed the tanks. Water rushed everywhere, and fish flopped on the floor. People fell on their asses trying to get out of the place.

The owner called Tiger the next day and cried uncle. From that point on, Big John and Marty stood at the door every weekend and collected the cover charge.

At the end of the night, they would hook up with Tiger and give him his money, but not before they skimmed a few bucks off the top.

"How does Lanni fit into this?" Sully asked.

"Lanni was a regular at Disco Mania. He told us that Tiger said he didn't have to pay the cover. That was fine with us, but then he started causing problems, insisting on free food and drinks. The owner says to us, 'What the fuck? I gave Tiger the door—now I've got to give his relatives free food and drinks too?'

"We calmed the owner down and pulled Lanni aside. I told him that he'd have to start paying for his food and drinks. The punk tells me to fuck off. He threatens to tell Tiger I've been hassling him. I decided it was time to go to Tiger. I told him about his cousin, and he tells me to take care of it.

"The problem is, I think 'take care of it' means make Lanni disappear, so the next time he comes in the club, Big John asks him to step outside. We get him out on the street, and John knocks him out with one punch.

"We throw him in the back of my car and drive him to some woods near a reservoir in East Providence. We pull him out of the car, and now he's starting to come around. Big John starts to punch him again. I grab a tire iron and hit him in the legs."

"How'd he end up dead?" Sully asked.

"Lanni is on the ground, moaning and groaning. He's threatening to have Tiger kill us both. Big John picks up a rock and smashes the punk's skull. I hear his head crack, and the fucker is finished."

"What did you do with the body?"

"I had shovels in my car because I never knew when Tiger was going to ask me to dig a hole. We buried him in the woods near the water."

"And his body's still there?" Griffin asked.

"We never heard that he was found. We figured since it was a reservoir, no one was going to be digging in there," Marty said.

"Go on," Sully said.

"The next day, we told Tiger what happened. He went fucking berserk."

"What did he say?"

"He said, 'You killed him! You killed him! I told you to take care of it. I meant rough him up, not kill the fucker. What the fuck do I tell my aunt? You are two of the dumbest fucks I've ever met in my life. Get the fuck out of here.' I thought he was going to kill us right there."

Marty told Big John to stay away from Tiger for a few days. After a week, he told him they should go to the club and face the music. When they did, Tiger told them if he did not need them for muscle, they would both be dead.

Tiger told them to go back to Disco Mania and start collecting his money. Marty sighed in relief, bought a round of drinks, raised his glass, and toasted Julio Lanni.

"Do you think you can show us where you buried the body?" Sully asked.

"It's been a long time, but I think so," Marty replied.

Sully turned to Gino. "Make security arrangements for tomorrow. We're going for a ride to East Providence."

"I'm on it," he said, and bolted to the phone.

CHAPTER 46

The James V. Turner Reservoir was a pristine water-shed that straddled East Providence, Rhode Island, and Seekonk, Massachusetts. The small reservoir was surrounded by acres of pine trees, which provided a natural barrier. The area was posted with No Trespassing signs, but the occasional nature walker or swimmer braved the notice.

Gino left Chepachet with Marty around nine and met with East Providence police officers on a narrow road that led into the reservoir. They waved Gino through the barricade, and he and Marty walked over to Michelle and the rest of the unit.

They began their search for the body, walking slowly through the towering pines with Marty in tow. At times, he appeared to be thoroughly confused but insisted that he was in the right location.

"If we find a body, it'll be a miracle," Gino whispered under his breath. The miracle occurred as they came up over a small hill. Located between two large trees was an area of pine needles slightly lower than the surrounding area. The sunken impression made by the needles was eerily shaped like a grave. Marty said it looked like the place.

"OK, we dig here," Michelle said.

"Gino, ask the East Providence guys to call the Department of Public Works and get a backhoe here as soon as possible."

By two o'clock in the afternoon, the area around the sunken ground was surrounded by uniformed troopers, detectives, and workers.

A large area around the trees had been cordoned off with crime scene tape. Only Quinn, the unit's forensic expert, and three members of the state police evidence collection team were allowed inside the tape. They went about their grisly work with the precision of an Indy 500 pit crew.

They started by slowly brushing away the pine needles, leaves, and other debris. Next, shovels were used to remove the first six inches of dirt. When it was obvious that they weren't making sufficient progress, the backhoe was called into service. The summer morning had drifted into late afternoon, and waiting for the equipment was a welcome reprieve from the humidity.

When the backhoe arrived, Quinn directed the operator to delicately remove soil by slowly scraping the bucket across the area at a depth of about a foot at a time. All eyes focused on the small patch of earth as each pile was deposited adjacent to the suspected grave.

After reaching a depth of about five feet, they saw what appeared to be human bones. Quinn and his team jumped into the hole. Using small spades, they slowly uncovered a skeleton lying perfectly in place. As they used brushes to wipe away the dirt, a large hole in front of the skull was exposed. Closer examination by Quinn revealed bone fragments gently resting against the rear of the skull.

By then, the sun was setting, and Michelle ordered all work at the gravesite stopped. The medical examiner was legally required to respond and pronounce what was left of Julio Lanni dead. He arrived an hour later and made the pronouncement.

Now Quinn's forensic team completed its work by carefully numbering each bone and packaging it for the medical examiner. Quinn would go to the medical examiner's office in the morning for the autopsy.

Michelle and Gino drove Marty back to Chepachet. After they tucked him into his cell for the night, Michelle called Renée.

"What's up?" she said.

"I guess we're not done with these guys, after all. We just found Lanni's body."

CHAPTER 47

Michelle called Gino into her office to tell him he would be working with Lou again, this time on positively identifying the body.

"Thanks. I appreciate the opportunity," Gino said.

"You can thank me by doing a good job," was her reply.

"What makes you think I wouldn't?" he joked.

"Get the hell out of my office before I change my mind," she said.

When they shared a glance or a smile, it was easy for Gino to forget they worked together—easier still to conveniently forget that on the Rhode Island State Police in 1983, supervisors and troopers could not be lovers. There was no time to think about the conflicts he faced. Gino had to switch gears and get to the work at hand.

Given the condition of the body, the only way to make a positive identification would be to match the teeth that remained in the skull with an old dental X-ray.

"We'll see if we can get a line on Lanni's dentist by going through our intelligence files. It's a long shot, but if his dentist is listed, we'll contact him and get the X-ray," Lou said.

"I'll grab the file and let you know," Gino said.

Julio Lanni's file was thin at best; he wasn't a wiseguy, just a street guy with a few minor arrests. There were numerous reports of Lanni being with Tiger's crew. No dentist was listed, but what jumped out at Gino were two reports of Lanni being stopped for speeding with a passenger identified as Gretchen Kluth.

Gino checked with the Registry of Motor Vehicles and got a hit on a Gretchen Kluth. Her address was listed as 124 Sheldon Street in Providence. Sheldon Street, located in the Fox Point section of the city, was a mix of Portuguese immigrants and students from Brown University.

They left Scituate to check out the Sheldon Street address. Even if Gretchen was not home, they could probably count on a nosy neighbor who was willing to talk.

As they walked to the door of the three-story house, Gino read the names under each doorbell: Mello, Silveira, and Kluth. He also jotted down two license plates of cars parked in a small lot adjacent to the house. He radioed dispatch, but neither plate came back registered to Gretchen Kluth.

"What do we do now?" he asked.

"Let's try the door and see if she's home. You never know," Lou said.

Gino rang the bell labeled Kluth, but got no response. Looking through the glass of the door, he could see a small hallway. Directly off the hallway was a door to the first-floor apartment, and then stairs to the other apartments. He rang the other bells, and an elderly lady opened the front door.

Lou explained that they were trying to locate Gretchen because a friend had been involved in an accident. In a heavy Portuguese accent, she told them Gretchen was at work and usually came home around four thirty. They thanked her and returned to their car. Lou decided to come back at four and wait for Gretchen to come home.

Lou and Gino stopped for lunch at a small sandwich shop on Chalkstone Avenue. It was famous for an Italian submarine sandwich made of salami, Italian ham, provolone cheese, hot peppers, and pickles on a half loaf of Italian bread. Lou and Gino washed down their sandwiches with a couple of Diet Cokes, got back in the car, and drove back to Sheldon Street.

Around four, they set up surveillance on the house. As if on cue, a 1978 orange Chevy Vega pulled into the lot at four thirty. A thin, leggy woman got out of the car, tugged at her keys, and headed for the front door. There was a weariness in the way she walked.

They approached and presented their credentials. "Miss Kluth, we're with the state police. My name is Lou Reynolds, and this is Detective Gino Peterson. We're just here to ask you a few questions. Can we come in?"

"Questions about what?" she responded in a German accent.

"Can we go inside? I'd rather not talk on the street," Lou said.

Gretchen was a quick study. "You want to talk to me about Julio, don't you?" Then in rapid fire, "Did you find him? Where is he? Is he all right? Why hasn't he called me? It's been four years; how long does he expect me to wait..."

"Slow down. Let's go upstairs. We'll explain everything," Gino said.

She led them to her third-floor apartment. It was sparsely furnished, meticulously clean, and decorated with the warmth of a hospital room.

"I'm sorry to tell you that we found what we think is Julio's body. I'm afraid he was murdered." Lou was steady and deliberate in his delivery.

"Those bastards," she said. "I knew they killed him. They lied to his mother. She died never knowing what happened to her son."

Gino noticed not one tear fell from the eyes of Gretchen Kluth.

"Who do you think killed him?" he asked.

"I always knew in my heart that if Julio was dead, it was Tiger's fault. Julio worshipped his cousin, but I knew that fat bastard would turn on him sooner or later. Julio was not a mobster. He just liked to hang around with his cousin—you know, feel important. That's what got him killed."

"I have to ask if you know what dentist he went to," Lou said.

"Dentist? Why do you need to know what dentist he went to?" She was obviously puzzled by the question.

"We need to match his dental records with the teeth left in his jaw. I'm sorry, but it's the only way we can be certain it's him," Lou said.

"We both went to Dr. Frank Saccocia on Reservoir Avenue in Cranston. I still go there; he's in an office building across from Cranston Hospital."

"Thanks. We'll follow up with the dentist. Do you want the medical examiner's number?" Lou asked.

"You can make arrangements with the examiner to give Julio a proper burial and put this part of your life behind you," Gino added.

"Arrangements? Are you kidding me? Now that I know what happened to Julio, I'm moving back to Germany. This country is fucked up; imagine killing your own cousin. Someone else can bury Julio. Maybe his asshole cousin will pay for the funeral."

So much for sentimentality, Gino thought.

"But we're going to need you for the grand jury and the trial," Lou said.

With a defiant stare, Gretchen said, "The only reason I've stayed in this country was to wait for Julio to come back to me. Now that I know he's dead, I'm leaving. You can ask me anything you want today, but then I'm gone. If you want me for anything else, you'll have to come to Germany."

Lou and Gino knew the best they were going to do was get a statement from her; there was no bullshit in this woman.

"We'll take a tape-recorded statement right here, if that's all right with you. Just let me get my recorder out of the car," Lou said.

The next day, Lou and Gino made a visit to Dr. Frank Saccocia. He turned over the dental records of Julio Lanni, and they brought them to the medical examiner.

Two weeks later, the medical examiner positively identified the body from the reservoir as Julio Lanni. The autopsy report indicated that Mr. Lanni of Providence, age twenty-five, suffered blunt force trauma to the skull, which caused his death. The manner of death was ruled a homicide.

CHAPTER 48

Michelle told Gino it was time to bring all the cases to the grand jury. The Dickie Calderone case would require the testimony of Moon, Billy, and Marty. Moon would have to explain why he lied to the state police and how that lie led to the cooperation of Billy and Marty. Billy and Marty would give their eyewitness accounts of the murder.

Officer Dan Kelly of Rehoboth Police, Massachusetts state troopers, crime scene investigators, and the medical examiner would also testify in the Calderone case. Michelle would testify about the bad blood between Tiger and Calderone.

For the James McDonald murder, Providence police detectives, the medical examiner, and Toby would testify. Billy would be the state's star witness.

Michelle wanted more work done on the Moron case. It would be hard to convince a jury that someone was shot in a restaurant full of people without producing one eyewitness who was not in protective custody. She told Gino to team up with Lou to track down a witness.

"Well," Lou said, "there's no way we're going to find anyone who was a customer. I don't even know where we'd start to look. Let's try to locate someone who was working at the restaurant."

Their first visit was to the Providence City Hall licensing bureau. They asked the unexpectedly pleasant clerk who held the license for Pita's Restaurant in 1982. She smiled and asked for a few minutes to search the records. Twenty minutes later, she returned to tell them that in 1982, the license was held by a Mr. Spiro Haritos, and added he still held the license.

"Thank you," Lou said. "Next stop, Pita's Restaurant. Let's go."

When they arrived at Pita's Restaurant, it was about ten thirty in the morning. The breakfast crowd was gone, and the place was empty except for two old men enjoying coffee and reading the paper. They approached a waitress, identified themselves, and asked for the owner. She nodded and left for the kitchen.

Spiro Haritos emerged from the swinging doors of the kitchen. Haritos, about fifty, sported salt-and-pepper hair, a large nose, and protruding front teeth that produced a slight lisp when he spoke. Lou explained why they were there, and the owner shook his head violently.

"Those sons of bitches almost ruined my business. If I was here that night, I would have called the cops. I talked to my help the next day, but they were so scared of Tiger, they made me promise not to report it."

"You should have called," Lou said.

"What was I supposed to do? I wasn't about to get anyone who works for me killed," Haritos said.

"Can you tell us who was working that night?" Gino asked.

"There's only one guy you should talk to, but he doesn't work here anymore," Haritos said.

"Why him?" Gino asked.

"Because he was behind the counter and saw the whole thing, and he's probably the only person stupid enough to talk to you."

"Why's that?" Lou asked.

"He's from Greece, only been here a few years. He hasn't been around long enough to be scared of these guys, still thinks everyone is on the up-and-up," Haritos answered.

"How do we find him?" Lou asked.

"These guys move from restaurant to restaurant. He could be working anywhere."

"Listen, Mr. Haritos, this is a murder investigation. If you know where he is, you better tell us," Lou said.

"Look, I'm in the food business, not the bullshit business. I don't know where he is. I'm telling you the truth."

"Then just give us the name," Gino said.

"Tim Karakides," he answered.

"What does he look like?" Gino asked.

"He's small, five foot six or seven, but everything else about him is big: head, belly, hands, and shoulders. He looks like one of those weightlifters in the Olympics."

The Greek community was as tight-knit as most ethnic groups. If they decided to hide Karakides from the police or help get him back to Greece, he would be gone. Lou knew a young federal agent named Theo Christopoulos who might be of help finding Karakides. Lou and Theo had become friends lifting weights at the YMCA, and Theo was tight with the Greek community.

Lou and Gino returned to the unit and explained the situation to Michelle. Overnight, she arranged for Agent Theo Christopoulos to assist the state police, unheard of under Colonel Smith's tenure. The colonel feared leaks and corruption, no matter the agency, and convincing him to let them work with Christopoulos was an indication of his burning desire to bring down the Mob. Gino also knew the success or failure of the cases would define Michelle's tenure as boss of the intelligence unit.

Lou had always spoken highly of Christopoulos, so Gino was looking forward to working with him. Lou gave Theo a call, and they agreed to meet at the federal building in Providence.

When Gino met Theo, he sensed self-confidence that belied his two years as an agent. Christopoulos was about five foot eleven and had jet-black hair, dark brown eyes, and the physique of a gymnast.

Lou proceeded to lay out the facts of the Moron Marchetti case.

"Theo, we need to find Tim Karakides," Lou told him. "We can't infiltrate the Greek community like you. If they think we're looking for him, they're going to hide him."

"I'll ask around," Theo said. "If he hasn't gone back to Greece, I'll get a line on him."

"Speaking of Greece," Lou said, "are your parents still there?"

"Yeah," Theo answered. "They tried it here for a couple of years, but my dad decided it wasn't for him."

Lou asked, "How much time do you need to find Karakides?"

"Give me three days, and I'll have an answer," he said.

"We'll wait to hear from you," Lou said.

Within two days of the meeting, Theo found Tim Karakides working in a Greek restaurant in Providence. Gino, Lou, and Theo approached him there and had an animated conversation. The interview was a wild game of English to Greek, Greek to Greek, and then Greek to English, but somehow it worked, and Karakides was convinced to cooperate.

Lou explained to Michelle that Theo had located Karakides and he was willing to cooperate. She wanted him interviewed that night, so Theo agreed to pick up Karakides and bring him to the intelligence unit office.

The duo arrived at the intelligence unit at seven, and the interview began quickly, before Karakides had a chance to change his mind. With Theo translating, Karakides explained that he knew Moron and Tiger's crew from their frequent visits to the restaurant. He then told them about the night of the Moron's murder.

Karakides was working on an order when he heard a commotion in the entryway. From the window at the end of the counter, he had a clear view of the struggle that took place in the vestibule. Karakides became more and more emotional as he described what happened to the Moron.

Karakides stopped speaking for a moment, and tears streamed down his face. Speaking in English for the first time, he said in a heavy Greek accent, "They pushed him up against wall, and they kill him. They kill him like chicken. I call my mother in Greece. I cry like baby."

Lou walked into Michelle's office and told her she could call Renée and tell her they had a witness who was not in protective custody.

Michelle nodded and picked up the phone; before she dialed, she looked at Lou and said, "Karakides is the last piece of the puzzle, it's definitely time to go to the grand jury."

CHAPTER 49

The cases were presented to a statewide grand jury at the Providence County Judicial Complex in Providence. Red brick wrapped itself around a huge seven-story building that stretched along Benefit Street for a full block. Atop the center of the building was a large clock tower visible throughout the city. Literally built into the side of a hill, the courthouse was adjacent to Brown University and the Rhode Island School of Design. Scattered around the courthouse were Victorian-style homes and small businesses catering to the student set.

Prior to the grand jury, Gino met with Renée and Arnold about the protected witnesses and their appearance before the grand jury. The primary consideration was their security as they were brought to and from the courthouse.

Gino developed a plan that included Providence police and state police. Together, they would be in charge of securing the perimeter and the doors of the courthouse. Pairs of officers would be stationed at the four corners of the building and all doors.

The outer perimeter would be manned by the state police SWAT team, taking positions on the top of the surrounding buildings. Once inside the courthouse, the security of the witnesses would be the responsibility of the intelligence unit.

On the first day of grand jury testimony, Gino woke early after a night filled with anxiety. Michelle's words ran through his head. *Gino, you'll handle security for the witnesses.* He knew that if the Mob was intent on stopping these cases, it would have to eliminate the protected witnesses.

The security detail was required to be at the Chepachet barracks at eight o'clock in the morning. Gino arrived at seven and got a cranky Moon showered. They dressed him in a conservative blue suit, white shirt, red striped tie, and black wingtips.

The security caravan made the forty-five-minute ride to the courthouse with lights flashing and sirens blaring. Moon and Gino rode in the backseat of one of the cruisers. The sounds of the sirens made for a private conversation.

"I envy you," Moon said.

"Why?"

"You got a straight job, people respect you, and you get to carry a gun."

They both laughed.

Moon told Gino he regretted not staying in the service and making it a career. "I know it's too late for me, but I think I could have made something of myself if I didn't get hooked up with these guys. I was young and stupid. I could have put in twenty years, retired, and still have been young enough to start another career. Instead, I came home and got suckered into the life."

He continued, "We're not very much different, you and I. We started in the same place, just took different paths."

"I wouldn't say this to anyone I work with, but I always admired you," Gino said. "The way you handled the Mob's books and still treated winners and losers fair and square. If you'd been a legitimate business-man, you'd probably be a millionaire."

"I'd like to think so." Moon paused and looked at Gino. "You know, it would've been nice having a sharp kid like you by my side."

They got off the highway on the outskirts of the city and wound their way through side streets to avoid the morning traffic. The caravan parked on Hopkins Street, a side street that ran along the south side of the building. There was a door to the courthouse about halfway down the street. As they pulled onto Hopkins, Gino could see pairs of offic-ers at each corner. The state police SWAT team was deployed, but only the team leader knew where or how many.

The Hopkins Street door was guarded by two familiar faces, Troopers Rick Schneider and Frank King, training academy classmates. They both gave him a quick nod as Moon was led into the courthouse. They hustled Moon into a small conference room for grand jury witnesses.

Michelle let out a sigh of relief when they entered the room. "Well, that's half the battle. Let's hope they get him into the grand jury fast. I want to get him back as soon as possible."

At ten thirty, there was a knock on the door, and in walked Renée St. Pierre and Arnold Bernstein. Moon stood and shook their hands. Renée and Arnold dumped legal pads and law books on the table.

"OK, Moon," Renée began, "the grand jury's ready to hear from you. We need you to explain how this all got started."

"You mean my call to the state police?" Moon asked.

"That and everything else," Arnold responded. "We'll start with you joining Tiger's crew and how you eventually ended up running his gambling operation. Then everything you heard them say about the Calderone murder."

"What about the Massachusetts beef?"

"Of course, tell them about that. How you ended up in prison and why you called the state police," Arnold said.

"I called them because I didn't beat that guy from Fall River. I already told you that," Moon said with a hint of agitation in his voice.

"We know that, Moon," Renée said calmly, "but you have to tell the grand jury. They have to understand that you used everything Marty, Tiger, Billy, and Big John told you about the Calderone murder. You used it to convince the state police that you were there the night he was killed."

"OK, but what about Massachusetts? When are you going to get the conviction tossed?" Moon asked.

An angered Renée answered, "Look, Moon, we've been over this before. We'll take care of Massachusetts after we're done with the Rhode Island cases. You just go in and tell your story, and we'll do the rest. Understand?"

"I understand," Moon responded.

Renée and Arnold gathered their books and pads. As she left, Renée said, "Michelle, give us five minutes and bring him in. When he's done, I need you to come in and give them an overview of the Pasquale Raimondi crime family and the feud between Tiger and Dickie Calderone."

Five minutes stretched into twenty-five, and then Sully stuck his head in and said, "Let's go, Moon."

Gino walked with Moon down a deserted corridor to the grand jury. Behind the ornate wooden door sat twenty-four jurors waiting to hear his story.

For the first time in his life, Moon was free to tell the truth. As he walked in, Gino thought, *They say the truth will set you free, but for Moon, it was a lie.*

CHAPTER 50

F or the next month, there was a steady stream of witnesses into the grand jury as the state presented the Calderone, McDonald, and Marchetti murder cases. Police officers, state troopers, forensic experts, medical examiners, and witnesses, protected and otherwise, testified.

Forty witnesses later, the statewide grand jury returned indictments against Frank "Tiger" Detroia and his crew: Big John, Marty, and Billy. The indictments gave Attorney General Thomas Morgan the press he needed to bolster his reelection campaign. His opponent, a former physician who gave up her vocation to pursue a career in law, was hammering him about his lack of organized crime convictions.

The headlines were better than paid political advertising: **MORGAN ANNOUNCES INDICTMENTS AGAINST**

RAIMONDI CRIME FAMILY, TIGER DETROIA CREW DISMANTLED, and **BEGINNING OF THE END FOR UP-AND-COMING MOBSTER.**

As soon as the indictments were announced, Renée was contacted by defense attorney Americo Salvatore, who told her he would be representing Big John Kazarian. Salvatore, a man of humble beginnings, was educated in Providence's public schools before attending Washington College and Revere Law School in Boston. He was tall and thin, with a penchant for custom-made suits and imported Italian loafers. At forty-five, he had a receding hairline, which he compensated for with mutton-chop sideburns. Thick glasses sat atop a large nose flattened as the result of a short stint as a professional boxer.

Jurors were drawn to his polished appearance and bellowing baritone. They perceived him as the outsider fighting the system, the quintessential antihero. When questioned by reporters about his Mob clientele, he consistently denied there was a Mafia. He would often say it was a figment of the press's imagination, stemming from Hollywood movies.

Tiger was represented by Boston attorney Richard Silverman. He was a little man standing about five foot five. What he lacked in height, he made up for with bluster. Silverman carried a chip on his shoulder as large as his client.

He was a walk-on player with the Massachusetts State University football team; he possessed catlike speed and the ability to hit like a sledgehammer, and he ended his football career a conference all-star.

Silverman attended a Catholic university law school; he applied only because he was Jewish and had been told by his classmates at State U he would never get accepted. Confounding expectations, he was accepted and graduated at the top of his class. He was offered a job at a premier law firm in Boston. He worked there for two years before deciding he preferred to fight for the little guy rather than represent corporate executives.

Silverman started out successfully defending small-time criminals from Boston's South End. He caught the eye of the Boston faction of the Raimondi crime family, and they sent him a capo that was jammed up on a RICO indictment based largely on the word of a cooperating witness.

Silverman had no respect for "weasels" who ratted on their friends, and the capo was acquitted largely because of Silverman's withering cross-examination of the cooperating witness. His destruction of the witness was the talk of the Boston legal set and duly noted by the Mob.

The Mob continued to send him clients, and Silverman joked to his friends that the Mafia, a centuries-old Italian criminal organization, needed a Jew to protect them.

Silverman contacted Renée and Arnold and gave the party line regarding his client. No testimony, no statements, only an appearance for an arraignment on the indictments.

CHAPTER 51

The defendants were scheduled to be arraigned six weeks after the return of the indictments. Until the trials began, the witnesses would be idle. Michelle gave Gino permission to take them golfing, jogging, weightlifting—anything within reason, as long as they were taken separately. Putting them together would offer the defense the opportunity to argue that their testimony was fabricated to be consistent.

Billy spent the downtime with his family. Moon and Marty dealt with their families differently. Moon wanted no visitors and had no contact with his family. His brothers and sisters lived on Federal Hill but had nothing to do with him since he flipped. To visit him would be a show of their support for his decision, and it would mean they would always live in fear of retribution.

Marty was constantly calling family and friends. He didn't give a fuck that he had turned state's evidence, and he let everyone know that his "friends" had tried to kill him in prison. Although divorced, he still kept in touch with his ex-wife, who was remarried but raising their two teenage sons.

Marty's ex-wife, Elaine Volpini, formerly Elaine Martelinni, worked at Vinnie's Pizza, a thriving pizza parlor on River Avenue in the Smith Hill section of Providence.

Her new husband, Aldo Volpini, tolerated the phone calls and the occasional visit from Marty when he was on the street. He certainly did not object when his wife suddenly possessed a wad of cash after a visit from her ex-husband.

On one occasion, while he was in custody, Marty got an urgent phone call from Elaine. Dean, his youngest son, nineteen, had fallen in love and decided to marry his eighteen-year-old girlfriend. Marty's son had no job, no prospects, not even a place to live when he got married.

Marty agreed to talk to his son, and Lou and Gino arranged for the meeting to take place at state police headquarters. They took Marty out of his cell at Chepachet and made the drive to headquarters around nine at night.

When they arrived at headquarters, Dean was waiting in the front lobby. He was tall and thin and dressed like John Travolta in *Saturday Night Fever*. Gino brought Dean from the lobby into the detective office. Lou and

Gino sat at one end of the room, and Dean and Marty sat at the other.

Marty started right in, no pleasantries or small talk. "Dean, your mother says you want to get married, right?"

"That's right, Dad," Dean said. "I'm going to marry Pat Malinson. Her dad owns the gas station on Plainfield Street. He said he'd give me a job after we get married. He probably thinks I got her pregnant, but she's not."

Marty started in on his son.

"Yeah, I know him, Dean, but that's not the point. He's only offering you a job because of his daughter. You don't know a fucking thing about fixing cars. All you're going to do is pump gas for the rest of your life."

"But Dad—"

"No, Dean," Marty said. "You're just a kid. What are you, fucking nuts? Are you out of your mind, marrying your first piece of ass? You think your mother was the first one?"

Gino and Lou turned away to avoid Marty seeing them laugh. Marty formed his thumbs and forefingers into an upside-down triangle, a rough representation of the female genitalia. He moved his hands up and down as he continued to speak in machine-gun-like fashion.

"This thing, Dean, this thing—it'll paralyze your mind. Don't you understand? They fight wars over this thing. They launched a thousand ships over this thing. Guys are doing life bids over this thing, and you want to throw your life away on the first one you've seen up close?"

By that time, Gino and Lou were bent over, snorting and giggling. Lou had tears streaming down his face, and Gino faked a coughing fit to disguise the laughter.

"But, Dad—" Dean tried again.

"No buts. No wedding. Enjoy getting your end wet with Pat Malinson for now, but believe me, she won't be the last. You're not getting married. Do you understand, Dean?"

"Yes, Dad," Dean said.

CHAPTER 52

Frank "Tiger" Detroia and John "Big John" Kazarian were arraigned at the Providence County Superior Court on September 28, 1983. Dressed in blue sports coats, open-collared white shirts, and khakis, they looked like schoolboys from Al Capone Preparatory Academy.

They stood before Judge Frances Kiley with their attorneys, Silverman and Salvatore. Tiger pled not guilty to the charge of first-degree murder in the case of Fredo "The Moron" Marchetti, not guilty to the charge of first-degree murder in the case of Richard "Dickie" Calderone, and not guilty to the charge of second-degree murder in the case of James McDonald.

As Gino watched Tiger enter his not guilty pleas, he studied him closely. He was of average height, with a round body, short stump-like legs, and a large chest that drew attention away from his large belly. Despite the shape, Gino could almost sense the strength; it radiated from the way he walked and stood. A pointed nose, thin lips, and bushy eyebrows turned up like out-of-control bullwhips dominated his face. He glared at the judge and everyone in the gallery. His response when asked to enter a plea was a contemptuous "not guilty."

Next came Big John, who pled not guilty to the charge of first-degree murder in the case of Fredo "The Moron" Marchetti, not guilty to the charge of first-degree murder in the case of Richard "Dickie" Calderone, and not guilty to the charge of murder in the first degree in the death of Julio Lanni.

Big John was a giant of a man who reminded Gino of Italian heavyweight boxing champion Primo Canera. Canera's title was bought and paid for by the Mob, and the irony of the similarities wasn't lost on Gino. Like Canera, Big John was all muscle and no brains, both puppets dancing from strings pulled by their Mob masters. Big John answered "not guilty" to each charge. He looked bewildered by the frenzied atmosphere.

Arnold Bernstein then made a motion to have the defendants held without bail. He argued that the judge should consider the defendants a danger to society by the very nature of the charges. The community was in danger every day Tiger and Big John walked the streets.

Silverman and Salvatore argued for bail. Despite knowing they were targets of a grand jury investigation, their clients had not fled and had appeared when summoned. They argued that both defendants had strong ties to the community and were not flight risks.

Judge Kiley gave little consideration to the defense and held both defendants without bail.

"Frank Detroia, you're hereby remanded to the warden of the adult correctional institution and held without bail until trial. John Kazarian, you're hereby remanded to the warden of the adult correctional institution and held without bail until trial. Court dismissed." Judge Kiley banged her gavel and left the bench.

The state marshals surrounded the defendants and, after cuffing them, led them out of the courtroom. As Tiger walked past the prosecution table, he turned toward Renée and Arnold and said, "Fuck you."

CHAPTER 53

Teresa had just finished laying out the strips of homemade pasta on her kitchen table. In a few hours, she and Gino would be feasting on a meal of pasta and meatballs covered with the sauce simmering on the stove.

As she washed her hands in the kitchen sink, there was a loud knock on the door.

"Who's there?"

"Mrs. Peterson, we have a gift for you, compliments of a friend."

She recognized the heavy Sicilian accent immediately. She opened the door to find two well-dressed men standing before her. Each wore a dark suit and black fedora. They were dressed like the "men of respect" of her native Sicily, and she knew instantly what kind of men they were.

One reminded her of the actor Anthony Quinn, with dark wavy hair and large features. He fingered a diamond pinkie ring as he spoke. The other was short and squat, like a fire hydrant come alive. His short arms held a large fish wrapped in white paper.

"Mrs. Peterson, this is for you, compliments of Mr. Raimondi. He wishes you and your family the best. His wish is that you enjoy this gift with your son, Gino."

The short one handed her the fish, and she received it with shaking hands. She knew it was a custom of the Mafia to leave a fish at the doorstep of someone who was about to be killed. "Tonight, you sleep with the fishes" was the message.

She mustered the courage to ask, "So this is for Gino?"

The big one spoke. "Although we wish your son was, should I say, not so zealous in his work, this is merely a gift for you."

As they walked away, she slammed the door, threw the fish onto the kitchen counter, and picked up the phone. With trembling hands, she called Gino.

"Detective Peterson."

"Gino, Gino, two men were just here, and they gave me a fish!" Her voice was rushed, and her words came between gulps of air. It was unlike her to be scared, and it unnerved him.

"Slow down, Ma. What are you talking about?" he asked.

She explained, and he tried to reassure her. "Mom, don't worry. I'll take care of this; no one is going to hurt you."

"Son, it's not me I'm worried about. It's you," she said.

Anger rose up inside him, but he didn't want to alarm her, so he spoke calmly. "Don't worry about me, and I don't want you to be scared. I told you, I will take care of this." He couldn't help growing angrier as he spoke.

"But Gino—"

"You won't be getting any more visits after today."

"Just promise me you won't do anything to get yourself in trouble. You've worked too hard to get where you are," she said.

"This has nothing to do with work. This is personal."

They knew each other well enough to know the discussion was over.

"I love you, Gino."

"I love you, Mom."

CHAPTER 54

Father Andre Messier heard confessions every Saturday from four to five at Our Lady of Mercy Church in West Warwick, a working-class town made up of French Canadians, Italians, and Portuguese. The stucco-styled church was built by French Canadian immigrants who came to the States to work in the mills that dotted the nearby Pawtuxet River.

As Father Messier entered the confessional booth at ten minutes to four, he stopped to say hello to the accumulation of old ladies, youngsters from the Catholic school, and a familiar figure.

Nicholas "Nicky" Gemma, acting boss of the Raimondi crime family, was a regular. Every Saturday, he would enter the confessional and confess his sins, but Father Messier choked on the words as he absolved the sinner and clutched at his scapular as he handed out Gemma's penance. It was the one time Messier felt a sense of hypocrisy for forgiving a sinner who had no desire to truly repent, but he had taken a vow to forgive sins without judgment.

After receiving absolution, Gemma left the confessional and sought a pew close to the altar to say his prayers of penance and reflect on the crucifix, which was the centerpiece of the altar.

Gino quickly moved into the pew behind Gemma. The movement behind him did not cause Gemma to stir; he continued to concentrate on the crucifix. Gino slowly pulled the snub nose .357 magnum from his shoulder holster and placed it firmly against the nape of Gemma's neck. Gemma tensed for a moment and started to turn. When he did, Gino slowly drew back the hammer, and it clicked into place. Gemma stopped moving, drew a deep breath, and slowly blew it out.

"Nicky, I promise you, if you ever send anyone to talk to my mother again, I will kill you. Not only will I take your life, I'll make it look like one of your Mob hits."

Gemma relaxed a bit. "For God's sake, Gino, you're in a church. What the hell is wrong with you?"

"What's wrong with me? You send two goons to my mother's house, and you want to know what's wrong with me? You crossed the line, and you know it."

"But Gino—"

"My mother has always shown respect to everyone in the neighborhood, and you send someone over to threaten her. What's the matter? Didn't you have the balls to talk to me?" Gino said.

"Put the gun down, OK? Listen, no one is going to hurt your mother. Just put the gun down, and give me a chance to explain." Gemma spoke calmly, but Gino could see his neck muscles twitching.

Gino placed him thumb firmly over the trigger and released it, slowly sliding the hammer back into place. He leaned forward and spoke directly into Gemma's ear.

"I'm listening," he said.

"The only reason those guys were sent to your house was because the Old Man wanted me to talk to you. He knew you wouldn't come if we just reached out to you, so we had to do something to get your attention. I swear, nothing will ever happen to her."

"And how do I know that?" Gino asked.

"First of all, if you got this close to me, you can do it again. Then there's the heat we would take from your friends if we ever hurt her—and you know the Old Man doesn't like heat."

"What's the Old Man want from me?"

"He remembers you and your family from the neighborhood, and he really admires what you've accomplished. I mean, an Italian on the state police— that's unheard of. You have to admit that," Nicky said.

"So you're telling me you threatened my mother so the Old Man could tell me how proud he is of me? You're kidding me, right?" Gino asked.

"No, no. Listen, he understands what it took for you to get where you are, and we'd never jeopardize that, but something has to be done about the Tiger situation. We know the guy's a loose cannon, but we have to protect our interests," Nicky said.

"Get to the point, Nicky."

"We think we can help each other," Nicky said.

"Help each other?"

"The Old Man knows you'd never take money, and we would never insult you in that way. All we're asking is that you let us know how the debriefings are going—exactly what these guys are going to say at the trial. If we know ahead of time, we can pass it on to our lawyers."

"I'd end up in jail when they find out. Did you ever consider that?" Gino said.

"It could never come back to you because all the testimony is going to come out at trial anyway. The lawyers would just be more prepared for cross-examination. It's perfect because no one ever has to know. No one would even question it."

"How does that help me?" Gino asked.

"In return, we will, shall we say, provide you with information about our rivals. You can take them off the streets, and you'd be golden at work—you'd be a superstar. Now what's the harm in that?"

Gino took the revolver out again and placed it against the back of Nicky's neck. Nicky tensed, and Gino could see his shoulder rise and fall rapidly as he took in each breath.

He imagined Nicky was saying a silent prayer as he waited for the hammer to drop and end his life. Gino used the opportunity to quietly slide to the end of the pew and leave the church.

CHAPTER 55

Robert Lee Nugent was warden of the United States Penitentiary in Atlanta. Carlo Ponzi and Al Capone were among its famous alumni, and now it housed the head of organized crime in New England, Pasquale Raimondi.

As warden, Nugent was notified whenever someone from law enforcement or a prosecutor requested a visit with a high-ranking member of the Mafia. Just before Labor Day in 1983, the warden approved a visit for Raimondi. He knew from past experience that most visits to mobsters were fruitless, but he approved them anyway.

The visitor would come into the glass-partitioned visiting room and wait patiently. The mobster would walk in, pick up the phone, listen for a minute, and walk away; rarely did the visitor leave with any valuable information. What he was not aware of was that

Pasquale was no ordinary Mafioso, and this was no ordinary visit. Pasquale had an iron grip on everyone he controlled, and he was about to demonstrate that control thousands of miles away from his fiefdom.

After presenting the proper credentials, the visitor was led to the visiting area and took his seat. The Old Man walked in wearing prison garb but looking as relaxed as if he had just taken a stroll down Atwells Avenue. He sat down and picked up the phone. The cold eyes locked on to the visitor.

"Listen, I'm only talking to you because I know your family."

"But you reached out to—"

"I'll tell you one thing. I haven't seen a good movie since I been in this joint."

"What?"

"Old movies. I like old movies. You know what movie I like? *Charge of the Light Brigade.* I think Errol Flynn was in that one."

"What does that have to do—"

"I like it because the general sends the soldiers into battle, even though he knows they're all going to die. He has no choice; they have to try and take the enemy out. It's the only way."

"But—"

"Listen to me, and try to understand. Sometimes a general has to lose a soldier or two for a greater cause," Pasquale told his visitor.

"Why would a general risk losing a valuable resource like that? It's suicide," the visitor said.

"You're right. It's a problem for the general, so instead of wasting a valuable resource, he makes him use an expendable associate. See, the valuable resource knows how to get the job done with someone who's disposable, so the general gives the order to the valuable resource, and it's done." Pasquale's eyes narrowed, and he cracked a small smile.

"But that could lead right back to the resource," the visitor said.

"He's too smart to let that happen—that's why he's so valuable. End of interview. Have a safe trip back."

Pasquale hung up the phone and walked away.

CHAPTER 56

On a Monday, four weeks after the arraignments, the beating death of James McDonald was the first case to be tried. The deputy sheriff bellowed the official greeting of the court: "Hear ye! Hear ye! Hear ye! All persons having business before this honorable court, draw near, give your attention and ye shall be heard. God save the State of Rhode Island and Providence Plantations."

Judge Robert Kruger banged his gavel and asked everyone to be seated. Kruger was a tall, gangly man with stork-like features. A former federal prosecutor, he controlled his courtroom with icy stares and an economy of words. The clerk called the case, "State of Rhode Island versus Frank L. Detroia, murder in the second degree."

"Will the defendant and counsel please identify themselves for the record?" Judge Kruger asked. Tiger and Silverman rose simultaneously.

"Frank L. Detroia, Your Honor," said the big man.

"Attorney Richard Silverman of One Twenty-Four Tremont Street, Boston, for the defendant, Your Honor," Silverman said.

The judge then continued with the formalities. "Mr. Silverman, would you please enter a plea for your client on indictment P1/9184-1508A?"

"Not guilty, Your Honor," Silverman said.

Judge Kruger then glanced over to the prosecution table. Renée and Arnold stood.

"Assistant Attorney General Renée St. Pierre for the state, Your Honor," she said.

"I'm Special Assistant Attorney General Arnold Bernstein for the state, Your Honor. May I make a formal motion at this time to allow Detective Gino Peterson to assist at the counsel table?"

"No objection," Silverman answered.

"Motion granted," the judge replied.

The first few days of the trial were taken up with pretrial motions and jury selection. Judge Kruger ruled on the motions quickly, and by Thursday afternoon, the jury was impaneled. He admonished the jury not to talk about the case, read about it, or watch television accounts of the trial.

On the following Monday morning, as the trial began, the courtroom was packed with the Detroia and McDonald clans. On the McDonald side of the courtroom, every shade of green known to man was displayed, and if freckles were currency, they would all be rich.

On Detroia's side, every shirt was unbuttoned to the belly, and there was enough gold jewelry and leather on display to sink a Spanish galleon.

Promptly at ten, Judge Kruger emerged from chambers, took his seat, and began the trial. The courtroom quieted, and all seemed to lean forward to hear Renée's opening remarks.

"Ladies and gentlemen of the jury, the state will present evidence which will prove beyond a reasonable doubt that on the night of August 23, Frank 'Tiger' Detroia beat James McDonald to death with a baseball bat. You'll hear from the victim's brother, who will testify that the defendant chased them down in a road rage incident that led to the victim's death. You'll also hear from cooperating witness William 'Billy' Franco. He'll testify that the defendant wrested a baseball bat from James McDonald and beat him to death. The state is confident that, once you hear the evidence, you'll return a verdict of guilty of murder in the second degree against Frank Detroia."

"Thank you, Miss St. Pierre. Mr. Silverman?" Judge Kruger asked.

"The defendant waives his right to an opening statement, Your Honor," Silverman replied.

Arnold explained to Gino that he wasn't surprised Silverman didn't make an opening statement. This case was all about Billy's credibility, and the quicker he could get to Billy on cross-examination, the better for his client.

"Very well, then," Judge Kruger said, looking at the prosecution table. "Call your first witness."

Arnold called Detective Wayne Sizemore of the Providence Police Department. Sizemore, a veteran of thirty years, took the stand. His testimony was right out of Police Testimony 101: he gave short, direct answers without a hint of embellishment.

Sizemore described the investigation of the baseball bat beating of James McDonald. He testified about the crime scene, the initial statement taken from Toby McDonald, and attending the autopsy. Sizemore concluded with the fact that the police were unable to identify the two individuals involved. The case remained unsolved until Billy came forward.

Richard Silverman asked Sizemore one question on cross-examination. He asked if, in 1982, Toby McDonald ever gave a statement identifying Tiger as one of the assailants. Sizemore answered the only way he could. "No, sir, he did not."

Arnold then called Dr. Richard Skolnick, the Rhode Island medical examiner. He testified that James McDonald was a healthy twenty-five-year-old male at the time of his death. The autopsy cited numerous skull fractures consistent with being hit with a blunt instrument.

"Did you determine a cause of death, Dr. Skolnick?" Arnold asked.

"Blunt force trauma to the skull," he answered.

On cross-examination, Silverman asked about the toxicology report. "Doctor, can you tell the jury what Mr. McDonald's blood alcohol level was at the time of his death?"

"Yes. Mr. McDonald's blood alcohol level was .20," Skolnick answered.

"And the legal limit, at least for driving, is .10, correct?" Silverman inquired.

"Objection, Your Honor, relevance. This isn't a drunken-driving case."

"Your Honor, if you'll permit me, I will demonstrate the relevance."

"Very well. Overruled; you may proceed," the judge said.

"Based on your training and experience, is it your medical opinion that a person who is over .10 is impaired?"

"That's correct."

"That impairment could alter a person's behavior as well as their driving, isn't that correct, Doctor?" Silverman asked.

"Yes, I suppose so," the doctor answered.

"Could it make someone violent, argumentative, or combative?" Silverman asked.

"Well, obviously, yes, but that would depend on the individual's reaction to alcohol. Not everyone reacts the same way," Dr. Skolnick answered.

"Nothing further, Your Honor." Silverman ended his cross-examination.

"Any redirect, Mr. Bernstein?" Judge Kruger asked.

"Nothing further, Your Honor," Arnold answered.

Judge Kruger dismissed the medical examiner. "You may step down, Doctor."

Gino could see the first of Silverman's strategies—to subtly imply McDonald was responsible for his own death.

CHAPTER 57

Arnold called Toby McDonald to the stand to testify about the encounter that led to his brother's death.

He told the jury how he pleaded with his brother not to confront the two men. He swallowed his pride and admitted that he hid under the dashboard when the duo approached.

Silverman started his cross-examination of Toby.

"Mr. McDonald, I know this is difficult for you, but can I ask a few questions about that night?"

"Yes," Toby answered.

"Did you and your brother have a few drinks that night?"

"Yeah, we had a few beers and a couple of shots."

"How many, would you say?"

"Maybe a six-pack between us."

"So you had at least three beers and a shot each. Would that be accurate?" Silverman asked.

"We had a few, but I could still drive," Toby answered defensively.

"Describe for me what happened right after your car stopped near the highway entrance ramp," Silverman asked.

"Jimmy grabbed the bat and jumped out," Toby answered.

"All right," Silverman continued. "What happened next?"

"The two guys started coming toward us, and Jimmy was hollering for them to keep coming."

"Did you hear exactly what he said to them?"

"Not really. Everything was pretty confusing."

"What happened next?" Silverman continued.

"Well, I was screaming at Jimmy to put the bat down and get back in the car. I wanted to get the fuck—oh, excuse me, Your Honor. I wanted to get out of there. I could tell these guys meant business, but Jimmy was out of control, and he wouldn't listen," Toby testified.

Silverman asked, "Two people were headed toward your brother, correct?"

"Yeah, that's correct," Toby answered.

"Who got to him first?" Silverman asked.

The second strategy revealed itself to Gino. Billy, not Tiger, killed Jimmy.

"Well, the skinny guy was first," Toby responded. You could almost hear Renée's and Arnold's hearts skip a beat.

"The skinny guy, as you testified—not my client, correct?" Silverman asked.

"Correct."

"Let me ask you again, which one of them got to your brother first?" Silverman continued. He waited for the answer he knew had to come.

"The skinny guy."

"Was it my client?" Silverman pointed to Tiger.

"No."

"The last thing you saw was the skinny guy headed for your brother, correct?"

"Yes," Toby responded meekly.

"Did you see the struggle for the bat?" Silverman asked.

"No."

"You can't tell this jury that my client took that bat away from your brother and struck him with it, can you, Mr. McDonald?"

"No, I can't," Toby answered, knowing quite well what was coming.

"And why was that, Mr. McDonald?"

"Because I ducked under the dashboard when they got close to the car," Toby said.

"So this other guy—the skinny guy, as you call him—could have struck and killed your brother with the bat, isn't that true, Mr. McDonald?" Silverman was driving his point home with a sledgehammer.

"Objection. Calls for conjecture on the part of the witness," Renée said, jumping to her feet.

"Denied. This is cross-examination; the witness can offer his opinion if he wishes," Judge Kruger said. "You may answer, Mr. McDonald."

"Yes," Toby said without much conviction.

"And this other guy, you have come to learn, is Billy Franco, is that correct?"

"Yes," Toby answered.

"Nothing further, Your Honor." Silverman sat down.

"No redirect, Your Honor," Arnold said.

"You may step down, Mr. McDonald," Judge Kruger said.

"Given the lateness of the day, we'll adjourn and start in the morning with Mr. Franco's testimony." Judge Kruger banged his gavel, and the courtroom emptied.

CHAPTER 58

Around five o'clock in the morning in the basement apartment of a run-down house on Messer Street in Providence, a junkie took his last hit of cocaine. As he dragged on his leather motorcycle jacket, he turned his back to the mirror and admired the gang colors.

He pawed at his greasy hair and unruly beard and looked into eyes that had not slept in forty-eight hours. Since meeting the man, he had gotten high and made love to his girlfriend like it was his last few hours on earth, because he knew it probably was.

Their "partnership" started a couple of years ago when he was jammed up for selling weed. Instead of arresting him, he let him go in return for a promise to provide him with the name of his dealer. He hated the dealer anyway, so it was an easy decision.

The problem was that the partnership never ended. Whenever he got jammed up, he turned to the man to solve the problem, and the man saved his ass every time. It didn't matter what the crime was; all that ever happened in court was a slap on the wrist. The payback was that he helped the man with information and anything else he asked him to do. Once, he asked him to beat up some guy booking numbers. He didn't ask any questions, just whacked the guy with a crowbar a few times. Whatever he did for the man, it kept him out of jail, and that was all he cared about.

This time, it was not about information on drugs, stolen cars, robberies, or even a simple beating. This time, the man approached him about taking out a rat.

He protested, but to no avail; the man told him he would do the deed or he would be found with a kilo of cocaine and go away for a long, long time.

The plan was simple. The junkie would ride his motorcycle past a police barricade, shoot the rat, and speed away. The man assured him he would create a diversion so that he could get away.

As he enjoyed the last of the cocaine buzz, the phone rang, and the man told him to head over to the courthouse. It was time.

CHAPTER 59

The next morning, the security detail was waiting at the training academy at seven thirty. Billy was dressed in a gray suit, white shirt, and muted red tie. He told Gino he was anxious because he was about to stand up in front of a courtroom full of people and turn on his former friends.

When they arrived at the courthouse, security was tight. Gino noticed his classmates had been replaced at the Hopkins Street door by another team. Gino was pleased, because his plan called for teams to be rotated so they did not become complacent.

As they started to escort Billy out of the car and into the courthouse, there was a flurry of activity on both Benefit and South Main Streets. The rest of the unit rushed Billy inside, but Gino remained on Hopkins Street, revolver drawn.

At the top of the street, two cars were involved in an accident that drew the attention of the detail on Benefit Street. At the same time, a motorcycle attempted to speed by the barricade on South Main Street. As the motorcyclist tried to roar past the security detail, the driver was hit by shotgun blasts and revolver fire. As the rounds found their mark, the driver was sent crashing into the side of the courthouse.

With the threat removed, Gino rushed to the witness room, where Michelle was glued to her portable radio, listening to excited voices. They reported that a lone gunman had been neutralized as he attempted to breach the security perimeter. A quick search of the dead man revealed a .38 caliber revolver, an ounce of cocaine, and a handwritten will leaving everything to an outlaw motorcycle club. They calmed Billy by telling him that the security plan had worked, but it only reinforced in everyone's mind that the Mob would do anything to stop these prosecutions.

A two-month investigation following the shooting revealed that a junkie motorcycle gang member, with no motive, had tried to kill Billy. The investigation showed no direct connection to the Mob, but the explanation was simple. The Mob was fond of contracting hits to loners, especially when the attempt was a suicide mission.

By ten o'clock, the courtroom was packed in anticipation of Billy's appearance. The commotion outside didn't deter anyone, and the gallery was filled with attorneys, prosecutors, press, and curious civilians.

"Call your next witness, Miss St. Pierre," Judge Kruger said.

Renée rose and said, "The state calls William Franco."

Gino escorted him as far as the gate that separates the gallery from the rest of the courtroom. Gino then sat at the prosecution table, and Billy took his place on the stand.

Once sworn in and on the stand, he locked his eyes onto Renée as he had been instructed. She asked him about his relationship with Tiger and his involvement with the crew. Renée then took him through the events that led to the death of James McDonald.

"Mr. Franco, did the defendant take the baseball bat away from Mr. McDonald?" she asked.

"Yes," Billy answered.

"Did the defendant beat Mr. McDonald with the bat?"

"Yes, he did. He hit him in the head several times. I heard his skull crack, and then the kid dropped to the ground," Billy said.

"Nothing further, Your Honor," Renée said.

"I have an unrelated matter to handle in another courtroom, so we'll stop here," Judge Kruger said. "We'll break until two o'clock and start with cross-examination. The jury is dismissed until then."

Once the jurors left the courtroom, Judge Kruger ordered everyone to remain seated until Billy was escorted from the courtroom. Gino took him out of the courtroom and into a small witness room across the hall.

CHAPTER 60

Promptly at two o'clock, Judge Kruger called the court to order, and Billy returned to the stand for cross-examination.

"Mr. Franco, you're presently in protective custody, is that correct?" Silverman asked.

"Objection." Renée rose from her seat.

"Overruled," Judge Kruger said. "I ruled on this during pretrial motions. It goes to the witness's motive. As long as Mr. Silverman doesn't ask any specifics, I'm going to allow it."

"Your Honor, I'd like my objection noted for the record," Renée responded.

"Very well. Your objection is noted. You may inquire, Mr. Silverman."

Billy turned to the judge and asked, "Can you please have the question repeated? I forgot what it was, Your Honor." The clerk read the question back to Billy.

"Yes, I'm in protective custody," Billy answered.

"Who's protecting you?" Silverman asked.

"The state police."

"So you're not in prison, correct?"

"No, I'm not," Billy replied.

"And you're not locked up, are you?" Silverman asked.

"No."

"And you're with your family, aren't you?"

"Yes."

"Well, let me ask you. You've been indicted on several other crimes by the state of Rhode Island, isn't that correct?" Silverman asked.

"Objection." Renée tried to stop Silverman's momentum.

"Your Honor, this all goes to credibility," Silverman countered.

Kruger looked over his reading glasses and said, "Objection overruled. You'll answer the question, Mr. Franco."

"Yes, I've been arraigned on this and other crimes," Billy answered quietly.

"Murder, gambling, robbery—just to name a few?" Silverman asked.

"Yeah, that's right."

"Mr. Franco, what has the government promised you in return for testifying against my client and your other friends?"

"What do you mean?" Franco was confused.

"Well, you're testifying against Mr. Detroia, and you've been charged with the same crime. If you plead guilty, I assume you're going to jail. After all, we are talking about a murder."

"No, no, no, I told them I wasn't going to jail and leaving my family," Franco answered, panic in his voice.

"Then I guess it's safe to assume that it doesn't matter who you accuse of committing this murder, isn't that right, Mr. Franco?"

"I wouldn't lie about something like this."

Silverman jumped. "So you have a deal with the government to testify. In return, you don't go to jail, no matter what crimes you've committed?"

Renée was up in an instant. "Objection!"

"Sustained. Don't answer that, Mr. Franco," Judge Kruger ruled, but the damage was done.

"Let me rephrase the question, Your Honor. Mr. Franco, what's your understanding about the charges you face?"

Silverman was doing a masterful job of turning the attention away from his client and to the deal the government made with Franco. The third strategy emerged: Billy was lying to stay out of jail.

"Renée and Arnold told me that when I was done testifying, they would speak to a judge on my behalf." Billy seemed proud of his answer.

"But it's your understanding that you're not going to jail for any crime?" Silverman asked.

"That's right," Billy said.

"Thank you, Mr. Franco. Let's move on to the night of August 23, 1982."

Judge Kruger interrupted, "Mr. Silverman, let me stop you right there. It's three forty-five, and I think we'll recess for the day before we move into that area."

"Yes, Your Honor," Silverman replied.

"Very well, then. Court is adjourned until ten o'clock tomorrow morning. Ladies and gentleman of the jury, please do not to discuss this case with anyone, read anything about the case, or watch any television accounts of the trial." Judge Kruger then dismissed them for the day.

After the jury was out of the courtroom, Judge Kruger turned to Billy and gave him a stern warning.

"Mr. Franco, I'll remind you that you're still under oath. You're not to speak to any member of the prosecution team about your testimony, do you understand?"

"Yes, Your Honor," Billy answered.

"You may step down, then." The judge banged his gavel. "Court is adjourned until tomorrow morning at ten."

The drive back to Scituate was slowed by a driving rain and afternoon traffic. The congestion made it impossible to move quickly, despite flashing lights and sirens, so they used breakdown lanes until they were out of the city and headed toward Foster.

CHAPTER 61

Billy took the stand just after ten the next day. After yesterday's attempt on his life, security was tightened. Every car was stopped and checked within a quarter mile of the courthouse. Everyone entering the courthouse passed through a metal detector, and uniformed troopers and Providence police officers were stationed in the hallways and directly outside the courtroom.

"Mr. Silverman, you may continue your cross-examination. Mr. Franco, I'll remind you that you're still under oath."

"Thank you, Your Honor, and good morning, Mr. Franco," Silverman said as he rose to his feet.

Billy acknowledged the greeting with a nod. For the next two hours, Silverman led Billy on a minute-by-minute retelling of the events leading to the death of James McDonald.

Silverman pointed out every inconsistency in Billy's statements to the state police and the grand jury and his testimony at trial. It was deliberate, meticulous, and effective.

"Now, Mr. Franco, when James McDonald got out of the car with the bat, what did he say?" Silverman asked.

"Come on, you bastards," Billy answered.

"But didn't you testify in direct that he said, 'Come on, you guinea bastards?'"

"Yes, but—"

"And didn't you tell the grand jury that he said, 'Come on, you fuckers?'"

"What I meant was—"

Renée rose. "Objection, Your Honor. He has to let the witness answer the question."

"Sustained. You may answer the question, Mr. Franco," Judge Kruger said.

Billy tried to explain, "What I meant was, he said something like, 'you bastards' or 'you guinea bastards.' I don't remember the exact words."

Silverman pounced. "Well, which of these three or four versions do you expect this jury to believe?"

"Objection," Renée said without even bothering to get up.

"I'll rephrase the question," Silverman responded.

"What is your testimony today as to what James McDonald said on the night in question?"

"He said, 'Come on, you guinea bastards.'"

Silverman struck at the weakness of Billy's story. "All right, Mr. Franco, who took the bat away from him?"

"Tiger."

"Are you sure?"

"Yes."

"But Toby McDonald testified that you were in front, headed for his brother, and surely he has no reason to lie."

Arnold rose this time. "Objection, Your Honor. That's not even a question."

"Sustained," Judge Kruger said.

"I'll withdraw it, Your Honor. Mr. Franco, who got to Mr. McDonald first?"

"Tiger," Billy answered.

"But we only have your word for that, isn't that correct?"

"Tiger got there first," Billy insisted.

"Are you sure?" Silverman asked.

"Yes, I told you that he took the bat away from the punk." Billy was losing his cool.

"Punk—is that what you just called Mr. McDonald?"

"Yeah, he was threatening us," Billy explained.

Silverman moved in. "Are you sure you didn't get there first, Billy? Take the bat away from Mr. McDonald and beat him? You were trying to show Tiger that you were a tough guy, weren't you?"

"No, no," Billy said.

"You beat James McDonald with the bat until his skull was bashed in. Isn't that what really happened?"

"No, I—"

"And wasn't my client shocked that you acted in such a vicious manner?" Silverman was asking questions in rapid-fire fashion.

Billy tried to fight back. "I'm telling you, Tiger hit him. I was just there. I didn't hit the kid. It was Tiger."

Silverman never let him off the canvas. "But my client doesn't have a deal with the government to keep him out of jail no matter what, does he, Mr. Franco?"

"I'm telling the truth," Billy said, shoulders slumping.

"Do you even know what the truth is, Mr. Franco?"

"Objection." Arnold jumped up.

"Sustained," Judge Kruger ruled.

Silverman wasn't about to stop, though. "Mr. Franco, what happened to the bat?"

"Tiger told me to get rid of it."

"Did you?"

"Yes," Billy answered.

"What did you do with it?" Silverman asked.

"I cut it up and used it for firewood," Billy answered.

"Mr. Franco, do you really expect this jury to believe that my client got to Mr. McDonald first?" Silverman continued.

"Yes."

"And that my client beat Mr. McDonald with the bat after he had already told you he wasn't going to get involved?" Silverman said.

"Yes."

"But after the beating, you ended up with the murder weapon. Don't you find that unusual?"

"No. I was doing what I was told."

"Just like today!" Silverman shouted.

"Objection!" both Arnold and Renée hurdled from their chairs.

"Sustained. Careful, Mr. Silverman," Judge Kruger said sternly.

"One final question, Mr. Franco. You've been promised that you won't go to jail, not even for a day, for your involvement in this murder, isn't that correct?"

"Yes," an exhausted Billy answered.

"No more questions, Your Honor." Silverman sat down. He whispered something into Tiger's ear, and his client smiled.

"Redirect, Miss St. Pierre?" Judge Kruger asked

"Nothing, Your Honor." There would be no rehabilitating the state's star witness.

"The witness is dismissed," Judge Kruger announced.

Billy left the stand a beaten man.

CHAPTER 62

After they brought Billy back to the training academy, Michelle told Gino he was done for the day and to report to the courtroom in the morning. Renée and Arnold had decided that there would be no other witnesses and that they would rest their case.

As Gino tossed and turned that night, he could only hope that the jury believed Franco, but trying to find the believability in Billy's testimony was as elusive as sleep.

The next morning, Renée rested the state's case. Richard Silverman told the judge the defense would not present any witnesses. It was apparent this was a case of credibility; either the jurors believed Billy or they didn't.

Silverman made a motion for judgment of acquittal, arguing that based on the evidence, no reasonable jury could find his client guilty and the case should be thrown out. Renée argued the state had presented more than enough evidence, primarily Billy's testimony, to allow a jury to decide the defendant's fate.

Judge Kruger ruled that this case was a matter of believability of the state's witness Billy Franco. He would not dismiss the case until the credibility of Franco was determined by the jury and denied the motion.

Judge Kruger then called for a recess. Gino and Arnold sat in the witness room and listened to Renée practice her closing. Somewhere, in another part of the courthouse, Richard Silverman was doing the same.

The jury was brought in, and Renée began, "Ladies and gentlemen of the jury, James McDonald was no mobster; he was a young man of just twenty-five years of age. He was killed because he ran into the wrong person at the wrong time.

"I'm not going to stand here and tell you Billy Franco is a saint; he's not. But I also remind you that Mr. Detroia isn't the kind of individual who surrounds himself with saints. Instead, he surrounds himself with sinners like Billy. Just because Billy has led a bad life doesn't mean everything he says is a lie.

"Billy is no liar. He told you exactly what happened the night of August 23, 1982, when James McDonald lost his life. If he hadn't come forward, the McDonald family still wouldn't know who killed James. Billy Franco deserves our thanks for putting a family at ease about what happened to their loved one. What he told you about how James was killed deserves to be believed.

"One truth remains, ladies and gentleman: Frank 'Tiger' Detroia beat James McDonald with a baseball bat until he took his last breath. I urge you to do your duty and return a guilty verdict."

Renée sat down, and Arnold gave her a gentle pat on the forearm. She poured herself a cup of water and took a sip with shaking hands.

"Mr. Silverman," Judge Kruger looked down from the bench, "your closing, please."

Silverman paused as he rose from his chair. "Ladies and gentlemen of the jury." He paused and put down his notes.

"I was going to begin with prepared remarks, but as I listened to Miss St. Pierre, something kept running through my head: 'beware of wolves in sheep's clothing.'

"Billy Franco is a wolf in sheep's clothing, make no mistake about it. He's a sheep when he tells you he had nothing to do with the death of James McDonald. He's a sheep when he tells you that he didn't beat James McDonald to death.

"But he's also a wolf, trying to stay out of jail by lying about who beat James McDonald to death. Ladies and gentlemen of the jury, my client didn't kill James McDonald. I think we all know who did.

"Please don't let this wolf pull the wool over your eyes. Return a not guilty verdict." Silverman ended abruptly. The jury looked like an audience wanting more.

Game, set, match, Gino thought.

After a short break, the judge explained to the jury the law of second-degree murder. He spoke about guilt beyond a reasonable doubt and their responsibility to render a fair and impartial verdict. It did not matter what he said; Gino could see in their eyes they had already made up their minds.

The jury was back in less than two hours. The foreman announced that in the case of state versus Frank L. Detroia, the jury had reached a verdict of not guilty.

As each juror was polled and repeated the not guilty verdict, there was much celebration among Tiger's friends. The McDonald family looked shocked and angered.

Gino watched as Tiger and Silverman hugged and congratulated each other. Judge Kruger dismissed the jury and left the bench. The sheriffs shackled Tiger and led him out of the courtroom.

As the sheriffs escorted him out of the courtroom, he looked squarely at Renée and Arnold. He said, for all to hear, "You ought to be ashamed of yourselves, putting that lying piece of shit on the stand."

When Gino got home, he called Michelle, and she agreed to come over. He thought he could comfort her because he understood what was at stake for her.

Sitting on his couch, they sipped Gino's version of the David Niven martini—chilled vodka poured into an ice-filled shaker. Vermouth was not added, but merely held over the top of the shaker for a second. Gino then shook the vodka twenty-one times and poured the libation into two martini glasses prepared with three olives.

"This isn't going well. If I can't get convictions on the other cases, I'm in trouble," she said.

"How do you know that? We still have two more bites at the apple." Gino tried to be reassuring.

"It's just the way the colonel reacted when I told him we lost. He was quiet and didn't say much. I would have felt better if he had a meltdown. I'm telling you, my ass is on the line."

"And a fine ass it is." Gino gently touched her leg, and the passion between them ignited. He placed their glasses on the coffee table and leaned into her as he kissed her neck and slowly moved his hand from her leg to her breast. Gino rested his head on her breast, and the rising and falling of her breathing excited him even more. She didn't resist as he lifted her sweater over her head and unbuttoned her jeans.

Michelle pushed him back and clutched at his clothes as every kiss and caress became more purposeful. They were soon naked, and arms and legs were moving in concert. What had begun slowly was now proceeding at a frantic pace. Once inside her, he slowed and enjoyed every thrust, which was returned with an equally slowed response. They stared into each other's eyes, aware they were making love, not merely having sex; both wanted this feeling to last as long as possible. Like two cars colliding, their lovemaking came to a halt as each climaxed.

After their lovemaking, they lay side by side covered by a single sheet, both staring at the ceiling. Not a word was spoken.

CHAPTER 63

T he not guilty verdict hung over the state police and the attorney general's office like a dark cloud.

MOBSTER ACQUITTED, read the front page of the Providence paper. When everyone thought the bloodletting was over, yet another article appeared. **MCDONALD FAMILY CRITICIZES ATTORNEY GENERAL.** The story featured Mrs. McDonald demanding to know why Attorney General Morgan had not prosecuted the case himself. She told the reporter that if Billy Franco was responsible for her son's death, she didn't understand why he wasn't going to jail.

The state police and the attorney general's office hunkered down and took the heat from the press. It was clear to all: presenting a case based only on Billy's testimony was a disaster.

They agreed the Calderone case would be different. Marty and Billy would both testify, increasing the odds of conviction. Two eyewitnesses to a murder had to be enough for any jury.

By late Friday afternoon, everyone in the unit decided to stop feeling sorry for themselves and decided to get something to eat and have a few drinks. Whenever the pressures of the day were overwhelming—a guilty verdict needed to be celebrated or, in this case, a not guilty verdict bemoaned—they headed for Michael's Bar and Grille.

Michael's was located at the intersection of Victory and Ventura Streets in downtown Providence. The combination bar and deli was conveniently within walking distance of the attorney general's office.

Michelle arrived with Renée and Arnold just after the rest of the unit had staked out a few barstools. Gino's plan was to drown his sorrows with a drink or two, and then try to convince Michelle to stop by his apartment. The bar was populated by state troopers, Providence police, prosecutors, and employees of downtown businesses. It wasn't unusual for the owner to lock the doors and continue to serve cops and prosecutors until the wee hours of the morning. Michael's was, without a doubt, a cop's bar.

On the street, as well as in the bar, there was a natural rivalry between the Providence police and the state police. It was fueled by New England's organized crime family using Providence for the base of their operations. Most of the unit's arrests, surveillances, and investigations took place in Providence, and anything the unit did in the city was perceived as a violation of the sovereignty of the Providence Police Department. They simply felt they were responsible for cleaning up their own city.

Usually, there was just an icy indifference between the two groups. Gino recalled times when too much alcohol led to a shouting match, but that was usually broken up by a prosecutor who had no desire to prosecute one cop for assaulting another.

Gino's sullen little group huddled in a corner of the bar, trying to make sense of the not guilty verdict. The Providence officers who were there that night were sympathetic to their plight and kept their distance.

Michelle downed her scotch and complained about Judge Kruger allowing Richard Silverman so much latitude during cross-examination. She finished her drink and left before Gino had a chance to ask her to stop by.

In a way, Gino was glad; it was difficult enough being around her at work without hiding his feelings. After a few drinks, there was no guarantee he wouldn't do or say something that would reveal their relationship. He would stay a little longer to prevent suspicion, leave, and give her a call.

Renée and Arnold bemoaned the fact that Billy was their only witness. They had no choice but to put him on the stand, and it proved to be a disaster. Lou agreed that with Billy as the only eyewitness, there was little chance of a conviction.

As the clock approached one o'clock in the morning, they all pledged next time would be different.

The volume of the jukebox seemed to rise in direct proportion to the amount of alcohol Gino consumed. There was no dance floor at Michael's, so the corner of the bar near the jukebox had to do. Gino would look on in amazement as cops, prosecutors, and cop groupies did their best disco dance imitation. Most "civilians" knew enough to steer clear of this collection of bumping and grinding bodies.

As "Girls Just Want to Have Fun" blared from the jukebox, Sully took a long string of pearls off his dance partner and started swinging it over his head. An unsuspecting civilian was hit in the face by the pearls. Sully apologized and continued to dance.

Sitting at the bar, Gino caught the look of anger on the man's face. He was about to sucker-punch an unsuspecting Sully when Gino shot out of his stool and put the civilian in an armlock. In an instant, Gino dragged him to the door and threw him out. Sully never missed a dance step, but out of the corner of his eye, he saw everything.

About three thirty in the morning, Gino left Michael's. The party continued without him, but he had the munchies and the beginnings of a terrible hangover. He ate a hearty breakfast at an all-night diner in the hope that a full stomach would absorb the alcohol.

It was about five o'clock in the morning when he pulled into his driveway; he unlocked the back door and headed up the stairs. Gino could hear Mrs. Ricci scurrying around in a valiant attempt to learn if he was alone.

With little, if any, balance, he stumbled to the medicine cabinet and prepared an exotic elixir. It was a concoction touted by his friends to prevent hangovers, but it rarely, if ever, worked. He downed four Excedrin, a multivitamin, and a banana, and drank three glasses of water. Tomorrow was Saturday, and with any luck, he wouldn't have to deal with protected witnesses, prosecutors, or a hangover.

As the bed began to spin, Gino cursed himself for not calling Michelle and asking her to stop by the apartment. Instead of holding on to her, he was forced to hold on to the sides of the bed and pray he'd survive the night.

CHAPTER 64

The next morning, Gino opened his eyes to an alarm clock that read eleven forty-five. His head ached as he shaved, showered, and consumed a gigantic bowl of Cheerios. As he tried to eat his way out of a hangover, he stared at a picture of astronaut Sally Ride on the box.

The rest of his weekend was spent reading the paper, watching sports, and napping. He ordered pizza for dinner on Saturday and made the obligatory visit to his mom's on Sunday.

Longing to hear her voice, Gino called Michelle, and they spoke, not of work but of their lives. Michelle told Gino what it was like growing up the daughter of a state trooper. How she felt that she always had to be better than the rest of the kids; getting in trouble was not an option. Oh, how she had longed to be able to just let loose as a teenager—to drink beer, smoke cigarettes, and raise holy hell like the others.

Gino confided to her about his struggles after his dad died and how easily he could have turned to a life of crime given his surroundings. Gino admitted how much he wanted to be one of the guys with all the money, the respect, and the power. He told her that even to this day, he sometimes felt the tug of the old neighborhood. It was something he was sure he'd never shake.

On Monday morning, Gino arrived at work, and Michelle called him into her office.

"Renée went to the chief judge of the Superior Court and asked for a quick trial date in the Moron Marchetti case. She told the judge that having three witnesses in protective custody was a drain on the resources of the state police." She lowered her voice. "You and I know the reason for the quick date is that there's only time for one trial between now and the election. A speedy conviction will wipe away the first acquittal in the public's mind, and Attorney General Morgan can still claim to be a crusading Mob buster."

Attorney General Morgan's opponent, Eileen Rose, was climbing in the polls, mostly by taking Morgan to task for the McDonald acquittal. The only way to fight back was to obtain convictions in the Moron case.

"You and Lou will continue to work with Billy and line up witnesses for the Moron case. Sully and Quinn will work with Marty and prepare him for testifying."

"Into the breach once more, my friends," he whispered under his breath as he walked out of her office.

CHAPTER 65

The Superior Court clerk notified the state and defense that it would be October when the murder case of Fredo "The Moron" Marchetti came to trial. The clerk asked each to present to the court a list of witnesses, and the state provided a list that included Billy, Marty, and Tim Karakides.

Gino felt that with two eyewitnesses, Renée and Arnold would finally be able to paint an accurate picture of how the Moron was shot in the early morning hours of May 15, 1982.

Renée was satisfied with the statements of Karakides and Marty, but she explained to Gino that merely directing Billy and the others after the shooting was, in her opinion, accessory after the fact, at best. She needed something more on Tiger to make a first-degree murder conviction stick.

Renée told Michelle she wanted to speak to Billy away from the academy. She arranged for Gino to bring Franco to a cabin on Waterman Lake.

Renée and Arnold followed as Gino traveled down the narrow dirt road leading to the cabin, which was owned by a retired trooper. When Renée got out of the car, it was obvious she'd dressed down for the interview. Blue jeans, a Providence College pullover hooded sweatshirt, and hiking boots. Arnold, on the other hand, dressed in a bright yellow polo, brown pleated slacks, and Sperry topsiders. A tan cardigan sweater was gracefully draped across his shoulders.

They entered the small cabin. Its wood-paneled walls were covered with amateurish oil paintings and police memorabilia.

Renée skipped the preliminaries and got right to her concerns. Why didn't Billy follow Tiger's direction? Why did he jump out of his seat and run over to the Moron? How the hell was anyone going to believe Billy tripped and shot the Moron?

"I told you a hundred times, Renée. I didn't wait like Tiger told me to. I jumped up, pulled my gun, tripped, and shot him."

"You said Tiger came out in the hallway, right?" Renée asked.

"Right," Billy answered.

"What else did he do when he got out there? He must have done or said something."

Billy answered, "Well, he was pissed, I can tell you that, but I don't remember anything special. The gunshot was still ringing in my ears."

"You shot him three times. Tiger was in the hallway after the first shot, right?" Renée asked.

Billy was obviously confused. He looked at Gino for help, but Gino said nothing.

Billy said, "That's right, but I told you that before."

"Well, did he say anything after the first shot? Did he tell you to do anything, direct you in any way?" Renée asked.

"He said, 'Shoot him again,'" he answered.

"He said, 'Shoot him again'?" Renée repeated.

"Yeah, that's right. He said, 'Shoot him, shoot him again.'"

"And did you shoot him again?" she asked.

"Yes, I shot him two more times," Billy answered.

Gino couldn't believe what he was hearing. This was the first time Billy had ever mentioned anything about Tiger telling him to shoot the Moron.

"Why did you shoot him two more times?"

Billy answered, "Because Tiger was the boss, and he told me to."

"Did Tiger do anything else while you were holding the gun after the first shot?" Renée asked.

"I was going to put the gun away, but Tiger grabbed my arm and pulled it down, pointed it toward the Moron, and said, 'Shoot him, shoot him again.'"

All three were shocked by what they had just heard. Renée broke the silence. "I think we're done, Billy." She turned to Gino. "Detective, I think we're ready to go."

Fear shot through Gino's body, and he thought no good would come of Billy's latest revelation. The defense was going to tear him apart with these new revelations, and hopes of a conviction seemed to be slipping away.

CHAPTER 66

The Fredo "The Moron" Marchetti murder trial began three weeks before Attorney General Thomas Morgan would face the voters.

The trial was assigned to Judge John Morton, a former public defender who was a veteran of many jury trials as an attorney and judge.

On a brisk October day, the usual cast of characters assembled for the trial. Renée, Arnold, and Gino were again at the prosecutor's table, and Lou sat in the gallery. Gino and Lou would handle Billy and the other witnesses; Sully and Quinn would handle Marty.

At the defense table, Tiger sat with his attorney, Richard Silverman, and Big John joined his attorney, Americo Salvatore.

Big John was out on bail as the result of an appeal to the Rhode Island Supreme Court of Judge Kiley's no-bail ruling. The Supreme Court felt it unreasonable and sent the case back to Superior Court. A more sympathetic judge set bail at $100,000, and John's mother posted her home. Today, and for the rest of the trial, he would arrive with his family and what seemed like most of the Armenian community in Providence.

Judge Morton called the case ready for trial. The clerk announced, "Trial in the matter of State of Rhode Island versus Frank L. Detroia and John Kazarian, one count each of murder in the first degree."

Judge Morton looked to the defense table and asked for the legal formality of a plea for the trial record. Tiger stood and said, "Not guilty." When Big John said, "Not guilty," his family and friends applauded. Judge Morton banged his gavel and ordered the courtroom quiet.

After pretrial motions and jury selections were completed, the judge ended the proceedings and scheduled opening statements for ten the next morning.

CHAPTER 67

The next morning, Renée began her opening statement by telling the jury that the state would prove, beyond a reasonable doubt, that on May 15, 1982, the defendants were responsible for the murder of Fredo "The Moron" Marchetti. This crime was committed in a crowded restaurant but not solved until Billy and Marty came forward. The jury would also hear from restaurant employee Tim Karakides, who witnessed the shooting.

Renée told them that this brutal slaying took place in the front foyer of Pita's Restaurant in the city of Providence. She showed them pictures of Pita's Restaurant and the small foyer where the murder occurred.

She finished by telling the jury that Marty and Billy would testify that the defendant Frank "Tiger" Detroia directed them in this murder and that Big John was an active participant.

Silverman and Salvatore waived opening statements.

The first witness was a Warwick detective who testified that in 1982, the Moron's body was found behind the Old Ranch Restaurant. The medical examiner testified that Mr. Marchetti died from three gunshots to the chest.

Renée's next witness was Tim Karakides, who testified with the aid of a court-appointed translator. He testified that in the early morning hours of May 15, he was working behind the counter at Pita's Restaurant, and he watched as a man ran into the foyer and shot the victim. Karakides ended his testimony by talking about hysterical customers running out of the restaurant when they heard the shots.

All of his testimony came under the watchful eye of Agent Theo Christopoulos. He sat in the gallery to bolster Karakides's confidence and to make sure the translation was accurate.

In cross-examination, Karakides testified Tiger and Big John were frequent patrons of Pita's Restaurant. When Silverman asked him to describe them, he said they both were "nice guys."

Silverman and Salvatore began a line of questioning that clearly established Karakides never witnessed either of their clients shoot the Moron. The only one he saw fire a gun was Billy Franco.

When Karakides's testimony ended, the judge adjourned for the day.

CHAPTER 68

G ino brought Billy to court the next morning, and security remained tight. The perimeter of the courthouse and surrounding streets was guarded by Providence police, state troopers, and the SWAT team.

Gino thought Billy sounded more confident testifying at a trial for the second time. Renée took him through the events leading to the shooting of the Moron.

When Billy testified that Tiger grabbed his arm and commanded him to "shoot him, shoot him again," there was a flurry of activity at the defense table.

Silverman and Salvatore began furiously writing and flipping through large black binders. When it was time for cross-examination, Gino could see an almost gleeful anticipation on Silverman's face.

"Good afternoon, Mr. Franco," Silverman began.

"Good afternoon, Mr. Silverman," Billy answered.

Silverman pounced on Billy's version of what went on in the foyer.

"Mr. Franco, did you say on direct examination that you rushed out into the foyer of the restaurant?" Silverman asked.

"Yes," Billy answered.

"You previously testified that my client told you *not* to go after Marchetti—to be cool and calm. Isn't that true?"

"That's right, Mr. Silverman," Billy responded.

Silverman pressed on. "But you rushed out and confronted Mr. Marchetti anyway, didn't you?"

"Yes, I did," Billy answered, "because I wanted to protect Tiger."

"Come on, Mr. Franco. Tiger didn't need protection. You just lost control. You shot the Moron in a fit of rage, didn't you?"

"No," Billy said.

Silverman hammered away. "And my client had nothing to do with your actions, did he, Mr. Franco?"

"Tiger told me what to do. I just jumped the gun."

"Interesting choice of words, Mr. Franco. Appropriate, wouldn't you say?" Silverman asked.

"Objection, Your Honor. That's not a question," Renée said. The judge sustained her objection.

"The night you shot Mr. Marchetti, you were carrying a gun, correct?"

"Yes," Billy said.

"Neither Tiger or Big John gave it to you, did they?" Silverman asked.

"No," he answered.

"No one ever told you to bring a gun that night, did they?"

"No."

"Mr. Franco, isn't it true that in an act of bravado, you rushed out into the foyer, pulled your gun, and shot Mr. Marchetti? Not once, not twice, but three times?" Silverman was on a roll.

"No, no, no... " Billy pleaded.

Silverman raised his voice. "Mr. Franco, did you or did you not rush out to confront Mr. Marchetti?"

"Yes."

"Were you alone when you rushed into the foyer?"

"Yes."

"And with a gun in your hand, you accidentally tripped and shot Mr. Marchetti. Isn't that your testimony?"

"Yes, but—" Billy was stuttering.

"Yes or no, Mr. Franco, nothing else. You tripped and shot him?" Silverman asked.

"Objection. He's badgering the witness, Your Honor," Arnold said.

"Overruled. This is cross-examination, and I'm going to allow it," Morton said.

"Yes," Billy answered, resigned to the beating he was taking.

"And no one told you to shoot the Moron, did they?"

"After I shot him, Tiger grabbed my arm, pulled it down, and told me to 'shoot him, shoot him again,'" Billy answered.

"Let's talk about that for a minute, Mr. Franco. This story about my client grabbing your arm and telling you to shoot Mr. Marchetti—isn't today the first time you've ever said that?" Silverman was going in for the kill.

"Yes."

"You've been in protective custody for almost three years, been debriefed numerous times, appeared before the grand jury—and suddenly, today, you remember that my client pulled your arm down and told you to shoot Mr. Marchetti. Is that what you want this jury to believe?" Silverman was looking right at the jury and connecting.

"The more I talked about it, the more I remembered," Billy said.

"But not when you gave a statement to the state police?" Silverman asked.

"No."

"And you didn't remember it when you first talked to the prosecutors, did you?"

"No," Billy answered.

"And you didn't remember it when you testified before the grand jury, did you?"

"No." Billy looked to Renée for help, but none was coming.

"Mr. Franco, are you telling this jury that, after you shot the Moron, my client miraculously appears, grabs your arm, and tells you to shoot him again?"

"Yeah, that's right," Billy answered.

"And, of course, this is after you accidentally tripped and shot him?"

"I already told you that." Billy's frustration was evident to Gino and everyone else in the courtroom.

"And you expect the jury to believe you?"

Billy answered quickly, "Yes, because that's what happened."

"You mean, it's what happened based on what you remember today?" Silverman was right in Billy's face.

"That's right."

"But it's not what you remembered for the three years leading up to this trial, is it?"

"Like I said, Mr. Silverman, the more I went over it, the more I remembered," a defeated Billy responded.

Even Gino didn't believe Billy; he couldn't blame the jury for not believing his testimony. All of the unit's hard work was beginning to look like a waste of time.

CHAPTER 69

Silverman had virtually destroyed any shred of credibility Billy had left, yet he continued his unmerciful cross-examination.

"Mr. Franco, do you have an agreement with the government?" Silverman asked.

"What do you mean?"

"You know what I mean, Mr. Franco—a deal. What has the government promised you in return for your testimony?"

"They haven't promised me anything," Billy answered.

"They promised you wouldn't go to jail, didn't they?"

"Yes, they said if I told the truth, they would recommend that I don't go to jail," Billy said.

"Recommend or promise, Mr. Franco?" Silverman asked.

"They promised me. I told them from the beginning I won't leave my family," Billy answered.

"And that promise is in return for testifying in three murder trials and other serious crimes, isn't that true?"

"I guess so," Billy answered.

"You wouldn't implicate people who weren't involved just to please the government, would you?"

"No."

"Really, Mr. Franco? You didn't implicate my client and Mr. Kazarian because you know the government wants to put them behind bars?"

"No."

"These men were your friends, weren't they, Mr. Franco?" Silverman asked.

"Yes."

"But today, as you stand in this courtroom, sworn to tell the truth, you're telling us they were involved in the murder of the Moron?" Silverman continued.

"Yes."

"Based on testimony, some of which we've heard for the first time, you want this jury to believe these men are murderers?"

"Yeah, like I said, that's what happened."

"I have no more questions of this witness," Silverman said.

"You may step down, Mr. Franco," the judge said.

When it was over, Gino escorted Billy from the courtroom into the security caravan and whisked him away to Foster.

CHAPTER 70

There was not enough time to be concerned about Billy's dismal performance because in less than twenty-four hours, Marty would be taking the stand. Gino could only hope that Marty was better prepared for what was coming.

The next morning, everything was the same, except for the witness. Marty entered the courthouse, escorted by Sully and Quinn. Gino sat at the prosecution table, and Lou was in the gallery. Judge Morton took the bench and called for the state's next witness.

"The state calls Frank Martelinni," Arnold Bernstein said as he rose to his feet. Arnold was dressed in a conservative blue pinstriped suit, but he couldn't resist adding a diamond stickpin on his tie and a red silk handkerchief.

Marty walked to the stand, enduring the glares of Tiger and Big John. He took the oath and began his testimony.

"In the early morning hours of May 15, were you in Pita's Restaurant?"

"Yes, sir," Marty answered.

"Who was there with you?" Arnold asked.

"Tiger, Billy, and Big John," he answered.

"Did you see Fredo 'The Moron' Marchetti at Pita's that night?" Arnold continued.

"Yeah, he came in about an hour after us. He comes over and starts talking crazy, says he's going to take Tiger out right there," Marty explained.

"How would you describe his demeanor?"

"His what?" Marty asked.

"How was he acting?" Arnold asked.

"Like a moron," Marty responded and shrugged his shoulders. The courtroom erupted in laughter.

"Order, order in the court." Judge Morton banged his gavel.

"What happened next?" Arnold asked.

"Billy wanted to make a move on him. Tiger told us to wait. He told us we would take him outside in the parking lot."

"Did you do as you were instructed by Tiger?" Arnold asked.

"I beg your pardon?" Marty asked.

"Did you do what he told you to do?"

"I did, but when the Moron headed out the door, Billy jumped up and ran after him," Marty answered.

"Then what happened?" Arnold asked.

"We jumped out of the booth and headed to the hallway to back up Billy."

"You said hallway, Mr. Martelinni. This is the area others have described as the foyer, is that correct?" Arnold needed to make the distinction.

"Correct," Marty answered.

"Who got out there first?" Arnold asked.

"Billy first, then Tiger," Marty said, looking right at his former boss.

"Then what happened?"

"I heard a shot, and I saw Billy and Tiger out in the foyer. Big John and I were right behind them when I heard two more shots," Marty answered.

"Did you see Mr. Franco shoot Mr. Marchetti?" Arnold asked.

"Yes, I saw him shoot the Moron," he answered.

"Did you hear Tiger say anything out in the foyer?"

"No, I couldn't hear much because of all the commotion."

"Did you see Tiger do anything at this time?" Arnold continued.

"It was hard for me to see. Four of us were crowded in that small—what did you call it?—foyer."

"Did Mr. Detroia say anything to you?" Arnold decided to move on.

"Tiger told Billy and me to get the cars. Big John helped drag the Moron out into the parking lot. We stuffed him in the backseat and took off," Marty replied.

"What did you do with the body?" Arnold asked.

"Tiger told us to drive to the Old Ranch Restaurant and dump him in the woods behind the restaurant," he explained.

"Did you and Big John do what Mr. Detroia told you to do?"

"Absolutely."

"Why?"

"Because if we didn't, we'd be next." Marty looked right at Tiger.

"Could you please repeat that?" Arnold said, hoping to bolster Billy's previous testimony.

"Tiger was the boss of our crew. If we didn't do what he told us to do, we'd be dead, just like the Moron."

Marty was suddenly unable to control the anger he felt for the man who tried to have him killed in prison. He looked right at Tiger and said, "Isn't that right, you fat bastard?"

"Objection." Silverman jumped up. "Motion to strike."

"Sustained. The jury will disregard the witness's outburst," the judge said.

"Mr. Martelinni, one more stunt like that, and you'll be held in contempt. Do you understand?"

"Yes, Your Honor," Marty replied.

"No more questions of this witness, Your Honor," Arnold said.

"Mr. Martelinni, we're recessing until two this afternoon. You're still under oath. Do not to discuss your testimony with anyone. Do you understand?"

"Yes, Your Honor," Marty replied.

"Court is adjourned until two."

Judge Morton waited for the jury to leave the courtroom, banged his gavel, and left the bench.

CHAPTER 71

They brought Marty to a conference room adjacent to the courtroom and spent the noon recess there. Gino thought he seemed relaxed for someone testifying for the first time.

Gino asked Marty if he was worried about being cross-examined by Salvatore.

"Gino, I know him because he's defended so many of my friends. I'm not worried."

At two o'clock, cross-examination began with Salvatore rising from his seat and greeting Marty.

"Good afternoon, Mr. Martelinni."

"How's it going, Rico?" Marty replied.

Judge Morton's face turned red. "No first names, Mr. Martelinni. It's Mr. Salvatore, counselor, or sir. Do you understand? This isn't a bar room; it's a court of law, and you'll act in an appropriate manner. Am I clear?"

"Yes, Your Honor," he answered.

"You may resume your cross-examination, Mr. Salvatore," Judge Morton said.

"Thank you, Your Honor. Mr. Martelinni, did you see Billy shoot the Moron?" Salvatore wasted little time.

"Yes," Marty answered.

"How many times did he shoot him?" Salvatore asked.

"Three times."

"Mr. Martelinni, did you at any time see Tiger grab Billy's arm and point it toward the Moron after the first shot?" Salvatore asked.

"Big John was in front of me…"

"Yes or no, Mr. Martelinni?" Salvatore asked.

"No," Marty answered.

"Did you ever hear Tiger shout, 'Shoot him again?'" Salvatore continued.

"No, I didn't," Marty answered.

"Now, Mr. Martelinni, you've testified that you and my client, Big John, helped get rid of the Moron's body, is that correct?"

"Yes, Mr. Salvatore, that's what we were told to do," Marty answered.

"And you want this jury to believe that you and my client dragged this body out of the foyer and across a parking lot and stuffed it into the backseat of a car?" Salvatore asked.

"Yes."

"In front of a restaurant full of people?"

"Yes."

"In front of how many people?" Salvatore asked.

"I don't know. Fifteen, twenty people," Marty answered.

"Fifteen or twenty people watched Billy shoot the Moron. They saw you and Big John drag the body outside, put it in the back of a car, and drive away, yet nobody comes forward?" Salvatore looked at the jury in disbelief.

"Yeah, that's what happened," Marty answered.

"And you really expect this jury to believe that?"

"Hey, Rico, what can I tell you? That's the way it went down. You know better than most what it's like on the street."

Marty obviously had forgotten the judge's warning.

"Motion to strike, Your Honor." Salvatore looked to Judge Morton.

"Granted. The jury is instructed to disregard the witness's last statement. I'll warn you one last time, Mr. Martelinni. No first names when referring to counsel."

"Yes, Your Honor," Marty said.

Salvatore continued, "All right, Mr. Martelinni, you've testified the car containing the Moron's body was driven from Pita's to Warwick, correct?"

"That's right."

"Then the body was dumped in the woods behind the Old Ranch Restaurant, is that correct?" Salvatore asked.

"Yes," Marty answered.

"And you expect this jury to believe that a murder was committed in the middle of a crowded restaurant, a body was driven to Warwick and dumped in the woods, and no one saw a thing."

"No one called the cops, if that's what you mean," Marty answered.

"Not only that, but no one ever implicated Tiger or Big John in the Moron's murder, did they?" Salvatore asked.

"No."

"Not until you and Billy turned state's evidence."

Arnold jumped out of his chair. "Objection."

"Overruled; you'll answer," Judge Morton said.

"Yes, not until we came forward," Marty answered.

CHAPTER 72

Marty had been on the witness stand for over an hour. He was calm and collected, but Salvatore continued to attack his credibility.

"Mr. Martelinni, do you have an agreement—a deal with the government—in return for your testimony?"

"No, I don't," Marty answered.

"Are you saying you're testifying out of some sort of civic duty?"

"Objection, Your Honor. That's ridiculous," Arnold said.

"Sustained." Judge Morton glared at Salvatore.

"Mr. Martelinni, what did the state offer you in return for your testimony?"

"They didn't promise me anything. They just told me to tell the truth, and they would speak to a judge on my behalf," he answered.

"Tell us about murders, robberies, baseball bat beatings, arsons—and don't worry about it; we'll take care of it. Is that your 'deal' with the government?" Salvatore asked.

"Objection."

But Marty answered before the judge could rule. "I guess so. I don't know. I just know they said they would take care of me if I told the truth," Marty responded.

"Objection withdrawn," Arnold .

Salvatore continued, "So, it really doesn't matter what you say, as long as you please the state."

"Objection." Arnold looked at Judge Morton.

"Sustained. Mr. Salvatore, I think you're about to cross the line, so let's get back on track."

"I apologize, Your Honor, and I have no further questions of this witness," Salvatore said.

"Redirect, Mr. Bernstein?" Judge Morton asked.

"May I have one moment, Your Honor?" Arnold said. He conferred with Renée.

"Just a couple of questions, Your Honor. Mr. Martelinni, have you been told you're required to tell the truth whenever you testify?"

"Yes."

"If you don't, the state won't make a positive recommendation for you regarding the crimes you've admitted to, isn't that correct?" Arnold asked.

"That's correct," Marty replied.

"Nothing further." Arnold sat down.

"Recross?" Judge Morton asked Salvatore.

"Mr. Martelinni, do you even know what the truth is?" Salvatore asked.

"Fuck you, Rico," Marty shot back.

There was a flurry of objections and motions to strike as four attorneys talked over each other.

Judge Morton put an end to Marty's theatrics quickly. "The witness is dismissed."

Judge Morton asked if the state had any other witnesses to present, and Renée told him they were prepared to rest.

"Does the defense have any witnesses for tomorrow?" Morton asked.

"No, Your Honor, no witnesses," Silverman and Salvatore answered.

Judge Morton turned his attention to the jury. "We'll adjourn until tomorrow at ten for closing arguments."

CHAPTER 73

Arnold delivered his closing argument in a gray flannel suit, a raspberry-colored shirt, and a black bowtie. He explained to the jury that the state had presented two witnesses who participated in the murder of the Moron and urged them to believe their testimony. Why would they testify to committing a murder in a restaurant full of customers unless it was true? No one would make up such a story.

If Billy was lying, it would have been so much easier for him to say someone else fired the fatal shots. Instead, he took the stand and said he fired the first shot.

He told them it made no difference that Billy had fired the first shot. The die had been cast when the Moron threatened Tiger in a restaurant full of people. The Moron would die that night, at the direction of Tiger, with help from Billy, Marty, and Big John.

Arnold explained that Tiger and Big John's active participation in the shooting made them guilty of first-degree murder.

"Ladies and gentlemen of the jury, the defense would have you believe that a murder couldn't take place in a restaurant full of people without anyone coming forward. But someone did come forward—a man who had the misfortune of working at Pita's that fateful night. Tim Karakides was brave enough to testify he witnessed the murder. Please ask yourselves what Tim Karakides has to gain by testifying. I submit to you, he's simply a man telling the truth. A man who told you that Billy, Tiger, Marty, and Big John actively participated in the murder of the Moron.

"This is no ordinary murder case. It's complicated because the state presented you with witnesses involved in the crime. It's your duty to judge their testimony based on their credibility. Please try to focus on what they said and not who they are.

"If you take all of the state's evidence and weigh it fairly, you'll come to an inevitable conclusion. Tiger ordered Billy to shoot the Moron twice after the initial shot and ordered Big John and Marty to put the body in the car. He then ordered his crew to dump the body. Both defendants willingly and knowingly engaged in a murder."

Arnold sat down, and Renée whispered, "Nice job."

Judge Morton looked at the defense table.

"Gentlemen, have you decided in what order you're going to present closing arguments?"

Silverman rose and answered, "Judge, Mr. Salvatore is going to close for both defendants."

"Very well, then, Mr. Salvatore."

"Yes, Your Honor." Salvatore stood.

Salvatore began by invoking the founding fathers. He told the jury the ancients were skeptical of placing too much power in the hands of a central government. They were concerned the government would overcome the rights of the individual merely at whim. They feared a government that could prosecute individuals based solely on a dislike for their religion, occupation, or associations. To protect us from such a government, they devised a system where the poor, the weak, and the least powerful would be judged by their peers.

So precious were these rights that the founders added them to the Constitution. The Bill of Rights guaranteed each individual the right to face his accuser, to be represented by an attorney, and, perhaps the greatest right, to require the government prove the charges it brings against an individual beyond a reasonable doubt.

"Mr. Detroia and Mr. Kazarian have been charged with the most serious of all crimes, murder, and they deserve your careful consideration of the evidence in this case. Reasonable doubt, ladies and gentlemen, as the judge will instruct you, is not a fanciful doubt or doubt based on whim or opinion, but doubt based on reason.

"I think it's reasonable to doubt Billy tripped, his gun went off, and the Moron was shot. I think it's reasonable to doubt that Tiger ran out into the foyer, grabbed Billy's arm, and directed him to shoot the Moron a second and third time. I think it's reasonable to doubt that, in a restaurant full of people, no one called the police after seeing the Moron's body dragged across the parking lot, put in a car, and driven away.

"Even the state's witness, Mr. Karakides, couldn't testify that Tiger grabbed Billy's arm, pulled it down, and ordered Billy to shoot him again. I would suggest to you that Billy's account of the events that night are not worthy of belief.

"On the other hand, what is reasonable to believe is that Billy deliberately shot the Moron. I submit to you that he did so because he wanted to be a gangster.

"There's no way to involve our clients in a first-degree murder unless you lie and testify Tiger pulled your arm down and made you shoot. Unless you lie and testify Big John dragged a body across a parking lot, stuffed it in a car, and helped dump it in Warwick. Unless you lie and say you tripped and your gun went off and struck the victim. How preposterous and insulting to this jury to suggest such a thing. I would suggest that Billy is the only one involved in this crime.

"Marty is just a trained parrot brought here to repeat the lies and please the state with his testimony. He has no more knowledge of Mr. Marchetti's murder than anyone who read the newspaper accounts.

"Ladies and gentlemen, I would ask you to carefully judge the credibility of the state's witnesses. Keep in mind: Billy has a promise from the government that he won't go to jail. Marty is relying on the goodwill of the state in disposing of the numerous criminal charges he faces. These open-ended promises are an abuse of the government's power. The kind of abuse our forefathers tried to guard against, the kind of abuse that compels men to lie.

"If you believe, as I do, that based on the illogical testimony of the state's own witnesses, there is reasonable doubt, then it's your duty to render two not guilty verdicts. Thank you, Your Honor." Salvatore returned to his seat.

Judge Morton took a short break and brought the jury back for his charge. He started with outlining the elements of first-degree murder to the jury.

"The state must prove beyond a reasonable doubt that the defendants were engaged in a plan, scheme, or design to kill Fredo Marchetti."

He emphasized that premeditation—that plan, scheme, or design—was an essential element. If lacking, there could be no first-degree murder. If there was doubt in their minds about whether the murder was planned, a doubt based on reason, they were duty-bound to render a not guilty verdict for each defendant.

Judge Morton finished by saying, "I trust that if you apply the law as I've explained it, you'll reach a just verdict."

CHAPTER 74

N ot guilty," the jury foreman said, not once, but twice. In the gallery, there were hoots and hollers and a few tears. Renée and Arnold slumped in their seats, and then stood and meekly congratulated Silverman and Salvatore.

Suddenly and without warning, the raw emotions that come with every murder trial came to the surface.

When Arnold walked out of the courtroom, someone from Big John's family screamed, "I hope you get cancer of the tongue, you son of a bitch!"

Silverman, trying to avoid a physical confrontation, stood between the family and Arnold. Standing face-to-face with Arnold, Silverman was unable to control his own emotions and unleashed his venom on the prosecutor.

"And you call yourself a Jew."

"What the hell does that mean?" Arnold asked.

"You're a disgrace to the Jewish race, Bernstein. For thousands of years, our people have been oppressed, and who do you lawyer for? The government—the great oppressor—which tries to throw innocent people in jail just because of who they are? Sound familiar to you?"

Arnold struck back, "You sanctimonious son of a bitch. How dare you? Who do you represent, Silverman? I'll tell you who—a bunch of thugs who prey on their own people, just like the Jewish guards in the concentration camps. And who helps them? You do. Your mother must be real proud of you, asshole."

Salvatore must have sensed things were getting out of hand and wedged himself between the two combatants. He took Silverman by the shoulders and turned him away from the fray. Gino stepped in and guided Arnold out of the courtroom as they continued to curse at each other.

Over the next few days, they were vilified in the press for the not guilty verdicts. The media was unmerciful in its condemnation of Attorney General Morgan's inability to convict members of the Mob. As each editorial appeared, it was apparent Morgan's reelection bid had been dealt a fatal blow.

On the first Tuesday of November 1983, Eileen Rose was elected attorney general. Much of the post-election analysis blamed the loss on Thomas Morgan's failure to convict members of the Mob.

As Thomas Morgan made his concession speech that night, Renée and Arnold polished up their resumes; both would resign before the new attorney general took office.

Renée joined the faculty of a small university, where she taught prelaw classes to undergraduates, and Arnold went to work as a legal researcher for the Boston branch of the Anti-Defamation League.

CHAPTER 75

November drifted into December, and then into January of 1984. As the transition from one attorney general to another took place, there was little to do but wait. The Dickie Calderone murder was the last case to be tried, but after two acquittals, no one seemed anxious to go to trial.

Gino wondered what Colonel Smith would do to uphold the suddenly tarnished reputation of the state police. Surely, he thought, Smith would come up with some brilliant strategy to convict Tiger and Big John for the Calderone murder.

Michelle called the unit together and told them Colonel Smith had decided to wait until Eileen Rose had a new staff in place before moving forward. In the meantime, Gino was on permanent security duty with the witnesses, and the rest of the unit returned to its regular duties.

During the holidays and into the New Year, Gino watched Billy become more withdrawn. He told Gino he was depressed by the two not guilty verdicts, and it caused him to question his decision to cooperate. The reality was that there was no turning back, and Billy told Gino he was going to see it through.

Marty gave off a completely different vibe, one that said he didn't give a fuck one way or the other. As for Moon, Gino got the impression that his only concern was getting his Massachusetts conviction overturned and being set free.

Gino spent the holidays babysitting Billy, Marty, and Moon. He managed an early Christmas Eve dinner with his mom and returned to the training academy around six to spend the rest of the night and Christmas Day guarding the Francos. Gino had volunteered for the duty so Lou, Sully, and Quinn could be at home with their families.

After the Francos went to bed, Gino walked over to the garage that had been converted into sleeping quarters for the security detail. He was about to turn on the TV when the door opened and Michelle walked in.

"Hi. I just visited my dad, and I thought I'd check on the Francos."

"They're doing fine. They just turned in for the night."

As he talked, something stirred inside of him, and he started to think about the unthinkable.

Michelle stood in the middle of the room between the desks and the bunks. Gino walked to the door and locked it, and she didn't say a word. As he moved toward her, he could smell the faint odor of wine and a hint of perfume.

"Gino, we can't do this," Michelle slowly protested as Gino left a trail of kisses from her face to her neck.

He wasn't listening; his only thought was that he had to have her now. Gino wrapped his arms around her, despite her halfhearted objections. They embraced, and he could feel her legs go limp for an instant. She recovered her strength, and as they kissed, she wrestled with his belt, and he began hiking her skirt over her hips. He pushed her down onto one of the bunks, and in an instant, his pants were around his ankles. Gino threw her panties across the room and clawed at her bra.

They made love without much thought about where they were, and when it was over, they dressed quickly, like two teenagers who had just screwed on a parent's sofa.

As Gino started to apologize, Michelle interrupted him.

"I'm a big girl. There's no need to say you're sorry. I knew exactly what I was doing."

"Are you sure?" he asked remorsefully.

"I'm not sure of anything anymore," she said, and as quickly as she had appeared, she was dressed and gone.

CHAPTER 76

In early March, Michelle called the unit together; she told them the new attorney general was fully committed to prosecuting the Calderone murder but that the colonel was not enthusiastic about their chances with the case. The colonel's orders were to dispose of the cases against Moon, Marty, and Billy, and then get them into the Federal Witness Protection Program.

Michelle explained, "The new attorney general has assigned two junior prosecutors, William Considine and Mike O'Brien, to the Calderone case. From what I understand, they're short on experience but very talented. Gino will be assisting them in the prosecutions and resolving Moon's Massachusetts case. Gino, you'll also be working with Considine and O'Brien to arrange pleas for Billy and Marty. After the Calderone trial, we'll put them into witness protection. Hook up with Considine and O'Brien as soon as you can. We want this nightmare over as soon as possible."

Urban's words left him numb. The colonel's decision to give him the case and team him with two green prosecutors shook him to the core. So this was the master plan: dump the whole thing in his lap and cut their losses.

Gino asked to speak to Michelle, and she called him into her office. He closed the door.

"With all due respect, what the fuck is going on?"

"What do you mean?"

"Well, I go from babysitting, to working the cases, to handling the whole thing. Don't you think that's a bit unusual?" Gino asked.

"I thought that's what you wanted—to be the big shot and handle a big case. Well, here you go, a big case, and it's all yours," she answered.

"You're kidding me. We lost two trials, and this case is just as bad. I thought the captain went down with the ship, not some rookie sailor."

Michelle tried to end the conversation. "Listen, I don't like this any more than you do. Do you think this is good for me? What do you think it's going to do to my career? You think I'm ever going to make lieutenant after this disaster? I'm sorry you feel that way, but it's the colonel's decision."

The ice that accompanied Michelle's words shocked Gino, and for the first time, he questioned their relationship. How could the passion they shared so recently be tossed aside so quickly? Was her career more important than what they had? To Gino, it appeared that she was answering yes. He lashed out at her.

"Your career? I thought we were in this together. I thought you'd fight for us, but you just rolled over when the old man told you how he was going to save his precious state police by throwing us to the wolves."

She struck back, "Is that what you think? You think that I don't care? You know I care; I risked everything just to be with you. We're both fucked, and there's no way around it. I did the best I could, but it's over."

"You know, maybe you're right. Maybe it is over."

CHAPTER 77

William Considine joined the attorney general's office after a stint with the Navy JAG Corp. He was about six feet tall, with a hockey player's solid build and the same tenacity. Considine had black hair and a small mustache that reached the corners of his mouth. It rested under a turned-up nose that accompanied blue eyes. His unruly hair was in constant need of being swept away from his forehead.

As a prosecuting attorney, he was known for his meticulous preparation and ability to thoroughly examine witnesses. Everything from Considine's opening statement to his closing argument was scripted and prepared long before the trial began.

Considine was preparing a sexual assault case when Winston Greene came into his office with an armful of case folders. Greene was the new head of the criminal division, the post previously held by Renée

St. Pierre. Greene, a former DA from Manhattan, was a no-nonsense practitioner of the law. He was tall and thin, with sparkling blue eyes that drew your attention away from a beard badly in need of trimming.

He dumped a bunch of files on Considine's desk and said, "Good luck." As he walked away, he said, "By the way, you can use Mike O'Brien as second chair if you want."

The files Greene left behind contained the case of the state versus Frank "Tiger" Detroia and John "Big John" Kazarian for the murder of Richard Calderone.

Considine flipped open the file, looking for a contact, and found Detective Gino Peterson listed as the lead investigator. He picked up the phone and made the call.

Gino arrived for a meeting with the new prosecutors at the AG's office on Pine Street. It was held in the same conference room where this strange odyssey started for Gino three years ago. Newly elected Attorney General Eileen Rose was there with Winston Greene, Considine, and O'Brien. Gino was the lone representative of the state police. Eileen Rose looked at Gino with the same disappointment he felt. He knew she must have expected a contingent of state police brass. Instead, she got a rookie detective.

Gino thought Attorney General Rose was an interesting study because she possessed an understated charisma. Your eyes were immediately drawn to her, and when she spoke, you felt like you were the only one in the room. Standing five foot two, she had closely cropped dark hair and wore large-framed glasses. There was an intelligence and fire in her eyes; it was a look that made you pay attention.

AG Rose asked Greene for an update on the cases; Greene talked about the two not guilty verdicts and said the last case to be prosecuted, Calderone's, had been assigned to Considine and O'Brien. Eileen Rose then asked Gino why Colonel Smith or Sergeant Urban wasn't at the meeting. He told her they were unable to attend because of a personnel matter that required their immediate attention. They both knew it was bullshit, but it's what he was told to say, and she was kind enough not to press the issue.

"The state police may have given up on these cases, and frankly, I don't blame them, considering the lack of convictions. So this is what *I'm* going to do. I have no personal investment in the Calderone case, but I do have an obligation to the people of the state of Rhode Island."

She looked directly at Considine and O'Brien. "Gentlemen, you have the full resources of this office to try the case. So I'm perfectly clear, let me say this. You concentrate on convicting those bastards, and we'll let the people decide in two years if I'm worthy of reelection."

Attorney General Rose then turned to Gino. "Detective, from what I've been told, you've been with these cases longer than anybody. Obviously, once they turned to crap, you were assigned to take the fall. Let me ask you something. Do you have it in you for one more good fight?"

"I'd prefer to go down fighting than with my tail between my legs, ma'am," Gino answered.

"Mr. Considine, Mr. O'Brien, you up for a good fight?" she asked.

"Absolutely," they both responded.

"Winston, whatever they need." AG Rose excused herself and left the meeting.

"Well, I guess that settles it," Greene said. "Clean this mess up so we can move on with our own agenda." Greene left, scurrying after his boss.

"This is either the opportunity of a lifetime or the end of three promising careers," Gino said.

The room filled with nervous laughter.

CHAPTER 78

G ino agreed to meet with Considine at the attorney general's Pine Street office the following day.
Considine's office was located on the third floor; prosecutors were packed into every office space, along with
secretaries, paralegals, and interns.

Gino arrived promptly at two o'clock, carrying
five binders that made up the Calderone case. He
made his way to Considine's office, which was remarkably neat for a prosecutor. The walls were covered
with diplomas and his certificate of appointment as
a special assistant attorney general. Arranged neatly
on his desk were several pictures of his wife and two
daughters.

O'Brien sat across from Considine, holding a legal
pad in one hand and a cup of tea in the other. Unruly
blond hair, nails chewed to the nub, and a day-old

beard made him look more like a college freshman than a prosecutor about to take on the Mob.

Considine and O'Brien were interested in Gino's take on the cases. He told them the state's open-ended agreements with Billy and Marty made it impossible for any juror to believe they were telling the truth.

Gino explained that it gave the appearance that the state would do anything to obtain guilty verdicts and that Billy and Marty would be based on their performance at trial, not telling the truth. What was needed was a written agreement between Marty, Billy and the state. An agreement that outlined exactly what sentence the state would recommend for each crime in return for their truthful testimony. He always felt that without a formal agreement in place, a juror would always assume Marty and Billy had great incentive to lie.

They all agreed that Salvatore and Silverman were talented attorneys, but, whether it was competitive juices or just plain ego, Considine and O'Brien felt they could beat them at trial. Gino found this new enthusiasm invigorating. He was on a sinking ship, no doubt, but at least he had found two shipmates who were willing to go down with him.

It was fast approaching four o'clock, and O'Brien suggested they head over to Michael's Bar. As they sat and talked, it became apparent that the three had much in common. They were all products of middle-class families, raised with encouragement and an occasional swift kick in the ass.

O'Brien and Gino were single, both living in apartments. After eight years of marriage, Considine was proud to say he owned a small colonial house in North Smithfield and a couple of beat-up Volvos.

After sandwiches and a few beers, O'Brien suggested they stop by his apartment in Pawtucket to talk strategy. O'Brien's apartment was on the second floor of his sister's two-family house.

O'Brien was born and raised in Pawtucket, and the O'Brien family was part of the strong Irish community that ruled Pawtucket socially and politically for decades. O'Brien had attended St. Peter's Academy, where he excelled in football, basketball, and baseball. After high school, he went to Boston College, and then Suffolk University Law School.

O'Brien graduated from law school, took the bar exam in July, and was sworn in as a prosecutor in September. He was only twenty-six at the time, one of the youngest prosecutors in the history of the department.

As Gino entered O'Brien's apartment, he thought for sure he was back in his college dorm because the furniture looked like it had been stolen from a frat house. The walls were decorated with wall-size posters of Fenway Park, Boston Garden, and Schaefer Stadium.

O'Brien led them into his living room, where the centerpiece was, as Considine described it, "the biggest television set in Rhode Island." He brought out three Budweisers and proudly said it was the only beer he stocked. Ever the elegant host, he brought out bags of Cheez-Its and Nachos and dropped them on a folding card table, which was strategically located between the couch and the TV.

Considine suggested they watch the Al Pacino movie *Scarface*. They were mesmerized by its parallels to the Raimondi crime family: it had the raw violence, betrayal, and struggle for power so evident in the Calderone case.

They watched it so many times together that in short order, they were able to repeat lines verbatim from the movie; it became their own form of communication and drew them even closer. Whenever nerves became frayed, a line from the movie delivered in a terrible Cuban accent broke the tension. "Say good night to the bad guy" became a common refrain at the end of the day.

That night ended like most they would spend together for the next year. Work, eat, and drink, work some more, and drink even more. They became brothers in a united cause: to confound those who had decided the Calderone case could never be won.

onsidine, O'Brien, and Gino made several strate-
gic decisions regarding the cases. They resolved to
have Moon's conviction overturned, and then get him
into the Witness Protection Program.

As they talked about Moon, O'Brien invoked the
words of Tony Montana. "You expect me to believe
that Moon is a stoolie because Tiger said so? You
bought that line." They laughed, but it was no line;
Moon was a stoolie, and he needed the program if he
were to survive.

O'Brien and Considine explained to Gino that it
was essential that plea agreements for Billy and Marty
be drawn up and executed. Under the agreements,
they would enter guilty pleas, and hopefully a judge
would accept the state's sentencing recommendation.

Gino met with United States Marshal Tom Parsons,
who outlined the process of getting Moon into the

Witness Protection Program. He told Gino that the state police and the attorney general would have to make a formal request for Moon to be placed in the program. If accepted, the Marshals Service would take Moon into custody.

Moon would then become the responsibility of the Marshals Service. He would be swallowed up in the federal bureaucracy known as the program, with a new identity, secreted in a state far from the Mob's influence. Richard "Moon" Capelli would cease to exist.

At the same time Gino was meeting with Marshal Parsons, Considine and O'Brien were meeting with District Attorney O'Hara of the Bristol County District Attorney's Office. O'Hara agreed to have Moon and Marty appear before the Bristol County Grand Jury and testify about the beating of Manuel Costa. Their testimony would lead to an indictment of Marty's actual accomplice, Albino Pontarelli.

The Massachusetts District Attorney would then ask a judge to overturn Moon's conviction and vacate his sentence, and then they would offer Pontarelli probation in return for a guilty plea, something he would willingly accept rather than risk a jail sentence.

They put their new strategy into action almost immediately. DA O'Hara presented Moon and Marty to the Bristol County Grand Jury on separate days. Their testimony of the events that occurred the night Costa was brutally beaten led to an indictment of Albino Pontarelli, as they had planned.

Once Pontarelli was indicted, they brought Marty to the court, where he stood before Judge Thaddeus Bulman, the same judge who had sentenced him five years ago. The judge agreed to reduce his previously imposed sentence of thirty years to time served because of his cooperation.

Two days later, Moon stood before Bulman. He listened as the judge vacated the twenty-year sentence. Essentially, Moon's conviction was wiped out; the time he spent in prison for a crime he didn't commit didn't seem to matter much to anyone. The only mention of it was a weak apology from the judge on behalf of the commonwealth. Moon didn't acknowledge the apology; he simply turned and walked out of the courtroom with Gino.

Within two weeks of their appearance in Bristol County, Colonel Smith received a letter from the Department of Justice indicating that Moon had been accepted into the Witness Protection Program.

In early March, Gino received a call at six o'clock in the morning from Marshal Parsons. Parsons told him to have Moon ready to travel by eight o'clock. Gino called the barracks and asked the trooper on the desk to get Moon up and ready to move. Gino jumped out of bed, took a quick shower, and made a high-speed run to Chepachet.

When Gino arrived, Moon was sitting with two troopers, a suitcase by his side. At exactly eight o'clock, two men walked through the door of the barracks and presented their credentials.

The marshals asked Gino to call US Marshal Tom Parsons to verify their identity. He called Parsons, who instructed him to ask the agents for a password. "Carrier pigeon," one replied. Gino repeated the password to Parsons and was given the go-ahead to make the exchange.

As Moon walked out the door, Gino shook his hand. He told him he was one of the few to escape the Mob.

"I appreciate that. But you have to understand, it may seem that way to you, but one way or another, they win. They always win."

"Just don't screw up, and you'll be safe. If there's a problem, all you have to do is call. You know that," Gino said.

"I know that, kid, but I'm not going to bother you. You've got the perfect life; don't blow it like I did. You might not know this, but people in the neighborhood are proud of you—the ones that count, not the shitheads you deal with. I'm talking about the ones that go to work every day and hope for a better future for their kids. You made it, and if you can make it, there's hope for them. Don't ever forget that, and don't let them down. I'm counting on you."

As he walked off with the marshals, Gino realized this was the last time he would ever see Richard "Moon" Capelli.

CHAPTER 80

With Moon out of the picture, O'Brien and Considine came to the same conclusion. Plea agreements for Billy and Marty were the first order of business.

In return for guilty pleas on all charges, the attorney general's office would be in a position to recommend a sentence of twenty years, with ten suspended and ten years' probation. No prison time for either, but the suspended sentence would become prison time if either committed a crime or lied. It was essentially a free pass, but it was a way to make good on the promise of no jail time the state police made to Billy when he first agreed to cooperate. They could then try the Calderone case with witnesses whose testimony wouldn't depend on performance.

They sat down with Billy and Marty and explained the terms of the agreement. The pleas would be contingent upon truthful testimony in every case. Any testimony determined to be false would make the agreement null and void.

Billy and Marty were told that they were exposing themselves to prison time if they lied on the stand.

The formal agreement would be drawn up by Considine and O'Brien, and then signed by the attorney general. Marty and Billy would then review the agreements with two court-appointed lawyers.

Considine explained to Gino that the court-appointed lawyers would ensure that Marty's and Billy's rights were not being violated and that they were entering into the agreements knowingly and willingly.

They both had the same questions. What judge was going to accept these pleas? How could they be sure the court-appointed lawyers weren't connected to the Mob?

Considine explained that they would approach Judge Antonio Tavares, a prosecutor-friendly judge, and ask him to appoint two lawyers. It would be Gino's job to make sure the lawyers weren't connected.

When they approached Judge Tavares, they would also ask if he'd accept the pleas. If he was receptive, they would return to him after the Calderone trial for sentencing.

"After the Calderone trial?" Billy screamed. "Then there's no guarantee?"

O'Brien jumped in. "No guarantees, Billy, just a commitment from the AG. That and a sympathetic judge, and I think we'll be just fine."

"But what if—"

"No buts, Billy, this is it. This is the way it goes down, or it doesn't go. All you have to do is tell the truth. That's what you've been doing, isn't it, Billy? Telling the truth?"

"Of course," Billy said meekly.

O'Brien continued, "You were made promises that shouldn't have been made, so just sign the agreement. It's the best you're going to do."

"Understood," Billy said.

The meeting with Marty went much more smoothly because he was happy to be safe; his satisfaction came from testifying against those who tried to kill him. The rest was irrelevant, so he asked a few questions and signed the papers without a fuss.

CHAPTER 81

They met Judge Tavares in his chambers at the Providence County Courthouse. He was about sixty years old, thin, with the sunken face of a lifetime smoker. He had jet-black hair combed straight back, dark eyes, and eyebrows as bushy as out-of-control hedges. He was known as a working man's judge, a man who toiled among judges with superior legal minds.

Tavares was proud of his Portuguese heritage. His chambers were decorated with photos of his ancestral home of Faial; he visited the island every August when the courts shut down for the summer.

There were few secrets in the Rhode Island legal community, and when they arrived, the judge already knew why. Gino sat in silence as O'Brien and Considine reviewed the plea agreement and made a formal request that Tavares appoint lawyers.

The judge sat back in his leather chair, put his reading glasses down, and brought his hands together.

"A court-appointed lawyer for Franco and Martelinni is easy; you could have gone to anyone for that. Why don't you tell me why you're really here?"

Gino admired the honesty and lack of pretense.

O'Brien leaned forward in his seat and looked Tavares in the eye. He knew this judge didn't require legal foreplay; O'Brien just needed to get to the point.

"Judge, we just want to try the case and be done with it, but we have to have the agreements in place, and then dispose of their cases after the trial," O'Brien said. "Would you consider accepting their pleas after the trial? We're going to be recommending twenty years, ten suspended, ten probation."

Judge Tavares placed one hand on his chin and said, "I know you inherited this piece of crap case, Mike, and it reminds me of a story they tell in my beloved Faial. If I accept the pleas, I'm going to be like that big pile of shit a dog leaves in the middle of the road. It stinks, so people walk around it. Nobody wants to have anything to do with it. But dog shit eventually dries up and blows away; so will the heat I take from the press for accepting these pleas. You can bring Mr. Franco and Mr. Martelinni to me after the Calderone case is over."

They thanked the judge and left before he changed his mind.

CHAPTER 82

Considine and O'Brien weren't in any rush to try the Calderone case until they were ready, but Silverman was pressing for a trial date because Tiger was still being held without bail. The only thing separating Tiger from freedom was one more not guilty verdict. If he couldn't get a quick trial date, Silverman would probably go to court for a reduction in bail based on the two not guilty verdicts.

Freedom for Tiger meant more than just returning home. It would enable him to vie for his seat back at the Raimondi crime family table—which might not be as easy as Tiger may have thought. Nicky and Pasquale would surely question his abilities as a leader, considering three of his crew turned state's evidence.

O'Brien and Gino decided to reinvestigate the Calderone murder from beginning to end in order to prepare for trial.

Since the body and Calderone's car were found in Massachusetts, the Mass State Police assigned Detective José Escobar to assist them. They started with a visit to the Calderone gravesite in Rehoboth. Officer Dan Kelly met them and pointed out where he found the body in 1974.

Considine asked Escobar what physical evidence the Massachusetts State Police had collected at the scene. He told them several soil samples were retrieved from the gravesite and Calderone's car. Gino added that he had a copy of the FBI analysis in his files.

O'Brien was interested in what had drawn Kelly to the area in the first place.

"Just boiled down to curiosity on my part, I guess. I'd like to tell you it was brilliant police work, but I can't," Kelly said.

"Well, I disagree, Dan," Gino said. "Most cops would have just driven by, and who knows if they ever would have found the body."

From Rehoboth, they travelled to Fall River and spoke to Sergeant Tom Beck, who had spotted Calderone's abandoned car. Beck told them how he thought the new Cadillac with Rhode Island plates was a bit out of place in an industrial section of his city. When he called in the plate, he was told that the Massachusetts State Police were looking for the vehicle in connection with a homicide.

Beck told them he was ordered by his supervisor to secure the vehicle and wait for the forensic unit. He explained that when they arrived, they examined the car, and then towed it away.

Gino thanked Beck for his assistance. They parted ways with Detective Escobar and headed back to Providence.

The trio decided to concentrate on physical evidence and identify several items they thought should be introduced at trial. They were looking for something besides testimony to link Tiger and Big John to the Calderone hit.

The best evidence was two sets of soil samples, one taken from the gravesite and one from Calderone's abandoned car. Gino produced the FBI lab report, which indicated soil seized from Calderone's car and from the gravesite matched. It wasn't a smoking gun, but it did corroborate Billy and Marty's account of Calderone's car being used to dump the body. O'Brien and Considine would be able to argue that whoever rode in Calderone's car that night was at the gravesite.

Turning their attention to trial preparation, they agreed to a structured approach. They decided that Mondays and Tuesdays, they would interview witnesses and visit locations of interest. Wednesdays would be devoted to working with Marty, and Thursdays with Billy. Fridays would be left open, with an eye toward happy hour at Michael's.

CHAPTER 83

The trio reinterviewed each police and civilian witness involved in the Calderone case. O'Brien and Gino would ask questions based on previous statements and grand jury testimony; Considine would make notes and suggest additional questions. Then, a list of questions for use at the trial was prepared for each witness.

With Billy and Marty, they used a different approach. Considine would ask questions during morning sessions, while O'Brien and Gino would take notes. During lunch breaks, the trio would refine the questions, adding and deleting whenever necessary.

In the afternoons, O'Brien would put Billy or Marty under mock cross-examination. He would start slowly and quicken the pace, trying his best to imitate Silverman or Salvatore. If they could get Billy and Marty accustomed to their styles of cross-examination, they would fare much better than they had in their previous encounters with the defense attorneys.

Both witnesses presented different challenges. With Marty, their goal was to keep him from losing his temper. O'Brien would hammer him with questions until he started to blow. Considine and Gino would then call a time-out and explain to Marty how he was being baited.

Billy's problem was trying to act like a good kid who fell in with the wrong crowd. They told him to drop the act and just answer the questions—he was a criminal, everybody knew it, and the only way to be believable was to just tell the damn story.

"Look at it this way," O'Brien explained. "They've got enough bullets to fire at you. Let's not give them a case of ammo with stupid answers."

After three months of constant work, Marty and Billy were ready.

In late August, Considine got a call from the clerk of the Superior Court. She told him *State v. "Tiger" Detroia and "Big John" Kazarian* was scheduled for trial on November 5 before Judge Brenda Leone.

In preparation for the trial, Gino had amassed four binders of notes and statements on just Billy and Marty. Four other binders contained police reports, lab reports, and witnesses' statements. They had prepared as if their professional lives depended on it—because in many ways, they did.

CHAPTER 84

Despite the time Gino spent with Considine and O'Brien, Michelle was never far from his thoughts. Their last conversation had not ended well. He tried to convince himself it was over, but his heart told him something else.

Gino was surprised when Michelle asked him to stop by her house after work. He pulled up to the white raised ranch in Warwick. Black shutters and flower boxes accented each window, and an American flag hung to the left of the front door. The landscaping was neat and trim, much like the owner.

Gino thought he should appear indifferent, but when she opened the door, his icy exterior melted away. Michelle greeted him with a warm smile and accepted his bottle of wine. As he climbed the stairs, he heard the strains of Grofe's Grand Canyon Suite playing in the background, a record his mother played for him often when he was a young boy.

He took in a deep breath and said, "Chicken piccata?"

"Good guess," she answered.

She was dressed in a peasant blouse sans bra, a jean skirt, and clogs. As she walked up the stairs, Gino admired the shape of her calves and the way the skirt accented her ass. If she was going to end their personal relationship, she certainly hadn't dressed the part.

As Michelle opened the wine, Gino took note of the tastefully decorated home with its fair share of state police memorabilia, mostly pictures of her father. It reminded him of his mother's house—not in style, but in the way it made you feel welcome.

When she offered him a glass of wine, he noticed the dinner table was set with linen and fine china. The table was illuminated by a single candle, which flickered as unevenly as Gino's heartbeat. She spoke, and he was smart enough not to interrupt.

"Gino, I thought I had to separate our professional lives from our personal lives. I found myself being especially hard on you, because I was torn between my career and us. Honestly, I didn't think we could have both.

"But after you told me it might be over, I thought about our careers and our relationship and realized it's time for the state police to wake up. They've got to realize that men and women on the job are going to have relationships. It's human nature, and they have to face it."

"Michelle, do you really think we can make this work?" Gino asked.

"I don't know, but I know it's worth the risk, whatever the consequences."

They agreed that if they went public, they would have to be prepared to give up one of the most precious thing in their lives, being members of the state police, but it would be for something more precious: happiness.

CHAPTER 85

On a brisk November morning, Gino arrived at the Providence County Courthouse for the first day of the Calderone trial. One hundred-year-old trees, silent witnesses to the passage of a thousand trials, lined Benefit and South Main Streets.

Gino met Considine and O'Brien on the second floor of the courthouse in a small office set aside for prosecutors.

They left the office and carried their binders and files into the elevator for the trek to the courtroom. Jammed together in the small elevator with lawyers and witnesses, they struggled to get out on the fifth floor, home to Judge Leone's courtroom.

The judge was assigned a spacious and ornate courtroom, and her bench stretched against the back wall of the courtroom. It looked down on the rest of the room like the top deck of an ocean liner. A door to the right of the bench led to the judge's chambers, and one to the left led to the jury room.

Beside her bench was an area for witnesses and a small desk for her clerk. To the immediate right of the judge's bench was the jury box, flush against three large windows extending from floor to ceiling.

As Gino entered the courtroom, his eyes were immediately drawn to the large gold seal of the state of Rhode Island above the judge's bench. On either side, flags of the United States and the state of Rhode Island stood in silent reverence.

Around nine thirty, spectators started to file in, and Considine took the lead chair. O'Brien sat in second chair, and Gino sat at the end of the prosecution table. Around nine forty-five, Silverman and Salvatore entered the courtroom. They coldly greeted the two prosecutors, and then took their places at the defense table.

The court clerk and stenographer filed in and out of the judge's chambers like worker bees preparing for the queen's flight to the hive.

The sheriffs and Tiger entered from a door directly opposite the jury box. Tiger was unshackled and seated next to Silverman. A few minutes later, Big John arrived with his usual entourage of family and friends.

At ten fifteen, the sheriff brought everyone to their feet with the words, "All rise." Judge Brenda Leone entered the courtroom, banged her gavel, and said, "Court is now in session. Please be seated."

The judge was in her sixties, and the word stunning came to Gino's mind. She had dark curly hair in a stylish cut that accented her gentle features. Her complexion was perfect and belied her years. As she walked to her seat, her oversize robe stretched out behind her like a bridal gown.

Judge Leone was the product of the Silver Lake section of Providence, another Italian American enclave in the city. Her father, Aldo, was the quintessential neighborhood lawyer, representing clients for real estate closings, wills, divorces, car accidents, and minor criminal cases.

As he toiled at his craft, he developed considerable political power as the chairman of the Seventh Ward Democratic committee. All Providence politicians knew the path to the mayor's office ran through the Seventh Ward; if you carried the seventh, you won the election. As chairman, Aldo's endorsement of a candidate ensured his or her election.

Brenda graduated from Brown University and Harvard Law. Her father cashed in a lifetime of favors to get his daughter a seat on the Superior Court. Aldo Leone would live long enough to see what he knew was her destiny: to become the finest jurist in Rhode Island.

CHAPTER 86

The first two days of the trial would be devoted to jury selection. Considine and O'Brien explained to Gino that the art of selecting a jury was a mixture of law and psychology. Prosecutors selected jurors with a strong sense of right and wrong. They loved blue-collar workers and women with families. The defense was looking for jurors who were cynical and questioned authority; college professors and young people were their favorites.

Under Rhode Island law, the prosecution and defense questioned each potential juror. A juror was removed if the prosecution or defense could demonstrate he or she couldn't possibly render a fair verdict. If this were the case, then the judge would dismiss the juror for cause. Failure to demonstrate cause would force the attorney to use a preemptory challenge. Each side was given twelve challenges, and no explanation was necessary when they were used to remove a potential juror.

On the first day of the Calderone case, Considine handled the questioning of the potential jurors. Silverman questioned the jurors for the defense. Over the next two days, it became a battle of demonstrating cause or using a peremptory challenge.

Whenever Considine found what he thought was a perfect juror, it seemed Silverman would use a preemptory challenge. A retired naval officer, a utility worker, and an emergency room nurse fell to Silverman's challenges. Likewise, a college professor, a psychologist, and a college student fell to Considine's challenges.

By late Wednesday afternoon, both sides were out of preemptory challenges, and the trio felt they had won the war of attrition. The remaining pool consisted of eight men and six women. Twelve would serve on the jury, and two would be alternates. They felt most of the fourteen fit the profile they wanted, and they were elated. The judge administered the oath of office to the jurors and dismissed them for the day. The trial would begin in the morning.

The next morning, Gino arrived at the courthouse to learn Considine and O'Brien had been summoned to the judge's chambers. He sat patiently outside her chambers until ten thirty, when Considine and O'Brien emerged. They were visibly upset.

Considine told Gino that Silverman was going to make a motion to have the jury dismissed, and the judge told them she was going to grant the motion.

As Gino started to ask O'Brien a question, the judge emerged from her chambers, and the sheriff announced, "Court is in session."

"Mr. Silverman, I understand you'd like to make a motion?" the judge said.

"Yes, Your Honor."

"You may proceed."

"Yesterday when you dismissed for the day, several jurors, as they crossed the courtyard, saw my client. He was shackled, surrounded by state marshals, and being escorted into the prison bus. Your Honor, it's impossible for this jury to render a fair and impartial verdict after what they witnessed. Seeing my client under those circumstances can only prejudice the jury against him. There's no instruction from this court that could overcome that prejudice. I respectfully request this jury be dismissed and a new one selected."

"Mr. Considine?"

"Judge, I'd like to renew the objection I made in chambers to the dismissal of the jury. I don't believe simply seeing Mr. Detroia being loaded onto the prison bus is fatal to the ability of this jury to render a fair and impartial verdict. Every day, the state marshals bring Mr. Detroia into the courtroom, and I don't think the jury is biased because of their presence. I believe an instruction from you on the presumption of innocence would be more than sufficient."

Silverman responded, "That's different, Your Honor. My client is unshackled and seated by the marshals before the jurors enter the courtroom. The marshals appear to be providing security for everyone—this is far different."

Judge Leone stopped him and ruled, "It is the decision of this court that the defendant has been prejudiced by the jury seeing him being placed on the prison bus. The bias against him is so overwhelming that no instruction could cure it. This jury is hereby dismissed from service, and we'll select a new jury."

"Please note my objection for the record, Your Honor," Considine said.

As she left the bench, she said, "Mr. Considine, your objection is noted. The sheriff will advise the jury their service is no longer needed. Court is adjourned until Monday morning at ten."

She was gone in a flash, and so was the perfect jury.

CHAPTER 87

Depressed wasn't an adequate description of how Gino felt about losing the jury. It was almost as if past failures haunted him, even now. The perfect jury had just slipped away—days of work gone in a five-minute motion.

Considine and O'Brien returned to the AG's office on Pine Street to lick their wounds and regroup for Monday. Gino left for headquarters to report to Michelle. The trio agreed to meet later at Michael's for something to eat and a few beers.

When Gino arrived, Considine and O'Brien were nursing a couple of beers at the bar. Gino grabbed a stool and ordered an Amstel Light. The conversation soon turned to the lost jury, and the beers started to fly across the bar at an alarming rate.

Around nine o'clock, O'Brien got up to go to the bathroom, and they didn't see him again for the rest of the evening. Maybe he found a friend or just decided to call it a night. It didn't really matter to Considine and Gino; they were glued to the bar.

They continued to drink and, as the clock turned to one, they were talking loudly and slurring even the simplest words. Finally, Considine decided it was time to head home; he'd drive.

The problem was, neither was in very good shape, and when Gino noticed they were headed north on Route 95 instead of south toward his apartment, he was sure Considine was toasted.

Gino told Considine he was going the wrong way.

"Fuck it, we're headed toward my house anyway. We'll just go there, and you can sleep at my house. I'll just bring you back to your car in the morning. My wife will understand."

When they arrived at Considine's house, his wife, Amy, was on the couch, watching television. Gino attempted to mumble something about being a state police detective and working with Billy. When she saw Considine practically carrying Gino into the house, she just sighed. "So tell me, what are you going to do with him?"

Considine said he was going to put Gino on the couch, let him sleep it off, and take him back to his car in the morning.

"The couch is barely big enough for you, never mind a guy his size," Amy said.

"All right, all right, I have an idea. I'll put Gino in our bed, I'll sleep on the couch, and you can sleep with the girls."

Gino thought it must have made perfect sense in Considine's alcohol-soaked brain.

"Fine," Amy said.

She tried to act mad, but Gino could see a smile cross her face. As Considine poured him into bed, some unknown compulsion forced Gino to reveal his soul—maybe he needed to unburden himself, or maybe he needed to brag about a conquest. He was too drunk to figure it out, and the words just came out.

"I love her, you know," he said, sounding as if he had just returned from the dentist's office after a root canal.

"You love Sergeant Urban, your boss? That's what you're telling me?" Considine asked.

"That's right. Michelle. She's beautiful, and I love her," he answered.

Suddenly, Considine broke into his Scarface imitation. "You're looking very beautiful tonight, Elvie."

"Stop busting my balls. I'm serious," Gino said.

"You work with a bunch of detectives and prosecutors. Did you really think you were fooling anyone? It's the worst-kept secret in the state of Rhode Island," Considine said. He became Scarface again. "With the right woman, I could go right to the top."

"You just won't stop, will you?" Gino said.

"You realize what you're risking. Smith will fire both your asses. You realize that, don't you?"

"Why? Why would he do that? We haven't done anything wrong." Gino was pleading, but to the wrong person.

"I know, but you have to realize, he comes from a different era. Lord knows he didn't even want women on the job. Now here's a woman; he makes her a supervisor, and she's banging one of her men. How do you think he's going to react to that?"

"Fuck him," Gino said, obviously bolstered by the booze.

"You know how many troopers are on the outside looking in for crossing the old man. Are you prepared for that?"

This was no attempt to make Gino feel better by Considine—only the delivery of a dose of reality.

"You bet your ass I am," Gino answered.

"Of course you are, because you're drunk, and you got beer muscles. Let's see how you feel in the morning."

"Considine?" he said.

"Yeah," Considine answered.

"What should I do?"

"I don't know. I just know that when I have doubts, whenever I'm searching for an answer, I talk to Amy, and when I'm talking to her, I never really have to wait for an answer. I just look into her eyes, and when I do, I can see the answer. Just look into her eyes, Gino, and you'll know."

Falling back into his Scarface persona once again, he added, "The eyes, Chico, they never lie. Now get some rest."

The next morning, Gino woke with a pounding headache and the feeling he wasn't in his apartment.

Lying in a strange bed, he was still in his shirt and pants. He was relieved when he recognized Amy's voice as she was getting the girls ready for school. In a fog, he struggled to formulate a game plan to make a gracious exit. Suddenly, Considine knocked on the door and came into the room.

He was wearing a T-shirt and boxer shorts, his eyes were slits, and he sounded like he'd smoked a carton of cigarettes.

"Gino," he whispered. "Sleep as long as you want. Amy is going to drive you to your car. I'm hung over and exhausted from all the time we've been putting in, so I'm going to go back to bed."

"Tell her I'll be ready in fifteen minutes," Gino said.

"Good. That'll give her a chance to get the kids off to school." Considine said a quick good-bye and returned to the couch.

Gino slowly walked downstairs to a grinning Amy. She offered coffee, which he declined in favor of some aspirin and a glass of water.

She finished her coffee and drove him to his car. Every bump along the way churned his stomach and shot pain from one temple to the other.

When they got back to Michael's, Gino thanked Amy, found his car, and drove home. He called work and said he'd be out sick. Gino crashed into his bed, hoping to wake to a better day, but his nap was interrupted by a call from Michelle.

"What are you doing home?" she asked.

"I'm sick. I think I got the flu," he said.

"The flu, really? It must be going around, because I just called the AG's office, and Considine's out sick too. The flu, my ass. You sure you didn't catch something at Michael's last night?"

The slamming of the receiver echoed in Gino's ear.

CHAPTER 88

G ino's hangover didn't release its grip until Sunday. On Monday, he returned to work, avoided Michelle, and headed to the courthouse.

Considine, O'Brien, and Gino made the trip from the AG's office to the courtroom to select another jury. The jury pool was brought into the courtroom, and the process of selecting a second jury began. At the end of two days, a new jury was impaneled, not as perfect as the last, but they'd do. It was made up of retirees, small-business owners, teachers, college students, and utility workers.

Judge Leone administered the oath to the jurors, and then had them wait in the jurors' room until Tiger left for his trip back to prison. Everyone was instructed to return on Wednesday for opening statements.

On Wednesday, they were greeted by a camera crew set up in the corner of the courtroom. The press decided this trial was worthy of gavel-to-gavel cover-age—mobsters were obviously good for ratings. The judge had only one rule for the camera: she would not allow them to show the jury's faces. This was a Mob trial; she deemed it a reasonable precaution.

Everyone was in place as Judge Leone assumed the bench and called the proceedings to order. She explained to the jury that they would hear opening statements and the first of the prosecution's witnesses.

Considine made his opening statement to the jury. He told them that the state intended to prove that in the early morning hours of March 18, 1974, Richard "Dickie" Calderone made the fatal error of walking into the Pineapple Social Club. He told the jury they would hear from two cooperating witnesses. The wit-nesses would testify that Tiger, after getting a gun from Big John, walked around the bar, stood behind Dickie Calderone, and fired six shots into his back.

They would hear from Officer Dan Kelly, who dis-covered the body in Rehoboth shortly after the mur-der. Also testifying would be officers involved in the first investigation in 1975 and those involved when Billy and Marty came forward in 1983.

He concluded by telling them, "Ladies and gen-tlemen, we will show that these defendants showed a callous disregard for the sanctity of life and viciously murdered Dickie Calderone. They shot him, stabbed him, and dumped his body in a shallow grave for one reason, and one reason only: to obtain what men like these covet, money and power. I am sure that once you hear all of the state's evidence, it will establish beyond a reasonable doubt that both defendants are guilty of murder in the first degree. Thank you."

Judge Leone asked Silverman and Salvatore if they wished to make opening statements, and both declined.

The state's first witness was Dan Kelly, who described the discovery of Calderone's body on that snowy night in March of 1974. Both the direct and cross-examination of Kelly was uneventful.

Considine followed up with officers from the Massachusetts State Police Forensic Unit, who testified about the crime scene and processing Calderone's car. He spent considerable time questioning them about the processing of the soil samples seized from the grave and car. Considine emphasized that all samples were sent to the FBI for analysis.

The day ended with Sergeant Tom Beck, who testified about locating Calderone's car in Fall River.

After court, Gino, O'Brien, and Considine quickly planned for the next day's witnesses. They didn't spend much time together because Considine was in a hurry to get home. His wife had invited new neighbors over for dinner.

When Considine arrived at home, he was greeted by Amy and his girls. His neighbors, newlyweds, were sitting on the couch, drinking wine and munching on cheese and crackers.

"Daddy, Daddy!" Considine's eldest, Jen, said excitedly. "They just said on the news they're going to show you at work today!"

Mary Beth, his youngest, sat glued to front of the TV. Amy brought Considine a glass of wine as they gathered around the TV. The anchor announced that the Calderone murder case had started in Superior Court earlier that day.

The screen filled with the image of Considine making his opening statement. The camera panned the courtroom and settled on the prosecution table, with O'Brien and Gino clearly in view. Jen jumped up, pointed at Gino, and said, "Mommy, Mommy! That's the man who slept in your bed the other night!"

Considine spit a mouthful of wine across the room, and Amy turned the color of the merlot. The young couple looked at each other in disbelief. Jen and Mary Beth jumped up and down, clapping and screaming, "We saw Daddy on TV with his friend who slept in Mommy's bed! We saw Daddy on TV with his friend who slept in Mommy's bed!"

The neighbors accepted Considine's explanation but politely excused themselves shortly after dinner. Considine thought it wise to sleep on the couch that night.

CHAPTER 89

The next morning, Considine continued the state's case with the medical examiner, Dr. Arnold Katz. Katz testified that Richard "Dickie" Calderone died from six gunshot wounds to the back and several stab wounds. The projectiles recovered from his body indicated a small-caliber weapon, and the stab wounds were consistent with those made by a large knife.

FBI Agent Terry Santos testified that the projectiles taken from Calderone's body were consistent with a .38 caliber weapon. Agent Walter Palmer testified that the soil from Calderone's car was the same soil recovered from the gravesite. The two agents' testimony was factual and professional, and the defense was unable to shake it.

Gino sensed Salvatore and Silverman wanted them off the stand as soon as possible. They only helped the prosecution, and spending a great deal of time on cross-examination only reinforced the importance of the physical evidence.

As the week ended, Considine, O'Brien, and Gino felt confident they had done a good job of prosecuting the case. The physical evidence showed that whoever was responsible for the murder used Calderone's car to transport his body from the Pineapple Social Club to the gravesite.

The difficulty, as always, would be getting the jury to believe Billy and Marty were telling the truth when they described the events surrounding the murder. Their testimony would be the key to the case. Gino could only hope that the work they had put in with them would pay off.

That night, Gino was watching news accounts of the assassination of Benigno Aquino, the political rival of Philippines President Ferdinand Marcos. He had always been fascinated by political assassinations and, shortly after getting into the unit, was selected to attend a two-day dignitary protection seminar taught by the Secret Service. The agent teaching the class analyzed every political assassination from Lincoln to Kennedy. Gino's concentration was broken by a call from Theo Christopoulos, and although his voice was calm, it carried a sense of urgency.

"Gino, sorry to bother you on a Friday night, but I couldn't get a hold of Lou. Tim Karakides is driving me crazy. He thinks the Mob is out to kill. I tried to explain to him there was no reason for the Mob to harm him because everyone was found not guilty and we couldn't try them again even if we wanted to. The wacko is starting to see a hit man behind every tree."

"What do you think? Do you think he's in danger?" Gino asked.

"I don't know, but you know how shaky he is. Even if he's wrong, he did stick his neck out and testify for us, so I think we should help him."

"I agree, but if he's never going to be a witness for us again, it would be hard to get him into protective custody," Gino said.

"Believe it or not, all he wants to do is go back to Greece. He just wants us to send him home," Theo answered.

"Let me make some phone calls, and I'll get back to you."

"I'll keep him calm till then. He's staying at a cousin's house, so he should be safe for now."

Gino was able to contact Considine, who authorized the purchase of a plane ticket for Karakides. Gino was able to book him on a flight from Boston to Athens that was scheduled to leave the following night at six o'clock.

The next day, Gino met Theo and Karakides at the federal office building at four in the afternoon. Karakides, dressed in a wrinkled suit, was carrying a small suitcase. Gino wasn't sure if they were helping him escape danger or if the state had just been scammed out of a plane ticket to Greece.

As they drove to Logan Airport, traffic was light, not the usual nightmare that led most people to use the Providence airport. Theo and Karakides spoke Greek in a rhythmic fashion that reminded Gino of a rollercoaster ride.

Gino called ahead, and the Massachusetts State Police had a parking spot reserved for him at the airport. When they arrived, a trooper escorted them to the ticket counter for Olympic Airlines. Once cleared by customs, Theo and Gino said good-bye to Tim Karakides, who, to say the least, looked relieved to be returning to his homeland.

Gino asked the clerk at the Olympic counter for a restaurant suggestion in the North End, the Italian section of Boston known for its fine restaurants and, like Providence's Federal Hill, mobsters. She suggested a restaurant on Prince Street called Uncle Tony's and gave them directions. Gino drove from Logan and luckily found a spot in front of the restaurant.

Over a feast of antipasto, pasta, veal, and sausage, and a bottle of Pinot Grigio, the conversation flowed much like the wine.

Theo asked Gino if he liked working Mob cases.

"I do because I don't think people realize how vicious the Mob can be. Everyone thinks they only harm their own, but that's bullshit. They prey on their own people and anyone who gets in the way. I haven't told many people this, but my dad was killed in a car accident when I was a kid. He was a straight guy, maybe a little gambling now and then, but a hard worker—worked two jobs to support us. Everything's going great for us, and one night, he has a run-in with a made guy; six months later, he's dead. I'll never know for certain, but I'll always wonder if those bastards were responsible."

"How'd he die?"

"He drove off the road and hit a pole. They said it was an accident, but I never believed it for a second."

"Is that why you joined the intelligence unit?"

"That's part of the reason. If I end up putting away the bastards that killed my father for some other crime, then so be it," Gino said.

"But there's got to be something more," Theo said.

"I just want to prove that an Italian cop from the Mob's neighborhood can do the right thing for his people. Show everyone that not all Italians are in the Mafia."

Theo let out a quiet laugh but said in a sarcastic tone, "Or you could go the other way. I'm sure Pasquale Raimondi would give you a boatload of cash to take out Billy and Marty."

Gino laughed and steered the conversation to more comfortable topics. They spoke about families, friends, and police work. The hours drained away like each glass of wine. After the meal, they returned to Gino's car and cursed the parking ticket left under the wiper blade. Gino threw it in the glove box with the rest of his collection. They drove back to Providence in the comfortable silence that comes with friendship.

CHAPTER 90

The drama of Billy and Marty's testimony was about to play out in Judge Leone's courtroom.

The security team arrived at the courthouse with Billy at ten o'clock in the morning, and Gino escorted Billy into the courtroom and onto the stand. He took his seat at the prosecution table, and O'Brien started his direct examination.

"Mr. Franco, you are presently in protective custody, is that correct?"

"Correct," Billy answered.

"And you're testifying pursuant to an agreement you have with the state, is that correct?" O'Brien asked.

"Yes, I've signed an agreement with the state."

"Your Honor, I'd like to introduce the agreement as a full exhibit."

"No objection," Silverman and Salvatore said.

"It shall be marked as State's Full Exhibit Number One," Judge Leone responded.

O'Brien continued, "Mr. Franco, can you briefly outline the agreement?"

"Yes. I've agreed to testify in return for a recommendation from the state. The recommendation to the judge will be a sentence of twenty years, ten suspended and ten years' probation," Billy said.

"And that recommendation is for a guilty plea for all the crimes you've committed?"

"Yes, for all crimes," Billy answered.

"Are there any conditions to the state's recommendation?"

"Yes. If I don't tell the truth, the state won't ask a judge to sentence me to what we agreed to."

O'Brien asked, "What else will happen if you don't testify truthfully?"

Billy answered as they had instructed him. "Then I could go to prison for the rest of my life."

"Let me ask you again. The state has agreed to recommend a sentence of less than jail as long as you tell the truth?" O'Brien reinforced the point.

"That's correct. If I want to stay out of jail, I have to tell the truth," Billy responded.

"Mr. Franco, you've signed the agreement, and it's also been signed by the attorney general. Correct?"

"Yes, Mr. O'Brien," Billy answered.

"All right, Mr. Franco, let's move on to the night that Mr. Calderone walked into the Pineapple Social Club."

Billy told the jury how Calderone wandered into the Pineapple in the early morning hours of St. Patrick's Day. He told the jury that Tiger sent Big John out to his car for a gun, that Tiger came out from behind the bar and shot Calderone six times. How Tiger viciously stabbed Calderon's body as it lay on the floor of the club. Billy testified that Tiger ordered Marty and Big John to get Calderone's car and about how he helped drag Calderone out to the car and dump him in the trunk.

As he testified, Gino took note of the jury; it appeared they were caught up in the story. They seemed fixated on Billy's testimony, and Gino allowed himself a glimmer of hope that maybe, just maybe, they believed Billy. O'Brien finished his direct examination of Billy, and before the defense could begin its cross, Judge Leone decided they would resume the next day. Gino escorted Billy off the stand and out of the courtroom. The next day would be the real test: cross-examination.

CHAPTER 91

Silverman, Tiger's attorney, began questioning Billy early the next morning, because the defense had decided that one attorney would cross-examine for both defendants. Gino thought it was a tactical error, that they'd have been better off each hammering away at Billy's story—he hoped it was a sign of overconfidence.

"Mr. Franco, are you telling this jury that the state hasn't promised you that you won't go to jail?" Silverman asked.

"No, I'm not saying that. I'm saying, if I don't tell the truth, they'll send me to jail," Billy answered.

"You've indicated in other proceedings that you were promised that you wouldn't have to go to jail. In fact, you testified that you wouldn't even cooperate with the state if it meant going to jail and leaving your family. Isn't that correct?"

"Yes, it is, Mr. Silverman," Billy said, "but things have changed."

"What's changed, Mr. Franco?"

"The new attorney general wouldn't make the same promise the state police and the other AG did."

"And you just accepted that?" Silverman asked.

"Mr. Considine and Mr. O'Brien explained to me that what the state police promised me was off the table and that this was the new agreement," Billy answered.

Silverman continued, "But if you lie, Mr. Franco, if you fail to tell the truth, you could go to jail for the rest of your life. Isn't that quite an incentive to tell the state what it wants to hear? What they want the truth to be?"

"No, Mr. Silverman, it's a reason to tell the truth. My life depends on it," Billy answered.

Silverman didn't appear to be scoring points with the jury by attacking the agreement, so he quickly switched his line of questioning. He asked Billy a series of questions about the night of the Calderone murder. Although there were plenty of times when Silverman confused him, Billy was consistent when it came to the significant facts of the case.

By late afternoon, Silverman had stopped his cross-examination. Gino thought Billy hadn't been shaken so badly that his credibility was in doubt. Considine and O'Brien whispered to Gino that they couldn't have asked for better testimony from Billy. Judge Leone adjourned court for the day. Billy talked about his testimony all the way back to Foster. He thought he'd done well—and, for the first time, Gino did too.

CHAPTER 92

The following day was Martelinni's turn to testify. The security team got him to the courtroom early enough for Considine and O'Brien to give him some last-minute instructions.

Once on the stand, O'Brien questioned him about the deal and the murder. Marty was solid. As with Billy, they'd been over his testimony a thousand times. The direct examination went exactly as they had rehearsed it. Gino held his breath as Marty was cross-examined by Salvatore; the defense had decided he would cross for both defendants. He was pleased when Tiger's attorney was unable to shake Marty about the deal or the night of the murder.

"Mr. Martelinni, are you willing to risk going back to jail for the rest of your life? Because I believe you're a liar."

"No, Mr. Salvatore, I'm not going to lie, because I know if I go back to prison, I'll be dead," Marty answered.

Salvatore shot back, "You've been in and out of jail your whole life. Why would you be in danger?"

"Because my *friends* in the Mob tried to kill me before, and I'm sure they'll try again."

"Objection, Your Honor," Salvatore said.

"Denied. You asked the question, Mr. Salvatore."

The questioning was like a tennis match. Salvatore would occasionally serve an ace, but most times, Marty returned the serve. When he was done testifying, Marty was whisked out of the courtroom. He was oblivious to what was going on around him, and he never heard the Kazarian and Detroia clans wishing him a horrible death.

Marty was quiet on the way back, displaying the same nerves of steel that had served him well as a mobster. He asked for a pizza as a reward for his performance.

Gino gladly took the ride to Vinnie's Pizza, and then back to headquarters. Gino was finally starting to feel a little confident. He thought maybe, just maybe, a guilty verdict was in their future.

With the possibility of a guilty verdict, Gino's mind drifted from the trial to thoughts of Michelle. If he brought home a guilty verdict, they'd both reap the rewards. They'd be considered superstars for convicting mobsters for a nine-year-old gangland slaying, and the colonel would have no choice but to accept their relationship—but there were many miles to go before this battle was over.

CHAPTER 93

The next morning, the state rested its case, and the defense indicated it would present no witnesses. The judge dismissed the jury and told them she would hear closing arguments in the morning. Tiger returned to the prison, and Big John left with his family.

Considine thanked Gino and O'Brien for their offer to help him with his closing but preferred to work on it alone. Gino went home expecting a quiet night, but that ended around seven o'clock, when he got a call.

"Gino, it's Sully."

"What's up? Everything all right?" Gino couldn't imagine why he was calling, but he knew it wasn't social.

"I want you to call a cop I know. His name is Tim Rego, and he's with Norwich PD. We went to a homicide school together, and we've stayed in touch since then," Sully said.

"Why do you want me to call him?" Gino asked.

"He says his wife has some information that could help you with the Calderone case," Sully answered.

"His wife?"

"Yeah, it's complicated, but I think you'll understand once you talk to her," Sully said.

Gino couldn't help but ask, "Sully, why are you helping me? It's no secret there's no love lost between us."

"I've seen how hard you've worked on this case, and if this helps you convict Tiger and Big John, you deserve the credit. Besides, we all know they've thrown you to the wolves with this case because they think it's a loser, and I don't appreciate them trying to fuck with your career. If they could do it to you, they could do it to any of us. The only way for them to know we're not stupid and we know exactly what they're doing is to convict these assholes."

Gino didn't know what else to say except to thank him.

"Thanks. I appreciate the call."

"And I appreciate you stopping that asshole from sucker-punching me at Michael's. Good luck with the call."

Gino didn't realize Sully had witnessed his stopping the attack, and now he thought that this was his way of protecting him.

Gino dialed the number. A female voice answered. "Hello?"

"This is Detective Peterson of the state police. May I speak to Joyce Rego, please?"

"This is Joyce Rego, and I know who you are, Detective Peterson. It's me, Gino, Joyce. Joyce Moradian from Norwich. Rego is my married name."

His coming-of-age summer with Joyce came rushing back to him. The awkward eighteen-year-old she turned into a man was at a loss for words.

"It's all right. I didn't expect you would recognize my married name. It's been a long time. We lost track of each other after Beach Pond, but I remember you always talked about being a trooper. I'm happy your dream came true."

Gino recovered a bit and tried to make small talk, still wondering what was so urgent about the call.

"Thanks. How's everything with you? How are the kids?"

"They're fine. I remarried, and my husband adopted them."

"That's great." Another awkward pause. "One of the guys I work with said you wanted to talk to me," Gino said.

"I've been struggling with something for a long time, but I've finally decided that I had to tell you. About a year after the summer we were together, I went to my cousin's wedding in Providence. I met a guy at the wedding, and we started dating."

She hesitated a bit. "Well, one thing led to another. I started spending a lot of time in Providence, and eventually, I moved in with him. We lived together in East Providence for about a year."

"Why are you telling me this?" he asked.

"I'm telling you because I lived with Big John. He was my boyfriend."

Gino was stunned. "Big John? Big John Kazarian? You were Big John's girlfriend?"

"There's more. I need to tell you I was living with John the night Calderone was killed."

"Are you trying to tell me you know something about the murder?" Gino asked.

"I do," she said. "That's why I called."

This has to be a dream, Gino thought, *could she actually be holding the key to a conviction?*

"Joyce, go slow, and tell me exactly what you know about the night Calderone was murdered."

"It was the middle of the night when I heard John moving around in the apartment. I got up and saw John and Marty standing in my kitchen. They were covered with dirt, and their hands and faces were scratched. John had blood on his pants, and Marty was leaning over the kitchen sink, washing his hands."

"Did you ask what was going on?" he asked.

"Of course I did. They told me they were hunting deer in the middle of the night—they called it deer jacking. John said the dirt and blood was from a deer. I didn't think much of it until the next day when I heard about Calderone's body being found in the woods. That's when I knew John and Marty were responsible," she said.

"Did you ever tell anybody about this?" he asked.

"No, never," Joyce said.

"What about your husband? Did you tell him?"

"No, I was ashamed to tell him. I was ashamed because of the kind of guy John was. He lied to me all the time. He was always out all night, never paid any attention to my girls. I just knew he and his friends were all up to no good."

"If you met your husband after John, why would you be afraid to tell him?" he asked.

"Because he's a cop, Gino, and I didn't think he would understand. But when I saw Big John was on trial for the Calderone murder, I told my husband everything. After I told him, he called Sully and found out it was your case. He said you lost the other trials, and you could lose this one if I didn't come forward. My husband explained to me that the right thing to do was to come forward. I know it's the right thing to do. I want to testify."

"Do you understand what it means to testify against the Mob? Are you ready for that?"

Gino's mind floated back to the first night they had spent together. He remembered how gentle and caring she had been when their lovemaking ended so quickly, and as much as Gino wanted her to testify, he cared enough to make sure she understood what was at stake.

"My husband explained it to me, and I'm not afraid. He'll protect me. I was around them for a year, and I know these guys aren't that bright. Let's face it, most of them couldn't find Norwich with three maps and a compass."

They both laughed, and it broke some of the tension.

"Joyce, if you're going to do this, it's going to happen fast. The trial is almost over, and I don't know if they'll even let you testify. I need to take a statement from you tonight."

"I understand," she said.

"Do you remember how to get to the Hope Valley barracks?"

"Sure I do. We used to drive by there all the time, just trying to get a glimpse of a trooper. I guess you don't remember how obsessed you were about the state police. Anyway, it's about twenty minutes from Beach Pond on Route 3, right?"

"That's right. Can you meet me and a prosecutor there in about an hour?"

"Sure. My husband can watch the girls."

"Thank you so much. You don't know how much this means to me."

"Oh, but I do. That's part of the reason I'm doing it. I've always had a soft spot in my heart for you." There was a slight pause. "One more thing," she said.

"What's that?"

"It's about my husband. All I told him was that you were a young lifeguard I met at Beach Pond, you know what I mean?"

"Yes, Joyce, I know exactly what you mean."

As soon as Gino got off the phone, he called Considine, barely containing his excitement as he explained his conversation with Joyce.

Considine said, "Pick me up, and we'll meet her at the barracks. Let's take a formal witness statement, and I'll make a motion in the morning to reopen the case."

He told Gino that Salvatore and Silverman would go berserk, but if they were lucky, Leone would allow her to testify.

Gino and Considine met Joyce at the Hope Valley barracks. Even now, in her early fifties, she was as appealing and sensual as she was the first time he'd laid eyes on her.

As they took her statement, it was hard for him to concentrate. Looking at her took him back fifteen years to the most wonderful summer of his life.

They finished around eleven that night, and Gino walked her to her car. He asked if she wanted to be picked up and brought to court.

"My husband's taking me. I'll be fine."

She kissed him on the cheek and told him she would see him in the morning.

He smiled and said, "Good night, Joyce Moradian."

Her face softened. "Good night, Gino the young lifeguard."

CHAPTER 94

The next morning, Considine briefed O'Brien, and they asked to see the judge and the defense attorneys in chambers. Once inside, they explained to Leone how Joyce had come forward the night before and that they wanted to make a motion to reopen their case.

Salvatore and Silverman raised holy hell. Rather than let the screaming continue, the judge ordered Considine to provide Joyce's statement to the defense. She would hear the motion in open court, without the jury.

"Your Honor, last night, Detective Peterson received a call from a witness who has valuable information about this case. It's vital that the jury hear her testimony. To not allow it would deprive them of having all the evidence before them as they determine the guilt or innocence of these defendants.

"As we explained to you in chambers, there was no way for the state to have known that the witness existed or that she was in possession of this information—information that clearly points to these defendants as having participated in the murder of Dickie Calderone. Her testimony also corroborates the testimony of the state's witness Frank 'Marty' Martelinni.

"We've provided to the defense a formal statement taken from the witness late last night. Therefore, Your Honor, the state respectfully requests to reopen its case and present Joyce Rego as a witness."

"Thank you, Mr. Considine. Mr. Silverman?"

"Yes, Your Honor, thank you. On behalf of my client, Mr. Detroia, I would argue that bringing this witness forward at the last minute is highly prejudicial at best and prosecutorial misconduct at worst. How is it that hours before closing arguments, this witness appears out of nowhere and has crucial testimony?

"Is it not, Your Honor, the obligation of the prosecution to present all of its witnesses in a timely fashion? We must be allowed to investigate and interview this witness. If Mrs. Rego possessed such valuable information, it was the state's obligation to find her and present her at the proper time. To spring her on us now would turn this trial into a mockery. I implore you not to let this last-minute trick deny my client a fair trial."

Salvatore rose. "Your Honor, may I be heard?"

"Of course, Mr. Salvatore, go ahead."

"Your Honor, I must go on the record with my colleague and object to the motion to allow the state to reopen its case. We've already rested, Your Honor. What are we going to do if we have a rebuttal witness? We need time, Your Honor, to investigate the validity of her statement."

"How much time do you think you need, Mr. Salvatore?" Leone asked.

"Two weeks, at least, Your Honor," Salvatore answered.

Gino slid to the edge of his seat in anticipation of her ruling. He didn't want her to give the bastards any time to prepare, never mind two weeks. Gino feared they would use it to find a way to intimidate or harm her.

He thought, *Please, Judge, deny the motion; don't let the bastards up for air.*

"Two weeks? I'm not going to delay this trial for two weeks to allow you to prepare for one witness. Either she testifies now, or we go to closing arguments," Judge Leone said.

"Your Honor, even your father, as great a lawyer as he is, would ask for as much time to prepare for such a witness."

A hush came over the courtroom, and a red hue crossed Leone's face. Salvatore had invoked the name of her beloved father to win a legal argument. Gino thought this was over the line, a cheap trick, a veiled reminder of her roots—call it what you will, it was a fatal error.

Leone didn't even recess to consider the motion; she simply ruled from the bench, "I'm granting the state's motion to reopen. Joyce Rego may testify before this jury. Mr. Salvatore and Mr. Silverman, you may have the morning to prepare to cross-examine the witness and do any investigation you deem appropriate." Anger hung on every word. She calmed a bit and turned to the sheriff. "Instruct the jury we'll hear from an additional witness at two o'clock. Closing arguments are postponed until tomorrow morning."

She turned back toward the lawyers. "Anything else, gentlemen?"

No one had the balls to say a word.

"Very well, then. Court is in recess till two."

Considine leaned over to Gino. "I think your witness may have just won this case for us."

He nodded and thought of how the woman who had ushered him into manhood many years ago had entered his life again. And this time, she may have just saved his career.

At exactly 2:00 p.m., Joyce Rego walked into the courtroom with her husband dressed in his Norwich Police uniform, his **REGO** nametag visible for all to see. Officer Rego took a seat in the gallery and sat stoically as his wife told of her life with Big John Kazarian and the night of the Calderone murder.

Her direct testimony was flawless. The jury was finally hearing from someone whose only mistake was getting involved with a wiseguy. Try as they might,

Salvatore and Silverman were unable to shake her with their cross-examination.

They tried to imply she really didn't know Big John that well.

"I have pictures of us together during holidays and other occasions. I think I have copies of a joint checking account we used when we lived in the apartment. I can bring it in if you want."

That she was lying and they were hunting that night.

"John never hunted a day in his life because he got lost in the woods when he was a small boy. It scared him to death, so I know he never would go deer hunting because he'd have to go into the woods."

That she came forward at Gino's request and made up the whole story.

"I came forward because my husband told me it was the right thing to do. I called Detective Peterson; he didn't call me. Besides, I know what kind of men John and his friends are, and I wouldn't be up here risking my life if I wasn't telling the truth."

They stopped asking questions; it was futile.

She walked off the stand more believable than any witness who had testified in three years. As she passed the prosecution table, she smiled and walked out of Gino's life once again.

Judge Leone asked the defense if they had any rebuttal. They didn't. Both sides rested. She dismissed the jury and asked them to return for closing arguments in the morning.

CHAPTER 95

Gino and Michelle took advantage of the time before the closing arguments to meet for dinner. They drove in separate cars to a small restaurant in Douglas, Massachusetts, just north of the Rhode Island border.

Dinner conversation was light but grew more serious as they lingered over after- dinner port.

"Gino, it's time we made some decisions about our relationship," she said.

"What kind of decisions?" he asked.

"Whether we're going to try to be together. I want to be with you, but I don't know how this will affect our careers. How's the colonel going to react if we go public?"

"What are you afraid of?" Gino asked.

"I'm afraid of losing everything I've worked for, and I'm afraid of losing you," she answered.

"You're not going to lose me. I'm not going anywhere."

"Really? What will you do if this whole thing blows up in our faces? If he fires us? What will you do then?"

He struggled for the words to reassure her, but he knew she had every reason to fear for their future.

"It's 1983, for God's sake. He can't keep us apart. I'll transfer back to uniform, and you won't be my supervisor, so we can be together."

"Really," she said, and he could hear the skepticism in her voice.

"This isn't the Stone Age. The state police has to face reality sooner or later. It's time for them to realize that men and women who work together can have a personal relationship."

The waiter approached and offered another glass of port. They declined because of the long day they were anticipating. Gino asked for the check.

He reached across the table for her hand, which she gave willingly. He looked into her eyes and spoke from his heart.

"Michelle, I love you, and I know that you love me. It's the only thing that should matter. I'm asking you to trust me to get us through this, because we're going to be together, and we're going to have lots of babies and grow old together."

"How can I be sure?" she asked.

The waiter appeared with the check before Gino could answer. He paid, and they left the restaurant and headed for their cars. Gino asked for a second to get something out of his car. He returned with a 45 record and handed it to her.

"What's this?" Michelle asked.

"Play it when you get home, and just listen to the words." He kissed her gently and said good night.

Michelle drove home as quickly as she could, opened the front door, and rushed up the stairs to the record player she kept in her bedroom. Carefully setting the record on the turntable, she placed the needle on the vinyl record, and it began to play.

It was *How Can I Be Sure?* by the Young Rascals—the record she and Gino picked up at the record store when he first started with the unit. How far they had come together since that time. So much had happened, almost all of it complicated.

As the song came to an end, she took in every word of the final verse. Those words were Gino's way of telling her they'd be sure about what the future held because they'd face it together.

CHAPTER 96

C losing arguments started at 10:00 a.m. in front of a packed courtroom. As the camera focused on Silverman, he began his closing, "Ladies and gentlemen of the jury, the thought of my client being found guilty of murder based entirely on the lies of two cooperating witnesses places a tremendous burden on me. I must convince you to return a verdict of not guilty, and if I fail, Mr. Detroia will suffer the consequences. I implore you to think carefully about this case.

"Please focus on the lack of evidence in this case. I submit to you, there is no evidence. Nothing more than two men who are lying to stay out of jail. Nothing whatsoever links Mr. Detroia and Mr. Kazarian to the death of Richard Calderone. No physical evidence. No fingerprints. No unbiased witness. The only thing linking them to this crime is two admitted criminals pointing fingers at their friends. Then, at the last possible moment, a former girlfriend comes forward. Her testimony is, at best, suspect. As the saying goes, hell hath no fury like a woman scorned.

"The only thing the state has proven is that Dickie Calderone met a violent death. What they want you to believe, but haven't proven, is that my client shot Mr. Calderone in a bar full of people.

"Ladies and gentlemen, gunshots in the middle of a city. A body, stabbed as it lies on the floor, carried out of a club and into the trunk of a car, then driven out of state and dumped.

"Does this sound like something that could happen and not draw anyone's attention? I submit to you that what the state has presented is a figment of the imagination. It comes from two witnesses who have sold their souls to stay out of jail.

"Please don't forget about this so-called agreement. The state would have you believe that they're going to jail if they lie. If that's the case, the state should be preparing perjury charges as we speak. As far as I'm concerned, all they did was lie during this trial. Lied to stay out of jail; lied to fool you into believing our clients were responsible for the death of Dickie Calderone. The only thing our clients are responsible for, ladies and gentlemen, is befriending two individuals who have no concept of the truth.

"Individuals, who, like the state's case, are weak, unproven, and unbelievable. Ladies and gentlemen, I suggest there is only one possible verdict for you to hand down, and that is not guilty. Thank you."

Silverman sat, and Salvatore rose and began his closing argument.

"Ladies and gentlemen of the jury, throughout this case, Mr. Silverman and I have attempted to demonstrate to you the absolute lack of evidence against our clients. Mr. Silverman has eloquently outlined the weakness of the state's case, and I need not repeat what he's told you. I think I need only remind you of your pledge as jurors to weigh all of the evidence and return a verdict that's true and just.

"The state's witnesses, Mr. Franco and Mr. Martelinni, can only be categorized as desperate men. So desperate to stay out of jail, they would have you convict a bar owner and one of his patrons, Big John, of taking part in a vicious killing. So desperate to save themselves, they accuse innocent men of murder. There isn't a shred of truth in any of their testimony." Salvatore bellowed, "The only thing my client is guilty of is being a friend to two men who have no concept of honor.

"They say common sense is not so common anymore, and the state is hoping that's true. I, on the other hand, believe you have the common sense to see through the lies and the deceit. Common sense tells you Dickie Calderone wasn't shot in a club full of people. Common sense tells you admitted criminals will say anything to please their keepers and stay out of jail.

"There seems little doubt if you use your common sense. You'll return a verdict of not guilty. Thank you."

He returned to his seat, and Big John gently patted his shoulder.

CHAPTER 97

Judge Leone waited until the courtroom calmed from the stir caused by the closing arguments of the defense. She told the jury that she would take a fifteen-minute break and resume at three forty-five. The day would end with O'Brien's closing argument.

The courtroom cleared, and Considine, O'Brien, and Gino retreated to the small witness room, where O'Brien rehearsed his closing argument. At three forty-five, he stood before the jury, pushed the blond hair off his forehead, and began.

"Ladies and gentlemen, I represent the state of Rhode Island in the case of State versus Frank 'Tiger' Detroia and John 'Big John' Kazarian. They're both charged with the murder of Richard 'Dickie' Calderone.

"I believe, when you analyze the evidence, you'll come to the logical conclusion that the defendants are guilty. I make no apologies for the case we've presented. The evidence is what it is, and the witnesses are who they are. I wish we could present you with a perfect case, but there's no such thing. This case is as imperfect as the men involved.

"You've heard from law enforcement officials that Frank 'Tiger' Detroia was the head of a crew involved in acts of crime. You've also heard about the friction between Mr. Detroia and Dickie Calderone. In this struggle for power, there could only be one winner. Like the unsuspecting fly caught in the spider's web, Dickie walked into the Pineapple Social Club, and his life ended.

"Ladies and gentlemen, let's not get fooled into believing Tiger was the kindly tavern owner who befriended some bad men. We've shown you through evidence and witness testimony that Tiger is a vicious killer, so vicious he shot Mr. Calderone in the back six times and stabbed him repeatedly.

"Big John wasn't just some patron enjoying a drink at his favorite social club. He was an active participant in this murder. We've proven Big John provided the gun to Tiger, helped bury Calderone's body in Rehoboth, and abandoned the victim's car in Fall River.

"We've presented you with two eyewitnesses. We understand they're not outstanding citizens, because outstanding citizens don't frequent the Pineapple Social Club. There are neither priests nor rabbis enjoying each other's company in the Pineapple. What you do find there are men like Tiger, Big John, Billy, and Marty. Billy and Marty are the individuals who told you what happened on that night, because they're the only ones who can.

"We've also presented to you a witness who has no stake in the outcome of this trial. Joyce Rego explained to you how she came here of her own free will. She needed to unburden herself of an ugly truth she's been carrying around for years: her former boyfriend and his friend were involved in the murder of Dickie Calderone.

"Ladies and gentlemen, these are criminals acting out of the most primal of instincts, kill or be killed. Our witnesses, flawed as they might be, told you the truth when they described the murder of Richard 'Dickie' Calderone."

O'Brien walked to the front of the defense table and looked at Tiger. His eyes narrowed. Suddenly, the frat boy disappeared, and a warrior stood before them.

"Mr. Franco and Mr. Martelinni testified this defendant asked Big John to get him a gun. He cowardly fired six times into the back of Mr. Calderone. He stabbed the victim numerous times after his bullet-riddled body thrashed about on the floor. He told Mr. Martelinni and Mr. Kazarian to dispose of the body."

O'Brien then moved over to Big John. "This defendant provided the murder weapon and disposed of Calderone's body, as he was told. He kept quiet about the murder, as he was told. These are not men betrayed by their friends. These are men betrayed by the life they've chosen."

O'Brien stood in front of the jury. Gino watched as each juror was completely captured by his words. "Ladies and gentlemen, I'm not asking you to put aside your common sense. I'm asking you to use it to judge the credibility of our witnesses. What is uncommon for us—murder, robbery, shakedowns—is common in their lives. I'm not asking you to decide whether our witnesses are good people or not. I'm asking you to determine whether or not they're telling the truth. I submit to you, if you use your common sense as the defense has asked, you'll come to the conclusion that they're telling the truth. I trust you'll return a verdict of guilty against both defendants because I, like Mr. Salvatore, trust in your common sense. Thank you."

CHAPTER 98

Judge Brenda Leone poured her morning coffee into a bar association mug. As she reviewed her notes for jury instructions, her attention drifted to thoughts of the trial.

Leone had presided over many murder cases, but never a Mob hit. She was familiar with the shady characters of her old neighborhood, those referred to as men of respect. As a young girl, she remembered seeing them hanging out on corners, whispering, laughing, and waving at passing cars.

She was curious why her father never represented these so-called men of respect. They were criminals of the worst kind, he explained, the kind who preyed on their own people. He wasn't willing to compromise his beliefs for a steady flow of clients. Salvatore implying that her father was like him in the way he practiced law offended her, and her emotions overtook her.

On the last day of the trial, Leone left her fashionable home on the east side of Providence at seven o'clock in the morning. She arrived at the courthouse at seven thirty, and Sheriff Henry Monte escorted her to chambers.

Leone told Henry she wanted to start at ten o'clock; he nodded and went about the business of calling everyone. Judge Leone took the bench at ten and instructed the jury on the legal elements of murder and the concept of proof beyond a reasonable doubt. She told them to take her instructions on the law and apply them to the facts. She closed by telling them that although she was the judge of the law, they were the judge of the facts.

She appointed Gerry Marley of Providence, a utility worker, foreman of the jury and sent them into their chambers to begin deliberations. Judge Leone then instructed the prosecutors and defense attorneys that they could leave the courtroom but remain available.

Jury deliberations began at 11:34 on Wednesday morning. Gino picked up lunch, and they ate quietly in the AG's office. The remainder of the afternoon was spent making phone calls, talking about the case, and listening to talk radio.

At five o'clock, Sheriff Monte called the office and asked that they return to the courtroom. Judge Leone told them that based on the late hour, she had decided to send the jury home for the night.

The judge brought them into the courtroom and instructed the jury to return at ten o'clock the next morning to continue deliberations. The sheriffs waited until the jurors left, and then took Tiger out of the courtroom. Big John left with his entourage.

CHAPTER 99

Newly appointed jury foreman Gerry Marley left the courthouse, got into his car, and drove home. He was still a bit confused as to why the judge had picked him, but he took the responsibility seriously.

During that first day of deliberations, he had asked each juror to give his or her opinions. As each juror spoke, he listened carefully but watched even closer. He saw fear in their eyes, the same fear he felt in his gut, the fear of retribution if they convicted Tiger and Big John of a Mob murder.

The fear caused them to speak robotically about the state's case. Some focused on the protected witnesses, others on the testimony of Big John's ex-girlfriend.

As Marley continued his drive home through the streets of the city, he thought of his job at Narragansett Electric and how service calls brought him to many houses on Atwells Avenue, the heart of organized crime in his city. He wondered how he could ever go back into those houses on the Hill after convicting two mobsters.

He recalled that the mobsters always made it a point to be home when he made his service calls. In the handshake he received when greeted at the door was the unmistakable message that he was in the home of a wiseguy—a handshake that put him on notice. It was that veiled threat of violence that bothered him, and it made him feel like less of a man.

It would be easy for him to guide the jury to where they seemed to want to go—take the easy way out and return a not guilty verdict. The criminal backgrounds of the protected witnesses were enough to plant reasonable doubt in anyone's mind.

But tugging at Marley was the oath that he had sworn, to apply the facts to the law. He thought about how the state had been straightforward with its protected witnesses, never making them out to be anything other than what they were. Then there was Joyce, the ex-girlfriend. What reason would she have to lie? She was obviously telling the truth, and it was hard to ignore her testimony.

As he pulled into the driveway of his house, he wondered which Gerry Marley would show up the next day. Would he be fearful or fearless? Only the verdict would answer the question.

CHAPTER 100

The second day of deliberations passed in much the same way as the first. At one point, there was a flurry of activity when the jury had a question. They were asking for a repeat of the instructions on premeditation.

Judge Leone called them into the courtroom. "A conviction of first-degree murder requires that you find the defendants had a plan, design, or a scheme to murder the victim. This plan need not be elaborate or dictated by time. It can develop in an instant or over a long period of time.

"If you believe that the defendant Frank 'Tiger' Detroia planned to kill Mr. Calderone by asking for a gun, then shooting him, there was premeditation. If you believe that defendant John 'Big John' Kazarian provided a gun to the defendant, knowing it was going to be used to shoot Mr. Calderone, then there was a plan in which he took part. I hope this assists you. I ask that you now return to your deliberations."

The courtroom emptied as quickly as it had filled. Considine, O'Brien, and Gino spent the rest of the afternoon trying to determine why the jury asked the question. Considine thought they were hung up on whether it was a planned murder or the impulsive act of a madman.

The second day of deliberations ended without a decision. Judge Leone dismissed the jury at six o'clock and sent them home with her admonition about their duty to not discuss the case and to avoid the media. The third day was more of the same until four o'clock, when all were summoned to the courtroom. The jury had reached a verdict.

When they arrived, the defendants and their attorneys were already present. The courtroom was full and completely silent. The judge came out of her chambers and took the bench, and everyone waited for the jury to come into the courtroom.

Gino looked into the crowd of onlookers and saw Michelle seated in the gallery. Would she champion him or be a shoulder for him to lean on?

Before the jury came in, Judge Leone told everyone that she wouldn't tolerate any outbursts in the courtroom, something every judge said and everyone ignored.

As the jurors filed in, Gino watched their eyes. If they were looking at the defendant, it could be a sign of a not guilty verdict. He believed jurors wanted to see the reaction of the defendant when the good news was delivered. If the jury had their heads down, it could be an indication of a guilty verdict. He didn't think jurors wanted to look at the man they were about to condemn.

To his delight, all jurors had their heads down as they found their seats. It was a guilty verdict, Gino could feel it—almost smell it in the air.

Judge Leone asked, "Mr. Foreman, have you reached a verdict?"

Gerry Marley stood and said, "Yes, Your Honor, we have."

"Will the clerk please call for the verdict?" Judge Leone questioned.

"Ladies and gentlemen, in the matter of State of Rhode Island versus Frank 'Tiger' Detroia on the charge of first-degree murder, how do you find the defendant, guilty or not guilty?"

"Guilty, Your Honor," Mr. Marley said in a strong voice.

Gino was sure his heart stopped and he went deaf, but he still heard the muffled moans and groans from the gallery.

The clerk continued, "Ladies and gentlemen, in the matter of State of Rhode Island versus John 'Big John' Kazarian on the charge of first-degree murder, how do you find the defendant, guilty or not guilty?"

"Guilty, Your Honor," he said again.

There was a second chorus of moans and groans, and then the wailing began. Judge Leone banged her gavel and asked for quiet.

Silverman rose and asked the jury be polled, and Salvatore made the same request. When called, each of the twelve jurors stood and said, "Guilty." The judge dismissed the jury after thanking them for their service.

The judge then looked into the eyes of men who showed no fear even in their darkest moment. Remembering the lessons her father taught her, she saw them for what they were: cold-blooded murderers.

"Mr. Detroia, would you please rise?"

Silverman stood at his side. Tiger displayed no emotion as he faced the judge.

"You've been found guilty of murder in the first degree. First-degree murder carries a mandatory sentence; therefore, it is the sentence of this court that you shall spend the rest of your life in the custody of the warden of the adult correctional institution. Mr. Kazarian, would you please rise?"

He rose from his chair with Salvatore by his side.

"You've been found guilty of murder in the first degree. Again, first-degree murder carries a mandatory sentence; therefore, it is the sentence of this court that you shall spend the rest of your life in the custody of the warden of the adult correctional institution."

Kazarian shook with anger.

"Both defendants are remanded to the ACI. This court is adjourned." Leone banged her gavel and disappeared into her chambers.

Silverman and Salvatore politely shook hands with Considine and O'Brien and left the courtroom. As they rode the elevator down to the second floor, Gino mustered as much discipline as humanly possible to hold in his emotions.

They walked into Considine's office and started jumping up and down like school kids. They hugged and screamed in delight as the tension and pressure of the last year were erased with the word guilty. Gino would never win a Super Bowl, World Series, or Stanley Cup, but this had to be as good a feeling.

The celebration was interrupted by a knock on the office door. Gino opened it and was greeted by Americo Salvatore.

"Detective, may I have a moment?"

Considering Salvatore had just lost his first Mob case, Gino thought he would have headed out to drown his sorrows at some watering hole, not stop by for a visit.

"Certainly, Mr. Salvatore. What can I do for you?" Gino asked.

"I have a message for you from my client."

"A message from Tiger? What does—"

"Not Tiger. One of my other clients—Mr. Raimondi," Salvatore said.

Gino was stunned but managed to compose himself.

"What's the message?"

"He just wanted you to know, that thing with your father, it shouldn't have happened. Someone got out of hand. You know how it is—some people are uncontrollable," Salvatore said.

"What are you saying?" Gino asked.

"I'm saying that after today, the individual responsible for your father's death is going to jail for the rest of his life," Salvatore said.

The question he had been asking since he was a child was finally answered.

"Tiger," Gino said.

"Tiger," Salvatore echoed.

CHAPTER 101

Warden Nugent of the Atlanta Penitentiary was annoyed but approved the visitor's request for a second meeting with Pasquale. Nugent had listened to the tapes of their first visit, crazy talk about an old Errol Flynn movie. The visitor wasn't going to get anything from the Old Man, so why was he back again?

The Old Man spoke first. "How's your family?"

"Fine," the visitor answered.

"Family is important, you know. Without family, we have nothing. We must protect our families at all costs."

"I know," he said.

The Old Man continued, "There are times when we have to make sacrifices for our families, even if that sacrifice costs us dearly. If there were people hurting your family, I would help you. If there were people doing harm to my family, you'd help me. It's because we understand how precious our families are to us."

A bead of sweat formed on the visitor's forehead. The reason for being summonsed didn't require the Old Man to say the actual words. The visitor understood exactly what was being asked.

"Have a safe trip back." The Old Man hung up and walked away.

CHAPTER 102

It had been three weeks since the convictions of Tiger and Big John. It was time for Marty and Billy to enter their pleas and be placed in the Witness Protection Program. It was the ending Considine, O'Brien, and Gino had envisioned when they first got together.

The conviction brought Gino praise from the members of his unit. Sully went out of his way to shake his hand in front of the entire unit. He even got an audience with the colonel—unheard of for a young detective.

At the attorney general's office, Considine and O'Brien enjoyed the same treatment. Attorney General Rose praised them in the press for bringing two mobsters to justice. Personally, they took great satisfaction in not only the convictions, but in what they had done to salvage their legal careers.

Gino and Michelle hadn't spoken much after the verdict. He had purposely avoided her, waiting for a Sunday afternoon to call her. She answered on the first ring, and he asked her to meet him on Atwells Avenue at Bond Street, not far from Pasquale's store. Gino told her he wanted to thank her for being there when the verdict was announced and to talk about the future.

At 2:00 p.m., he parked the undercover Caddy on Atwells and waited. She pulled up a few minutes later and jumped out of the car.

"I appreciate you wanting to thank me, and I know we have a lot to sort out, but did you have to drag me out of my house on a Sunday afternoon? We could have planned this a little better, don't you think?" she asked.

"Please just follow me, and you'll understand completely."

She followed him to Spruce Street, a narrow roadway with three-story tenement houses on either side. He opened the first floor door of 28 Spruce and quietly started up the stairs, Michelle close behind. The hallway was filled with the aromas of meats, sauces, and espresso.

When they reached the second landing, Gino stopped and raised his hand to knock on the door.

"State police! Open up!" Gino bellowed.

The conversation and laughter going on behind the door ground to a halt, and the door swung open.

"Gino, why do you do that all the time? You're going to give me a heart attack someday," his mom said.

She hugged him and at the same time looked past him to the puzzled woman on the stairs. Teresa released her son from the hug and faced Michelle.

"Mom, I wanted you to meet Michelle. She's the girl you said I'd never find. You know, the one who would never be good enough for me."

"Gino, stop it," she said, hitting him playfully with the dishtowel she carried over her shoulder. "Michelle, welcome to our house. Our family and friends are here, and they would love to meet you. Gino has told us so much about you. Please, please come in."

A bewildered Michelle entered the Peterson home. Gino's mom introduced her to at least twenty family members, friends, and neighbors. It was a typical Sunday afternoon, and she was about to be treated to a wondrous feast and a large dose of Italian hospitality.

During the meal, there was much laughter and stories about Gino as a child. Michelle seemed to enjoy herself, but Gino waited for a sign that this meant more to her than good food and welcoming hospitality—that she felt the love of his family and would allow him to provide her with the same kind of devotion.

After dinner, the men sat at the dinner table, eating Italian cookies and sipping on espresso laced with a healthy dose of anisette. He glanced over at the kitchen sink watching his mother doing the dishes, but something was different—by her side, carefully wiping each dish, was Michelle. Gino watched in silent joy as the two most important women in his life stood side by side, breathing life into the most mundane of tasks. Michelle looked to him and nodded. He looked into her eyes, and they told him she had found something worth being a part of, no matter what the future held. Considine was right: the eyes never lie. He took a sip of his espresso and said a silent prayer of thanks.

CHAPTER 103

The first step in getting Marty and Billy into the witness protection program was disposing of their criminal cases. Judge Tavares agreed to take their pleas on Tuesday morning.

They decided to bring Marty and Billy to court on the same day and double the security detail. Four unmarked cruisers and four uniform cars left for the courthouse.

They arrived and parked their cars on Hopkins Street. Again, the SWAT team was manning the building tops, and Providence police and troopers manned the perimeter and doorways.

As Gino led Billy and Marty in the side door on Hopkins Street, he saw a trooper standing alongside a Providence officer. He exchanged quick glances with them as he hustled Billy and Marty into the courthouse.

Everyone was in place as the judge entered the courtroom from his chambers. Marty and Billy sat at the defense table with their court-appointed attorneys. Gino sat with Considine and O'Brien at the prosecutor's table.

Judge Tavares called the court into session. Considine rose from his seat and outlined the plea agreement for each of the defendants. The court-appointed attorneys indicated they had reviewed the pleas with their clients and each wished to enter a plea of guilty. Judge Tavares asked Marty and Billy to stand. They pled guilty, and he sentenced them to ten years' suspended and ten years' probation. In twenty minutes, it was over.

Gino led the way as they exited the courtroom, traveled down a corridor, and exited the Hopkins Street door. His eyes were immediately drawn to Agent Theo Christopoulos. The trooper and the Providence officer were nowhere in sight.

His mind couldn't process why Theo was there, and as he searched for an answer, shots rang out. He turned back toward Marty and Billy and watched helplessly as Theo fired two bullets into Billy's head. Marty turned instinctively toward the sound, and when he did, Theo calmly pumped two shots into his chest. As bodies fell to the ground, Gino's world suddenly went into slow motion. He pulled his gun and pointed it at his friend and looked into eyes that reflected regret, fear, and resignation. Gino's gun hand shook as he started to squeeze the trigger. Suddenly, a sniper's bullet passed through the head of Agent Theo Christopoulos. The SWAT team had ended his life, but not before he carried out Pasquale's order.

CHAPTER 104

As the Georgios II steamed toward its homeport of Visiliki on Greece's Lefhada Island, Captain Theo Christopoulos Sr. watched with pride as his young son washed down the deck and secured the lines of their fishing boat. As they approached the docks of their village, he joined his father on the bridge.

"Papa, I have scrubbed the boat from stem to stern and no traces of drugs remain." He was twenty-five, thin and wiry like his brother, Theo, an uncomplicated young man who enjoyed the simple yet hard life at sea.

"That's good, Ari; we must never expose ourselves to the authorities. Life is going so well for our family—"

The old sailor's attention was drawn suddenly to the docks. As his boat drew closer he could see his wife pacing, arms pointing to the boat and then to the sky.

Frenzied, they docked the boat and she approached screaming the name of her eldest son, Theo. The old woman walked and cursed her God as she told them that Theo had been shot and killed by the police in America.

"Why, Papa? Why? Why would they kill Theo? He was one of them, he was on their side." Anguish hung on every word and sorrow crossed his face like a cruel mask.

The old sailor tried to compose himself but it was nearly impossible. He sobbed uncontrollably as his worst nightmare had just become a reality. Selling his soul for the riches of the drug trade had come with the ultimate price—his son.

"I am so sorry, my beautiful family, so sorry. I thought if I did this man's bidding, no more would be asked of me but I was wrong, so very wrong."

As he held his wife and only remaining child in his shaking arms he looked up to the heavens and screamed in Greek, "They Win! They Always Win!"

Made in the USA
Las Vegas, NV
16 July 2022